DATE DUE

Tales of Judge Dee

Tales of Judge Dee

Zhu Xiao Di

iUniverse, Inc.
New York Lincoln Shanghai

Tales of Judge Dee

iUniverse books may be ordered through booksellers or by contacting:

iUniverse
2021 Pine Lake Road, Suite 100
Lincoln, NE 68512
www.iuniverse.com
1-800-Authors (1-800-288-4677)

ISBN-13: 978-0-595-38438-9 (pbk)
ISBN-13: 978-0-595-82816-6 (ebk)
ISBN-10: 0-595-38438-2 (pbk)
ISBN-10: 0-595-82816-7 (ebk)

Printed in the United States of America

Acknowledgement

The main character in this book is a historical figure in 7th century China known to the West many decades ago as a character in stories by the Dutch author, Robert van Gulik. Like van Gulik, I use old Chinese crime literature to create baffling cases for the judge to solve, and the solutions to these cases are also found in old Chinese literature.

I accomplished what van Gulik was unable to do. A key solution to one old case lies in a play-of-words hidden in an old man's will, which van Gulik was unable to translate into English. Instead, he created a map of a maze as the puzzle in the will. Now the play-of-words is just as entertaining in English as it was written in Chinese.

I am grateful to van Gulik for his appreciation of ancient Chinese traditions and culture. While most China watchers of his day saw the sweeping ideological change in mainland China after 1949 as irrevocably fundamental, he wrote detective novels to help reveal Chinese culture, tradition, and philosophy as having a more enduring power. Even in China today, many people continue to hold characters like Judge Dee as their heroes. Several long TV series of movies based on Judge Dee stories were aired in China during the past years.

Considering the source, it is appropriate and authentic that an ethnic Chinese rather than a Dutchman write Judge Dee's stories. Many individuals have helped me to achieve this through valuable comments, editing, and suggestions. Without them, the book would not have been written. Particularly I want to thank three friends who contributed the most: Nick Herman, Louisa Birch, and Ted Braun. Other friends who helped review and edit some of the drafts are Seymour Katz, Patti Grossman, Nancy McArdle, Kate Hartford, and Dave Golber. Last but not the least, I benefited from a group of writers known as the Porch Table Group hosted by Elena Castedo in Cambridge, Massachusetts, many of whom gave me valuable feedback and input. Among them I want to thank Richard Hoffman for reviewing and editing over half of the early draft.

My thanks also go to my dear family members: my wife Meirong, our elder son Alexander, and our younger son Jefferson, for their indispensable encouragement and support.

CHAPTER 1

▼

THE OLD MAN'S WILL

"Someday I'm going to teach these greedy people a lesson," said Judge Dee, a tall broad-shouldered man with a foot-long black beard and matching side-whiskers.

The last tribunal session had been unexpectedly short, and it was too early for dinner. The judge did not want to go to his three wives, because his unanticipated presence at the ladies' quarters would interrupt their afternoon routines. At this hour his First Lady would be reading the classics and his Third Lady would be practicing painting or calligraphy. As to what his Second Lady might be doing, he wasn't quite sure. She was less educated, and perhaps still talking with her maid about the day's shopping, or yet still doing it.

The judge's office was adjacent to the court-hall, separated from the ladies' quarters. The two buildings were connected through a narrow corridor with a tiled roof. If the judge had wanted to join one of his wives, he had to walk through the corridor, likely to be noticed by the servants in the main kitchen. Not wanting to alarm anyone unnecessarily, or to disturb the preparation of his dinner, Judge Dee decided to stay in his office with his confidential advisor, Sergeant Hoong Liang.

Sergeant Hoong helped him take off his ceremonial robe of shimmering green brocade, and put away the magistrate's official cap of black velvet with stiffened wings spread out to each side. Judge Dee changed to his blue house robe and put a small black skullcap on his head. All civilized men wore caps, even indoors, except when sleeping.

It was early spring in a Year of the Snake and Earth, according to the Chinese calendar, approximately 669 AD. For a year now, Judge Dee had held the position as Magistrate at the tribunal of Poo-yang, a small but flourishing district of about twelve thousand people, located on the Grand Canal in middle-eastern China's Kiangsu Province.

As the judge spoke to Sergeant Hoong he referred to a case brought in earlier that afternoon. A tailor named Bao Yuan had complained that one of the wealthiest merchants in Poo-yang named Yang Feng had refused to pay for an expensive wedding suit he had ordered for his son. The tailor had tried once more to collect his money that very afternoon. According to him, the greedy merchant had shamelessly claimed that he had already paid for it. The wedding would take place that evening, and the angry tailor had appeared in court. Although his sympathy went initially to the tailor, Judge Dee did not bring the merchant to court. On his wedding night, an innocent young man should not be hurt by his father's greed. Judge Dee promised the tailor that he would investigate the case the following day.

Quite relaxed in his private study, the judge sat in his chair, slowly stroking his beard from his chin to its tip. His sergeant poured him a cup of tea. Hoong had been a long-time servant, who had for years been in the household of Dee's father and had known the judge since he was nine years old. Poo-yang was Judge Dee's third post as district magistrate and Sergeant Hoong had followed him from his very first posting. Although a small elderly man with a slightly bent back, the sergeant was courageous and had a natural gift for detective work. Judge Dee had appointed him sergeant of his constables, and treated him as his most confidential advisor.

Judge Dee walked across his private office to the window to glance into the courtyard, where Ma Joong, one of his lieutenants, a big, tall man and an excellent boxer, was drilling his constables. The night before, Judge Dee had sent his two other lieutenants, Chiao Tai and Tao Gan, to Magistrate Lo of Chin-hwa at the neighboring district to the east to give him some desperately needed help with a recent rash of pick-pocketing. These three lieutenants of his own choice and Sergeant Hoong formed Judge Dee's inner circle, and the judge held the absolute power in Poo-yang.

The judge's full name was Dee Jen-djieh, Dee as his family name and Jen-djieh as his own given name. It was composed of the two Chinese characters his late father had chosen for him: benevolence and prominence, hoping that the son would grow up to fulfill such lofty expectations. The magistracy was the lowest level of imperial administration to be appointed directly by the Emperor, who was referred to by all magistrates with much awe as "our August Throne."

As the sergeant began to serve the judge his tea, Ma Joong came in and reported that a Mrs. Woong had come to see the judge and that she was waiting outside. Judge Dee couldn't remember anyone by that name, but agreed to meet her anyway since he had so much time left before dinner.

"Bring her in," Judge Dee ordered. Ma Joong left the room, followed by Sergeant Hoong. As Ma Joong showed Mrs. Woong in, he leered at the judge. The woman looked almost forty years old, but the judge quickly apprehended Ma Joong's overt interest. His lieutenant was not necessarily a womanizer, but this was truly a beautiful woman. Her cherry mouth and almost apricot-shaped eyes modeled precisely the male ideal of female beauty. Even more remarkably, she achieved this beauty without any makeup, and indeed she was dressed very plainly.

She knelt in front of the judge and introduced herself. "This humble and insignificant woman, Woong *yoo* Mei, r-r-respectfully greets the Magistrate of Poo-yang."

"We are not in tribunal session, Madam." Judge Dee noticed her timid voice as he gestured her to stand up. "There is no need for formality here. Please rise and be seated."

Mrs. Woong rose slowly and sat down on one of the drum-shaped footstools in front of the judge's desk. She spoke in a quiet but sad and nostalgic tone. "On his deathbed twenty years ago, my late husband handed me this note with a gold bar." The woman took out a piece of paper from her sleeve and placed it on the desk.

"My husband said that he would bequeath the gold bar to me and my son, leaving all the rest of his assets to my step-son-in-law. That included a mansion with a hundred rooms and three hundred acres of land."

"I find it most peculiar, Madam," Judge Dee said, tapping the desk with his hand, "that your husband should have given almost all of his possessions to his son-in-law instead of his son!"

"I thought that way too," the woman mumbled, barely opening her cherry-sized little mouth, "especially as his daughter had already passed away. But my husband also told me that I should bring this piece of paper to the tribunal and show it to the magistrate when my son became twenty years old. 'If he does not understand it, show it to his successor, until a wise judge knows what to do,' he said."

Judge Dee picked up the piece of paper and read carefully. Written Chinese did not yet then have punctuation. A writer could employ line breaks to help his readers understand his meaning, but this old man had deliberately written his message in an uninterrupted long line. *This old man is sixty nine his wife has just delivered a son no one believes that it is truly his all of his properties shall be given to his son in law and others shall get none.*

"That is his will," the woman spotted Judge Dee's puzzled face and added, "and he also gave a copy to his son-in-law. My husband read his will to both of us from his death bed." The woman recited the will exactly the way her husband had read it twenty years before:

This old man is sixty-nine
His wife has just delivered a son
No one believes that it is truly his
All of his properties shall be given to his son-in-law
And others shall get none.

"His son-in-law said I had deceived my husband and kicked me and my son out of the house. I don't know why my husband said my son was not his. He only pressed my hand to remind me what he had told me earlier. Today is my son's twentieth birthday, and it is my duty to execute my late husband's instructions."

"How old was your son when your husband died?" Judge Dee asked.

"Only a baby, less than a month." The painful recollection made the woman weep, and she took out an old silk handkerchief to wipe her eyes.

"I see," Judge Dee stroked his black beard. He waited until she had put her handkerchief back in her pocket. The woman must have endured great deprivations during the past twenty years, Judge Dee thought, since she was still using an old silk handkerchief that her husband must have given her!

"Madam, there must be some deeper meaning in this will. I shall study it more carefully. It is my duty to warn you, however, that I have to keep my mind open. I may find in your favor, but I could also find you guilty of adultery. In either case I shall take appropriate steps, and justice will take its own course. If you prefer to take back this note and withdraw your request for a public intervention into your domestic affairs, it is not yet too late. But personally I appreciated the fact that you have truthfully followed your late husband's instructions."

Mrs. Woong rose promptly. With quiet dignity she said: "I beg you to keep this for study, and pray to Merciful Heaven that it will grant you all the wisdom needed to solve the puzzle." After a pause, she added: "Perhaps I should let you know that my step-son-in-law is one of the wealthiest merchants in this town and his name is Yang Feng."

"I've already guessed that. I didn't know he had inherited so much of his wealth from his father-in-law," Judge Dee said.

The woman bowed deeply and took her leave.

Sergeant Hoong and Ma Joong had been waiting outside in the corridor. "Indeed a very wise man!" Sergeant Hoong commented as he came in. "And evidently a most potent old man, I should say," Ma Joong laughed mischievously as he sat down on the footstool that Mrs. Woong had been sitting on, finding that her bodily warmth gave him quite a lively sensation.

While Sergeant Hoong was making a new pot of tea for the judge he continued his comments and speculations. "The old man realized that his wicked son-in-law was violently jealous of the newborn baby. If the old man divided his property equally between his son-in-law and son, the former might have killed the infant to get his part of the inheritance."

"Exactly!" Judge Dee said. "So the old man has made it appear that he disinherited the baby." The judge shook his head disapprovingly as he reflected on the age gap between the old man and his young wife. To him, that was a sure way to destroy a family. One had to be very careful in adding a wife, Judge Dee thought. He had only three wives, although he could have four according to the law. It was under very unusual circumstances that he had even taken his third wife six years before. Personally he held the view that two ought to be sufficient, unless both proved barren, and that any additional ones would be likely to cause more trouble than not in a harmonious household.

Sergeant Hoong picked up the will from the desk and read it word by word, following with his fingers. "I don't get it," he said, putting down the paper on the desk. "It's straightforward. What's its secret?"

Ma Joong picked it up, and held it against the sunlight. "No. There's nothing underneath either." He put it back, crestfallen.

A servant came to the door and announced: "The First Lady says that dinner is ready."

To their surprise, just at that moment, the gong at the tribunal's entrance sounded urgently. Normally this large gong on an ornate wooden frame at the tribunal entrance was sounded only for the opening of the morning, noon, and afternoon sessions; to have it struck otherwise made known that someone needed to report an emergency case.

"Please tell the ladies to proceed without me," Judge Dee told the servant, donning his official robe and winged cap in front of "the Mirror for Adjusting the

Cap" made of polished silver with a lacquered frame and mounted on top of a square box. It was particularly important for an official to wear his winged cap properly straight and forward.

As he was waiting for his name to be officially announced in the court-hall, the judge smoothed the front of his robe and pulled it around to the back. After he entered the court he gracefully ascended the dais and seated himself behind his high bench, the top of which was covered in a width of red brocade. In front of the high bench, two clerks, six constables and other such minions of the law had lined up in separate rows to the left and right. The constables carried iron chains, bamboo clubs, hand screws and other intimidating paraphernalia of the tribunal.

Behind the high bench, the entire back wall of the court-hall was covered with a dark-violet curtain. In its center a large image of a unicorn, the symbol of perspicacity, was intricately embroidered in a shimmering thick gold thread. The fundamental rule of imperial justice was that everyone appearing before the .bench was considered guilty until proven innocent. Everything in the tribunal was calculated to impress the public with the majesty of the law, and the awful consequences of opposing it. With no exceptions, everyone appearing there, old or young, rich or poor, man or woman, complainant or accused had to kneel on the bare flagstones. If the magistrate so ordered, they would be harshly beaten or tortured on the spot.

Sergeant Hoong and Ma Joong stood behind the judge, holding signs that read "Be serious" and "Be silent." Usually this was Ma Joong and Chiao Tai's job. Today, Sergeant Hoong substituted for Chiao Tai, and the sight of his puny figure sharply contrasted with the very large size of Ma Joong. This made it hard for spectators in the court to be silent or serious. They would all giggle or laugh.

It was the tailor who had hit the gong again. Kneeling in front of the high bench he panted: "This insignificant person is named Bao Yuan. My daughter is murdered. After I left the court this afternoon I walked straight home. To my surprise, my front door was open. I rushed inside and found my fifteen-year-old daughter lying on the floor. She is my only daughter; my wife passed away three years ago. I'm all alone in this miserable world and I'm not even sure why I'm still alive," he sobbed as his voice trailed off.

Judge Dee felt disturbed with this distressing news, particularly because the tailor had been here before, asking for help with the wedding suit and he had given none. Judge Dee offered prompt action. "Let's go to your house right now," the judge said. "Where do you live?"

"My house is inside the South Gate, the ninth on the Fifth Street counting from the east."

That was quite a distance from the tribunal, which was in the center of the city. Judge Dee sent a constable to have the coroner meet him at the tailor's house. Half an hour later, Judge Dee arrived in a palanquin, a comfortable seat enclosed by curtains and carried by two strong men on their shoulders.

The coroner was waiting at the front door. He was a thin middle-aged man, having his own pharmacy business when he was not serving as coroner to the tribunal. Judge Dee followed him and entered the house. The body of a slim girl with a beautiful figure stretched out on the hallway floor. Her robe was open and her underwear pulled down. The coroner reported that she had been raped and died of suffocation, perhaps only a couple of hours before. There was no sign of struggle, but the front of her robe was soaked with blood.

"Look what I've found!" Ma Joong exclaimed, holding up something half an inch long, soft and twisted. Both Judge Dee and the coroner frowned. They looked at each other in a quick silent confirmation before they exclaimed loudly in bewilderment: "A cut-off tongue?"

"Holy Heaven!" Ma Joong flinched. Tongue was his favorite food, but a cut-off human tongue made him feel sick. He had to cover his mouth with his left hand, while with his right hand he was still shaking the gruesome remains in the air, not sure what to do with it. Judge Dee silently wrapped it in a piece of oiled paper and put it carefully in his inside sleeve pocket.

It had become dark outside. Judge Dee ordered two of his constables to guard the house and body overnight. He said he would come back the next day to take another look at the murder scene in the daylight. The following day, however, none other than the wealthy Merchant Yang himself, an elderly man of about sixty with graying hairs, brought a new case in the tribunal's morning session.

"This insignificant person is Yang Feng. I had two hundred guests last night for my son's wedding. But this morning my fortune has completely changed. I woke up to find my daughter-in-law has killed herself and my son is missing."

"When did you last see them?" the judge asked.

"I saw her after dinner at about nine. As custom required, she retreated to her room after dinner, waiting for my son to join her later. But, as you know, the guests always try to prevent the bridegroom from joining his bride, and that is part of the fun of a wedding. So my son and I entertained our guests in the hall until the last guest had left at midnight. That's the last time I saw him."

"Did you search your house? Have you found anything suspicious or missing?"

"Nothing is missing, except for a servant named Nee. No one has seen him since yesterday mid-afternoon."

Just then a commotion arose at the tribunal gate. Judge Dee raised his hand, and a constable came and took the old merchant by the arm and helped him to his feet. Other constables brought in three men and made them kneel in front of the judge. The number of spectators in the courtyard quickly redoubled. Judge Dee looked at the three men kneeling in front of him. The man in the middle was obviously a night watchman, for he still had his wood bell in his hands that he used for his job. The man on his right was covering his mouth with his hand and Judge Dee couldn't see his face well. Pointing to the third man the judge commanded, "Speak up."

"This insignificant person is Yang Hua."

"Son! Where have you been?" the old merchant cried.

Judge Dee raised his hand to interrupt the merchant. To the son, he ordered: "Proceed now!"

"The most unfortunate thing happened to me last night. My bride was waiting for me in our bedroom after dinner. At midnight I went to my wife and found her sleeping on my bed, facing the wall. That was odd, I thought, for she was supposed to sit on my bed waiting for me. I hadn't yet removed her head-cover."

The man paused to catch his breath. Judge Dee found his story most striking. According to an age-long tradition, the bride wore a head-cover of red silk or brocade throughout the entire ceremonies of her wedding. As most marriages were arranged by others, usually parents, most newly weds had never even seen each other before their wedding day. When he took off that head-cover was the husband's first chance to look at his wife.

"When I approached her in bed," the young man continued his story, "she turned her face to me and screamed. 'Who are you? Get out of here!' Surprised and confused, I said, 'What do you mean? I'm your husband.' 'No, you are not! He was here about an hour ago,' she yelled. 'Don't talk nonsense! I am your husband, and I'm the only man who is supposed to enter this room, for Heaven's sake. Look at me, and look at this expensive wedding suit!' She stared at me and mumbled suspiciously, '*You* are my husband?' and then her voice trailed off. The next moment she screamed hysterically, 'What a shame! An imposter has slept with me! I don't want to live any more!' She threw herself off the bed, and I had to restrain her from hurting herself."

Poor woman, Judge Dee thought. It reminded him of his own third wife. Six years before, the girl had been taken hostage and raped. Her father and fiancé had both refused to take her to their homes, for such a rape victim had been stigmatized as unworthy to be any man's first wife. Seeing she had no place to live,

Judge Dee had taken her into his house as a chambermaid to serve his First Lady, who later developed an affection for the girl and insisted that the judge take her as a third wife.

"Proceed!" Judge Dee couldn't wait to hear the rest of the story.

The young man resumed. "Having heard her words I felt as if I had been struck by a bolt of lightning. How could I have such bad luck?" Self pity made him break into tears.

"Did she mention any specifics about the imposter? His height, weight, accent, and so on?" Judge Dee asked.

"She mentioned a big hairy mole on his right buttock."

A laugh broke out among the spectators in the courtyard. Judge Dee rapped his bench sharply with the "wood that frightens the hall," an oblong piece of brown hardwood specifically designed to keep order in the court. When silence resumed he commanded: "Proceed!"

The man continued. "I was so upset I couldn't sleep. All night I sat on the couch while my wife crouched on the bed weeping. I left the house before dawn and wandered the streets. I didn't know what to do or where to go. In my confusion, I walked to the Temple of Confucius. At its front gate, I saw the night watchman and him," Yang Hua pointed at the man kneeling with him who had been using his hands covering his mouth all the time. "I don't know why I followed them, but here we are."

"That's my missing servant, Nee," the old merchant cried from the side. The spectators in the courtyard became very excited as they heard that.

"Your Honor, this insignificant person is named Koong Ren," said the night watchman. He obviously took ardent pride in his family name, Koong, for it indicated one of his forefathers had been related to Confucius, the great master of a school of philosophy that had endured for over a thousand years. "I heard the rumor about the rape and murder at the tailor's house. The half tongue found on the floor must belong to the murderer. Look what I've found! A man who can't talk! He was crouched under the table where we put our altar and place our incense for the Great Master. No matter how I questioned him, he wouldn't talk. This man must have lost his tongue!"

Nee, who was kneeling on the floor, looked up at the judge with great pain and he couldn't speak a word.

"And I also found this in his pocket," the night watchman handed a golden nugget to the judge. Although it looked like gold, it was a fake and much lighter than real gold.

"Do you confess now to the murder of the tailor's daughter?" Judge Dee asked Nee in his loud voice that conveyed all the power and authority of a tribunal.

The man denied it violently, shaking his head from side to side.

"Strike him twenty times on the bare behind," Judge Dee ordered. "I'm sure he deserves much more," he quickly added.

Two constables with five-foot-long bamboo clubs pulled down Nee's underwear, and were dumbfounded. One of the constables knelt down before the bench and reported: "Your Honor, this man has a big hairy mole on his right buttock."

A huge roar broke out among the spectators. "Kill him!" "Kill him!"

This new discovery was startling and unexpected; Judge Dee didn't like it at all. He ordered the warden to jail Nee, and straightaway concluded the session.

Inside the judge's private office, Ma Joong asked eagerly: "Your Honor, why didn't you torture the servant Nee and make him talk?" "How could I? He has lost his tongue!" Judge Dee gave Ma Joong a reproving smile; his lieutenant still had much to learn!

While Sergeant Hoong was preparing tea for the judge, he offered his comments freely, and with his usual keen judgement. "That poor servant seemed still badly hurt. After losing his tongue he couldn't have enjoyed posing as a bridegroom." "Right!" Judge Dee exclaimed, "and for the same reason he couldn't have raped the tailor's daughter either if he had lost his tongue."

"Why didn't I think of that before!" said Ma Joong, whose pride was badly hurt, as he felt he knew everything about lovemaking.

"I don't follow you, Sir," Sergeant Hoong protested. "How did you know he lost his tongue before the rape?"

"Didn't you see the blood on the upper portion of her robe? That suggests quite strongly that someone raped her *after* she had bit the tongue off. Her robe was not removed during the kissing, which usually occurs before a rape, not afterwards. If she had bitten off his tongue, the man wouldn't have been able to complete the rape, for he would have been badly hurt," Judge Dee explained.

"Then who raped her?" Sergeant Hoong blinked.

"There must have been a second intruder in the house," Judge Dee said. "In fact, I already have a theory. I just need to verify a few minor points. This is really a fairly simple case," he stroked his long black beard.

"Who is the murderer then?" Ma Joong asked eagerly, clenching his hands so tightly that the joints crackled.

"I haven't seen him yet. But you'll discover him, Ma Joong. I want you to go to Yang's house, which is not far from here. Ask Yang Feng if he had a wedding guest who is young, single, male, and lives in the southeast corner of the city so that he passed the tailor's house on his way to the wedding. There shouldn't be too many guests from that part of the city, for most of the guests were probably Yang's neighbors. The southeast corner is not a rich neighborhood and Yang can't have many acquaintances there. If Yang Feng can identify such a person, go and arrest him immediately."

Ma Joong gave the judge a bewildered look; Sergeant Hoong was also mystified. Judge Dee spoke a few words in the ear of Ma Joong, who leered, and then left.

The judge looked blankly at his desk with its "Four Treasures" on top: a brush-pen made of sheep hair and bamboo, a compact black ink-stick, a pile of white blotting paper as soft as silk, and a black ink-stone that looked delicately smooth but was actually as hard as steel. Scholarly administrators were disciples of Confucianism, and they all had these four items on their desks.

"Sergeant Hoong," Judge Dee called his advisor as he took out Mrs. Woong's note, "we still have the old man's puzzle to solve. There are two tricks in the will, and I've already found the first one." "You did?" the sergeant exclaimed. He couldn't help but admiring his young master's intelligence, even without being told what exactly the judge had figured out. And he didn't ask for the information because he knew the judge loved to hold back critical evidence until the final moment when he announced how he had solved the case.

Judge Dee, with his hands behind his back, paced slowly around the desk to sip some tea and look at the will repeatedly.

Suddenly he stopped. "Yes, I've got it!" Judge Dee quickly walked to the desk and picked up a big brush-pen. Sergeant Hoong laid a large piece of paper on the desk, preparing the ink by rubbing the ink-stick against the ink-stone. It took only a minute before the ink was ready, while Judge Dee kept pacing, impatiently.

The judge quickly wrote down a few words in a big bold hand. His sergeant stood silently behind him watching. When the judge put down his brush-pen, the two men looked at each other and smiled. The sergeant was just about to speak, but Judge Dee put a finger on his lips, gesturing him to remain silent.

Before the noon session began, Judge Dee asked a constable to fetch Mrs. Woong and her son, and had them wait for him in his private office. He also sent for Yang Hua, the son of the wealthy merchant. Ma Joong had not returned when the session opened. The judge began with routine matters. When the son of the merchant was brought before him, clad in a mourning robe, the judge spoke to him in an amiable voice. "The coroner has proved that your wife killed herself. I'm terribly sorry about your loss. Since every detail is important, I want you to repeat her words exactly as you remember them. Proceed now."

The young man hesitated for a second before he opened his mouth. "She said: 'I waited for you in bed, and you came. No, that imposter came. He undressed me, but didn't speak to me at all. Even when I asked him if he wanted tea, he just shook his head. That was odd, wasn't it? I should have thought of it. After I became his woman he left the room and never returned. Oh, I nearly forgot. My right hand touched a big hairy mole on his behind.'"

"Stop!" Judge Dee interrupted. "That's exactly what I've thought." He caressed his long side-whiskers contentedly.

"See, the mole is actually on the *left* side of the imposter, for she touched it with her right hand." Judge Dee said.

The spectators in the courtyard murmured, excited at the new finding. Yang Feng, who had followed his son to the tribunal, also stood among the onlookers. Judge Dee watched him out of the corner of his eye as he addressed the son: "When I find the imposter, I'll make him pay dearly. As he is responsible for your wife's death, some of his properties should be confiscated and transferred to you as compensation." At that moment, Judge Dee thought he had detected a smile on the face of the elder Yang.

"Now, bring back that disgusting Nee." While waiting, Judge Dee surveyed the tribunal to see if Ma Joong had returned. Not seeing him, the judge looked disappointed and impatient. As the constables forced Nee to kneel down, Judge Dee roared at him: "I know you can't talk, but I'll get a confession from you anyway. See the tools of torture in the hands of those men? You'd better behave!"

The man on the ground quivered in fear, as he glimpsed the five-foot-long bamboo clubs, the half-inch thick whips made of snakeskin, and the hand screws that looked innocent and delicate, but whose power everyone knew. At that moment, Ma Joong appeared at the gate with a young bookish-looking man in tow. Judge Dee's face lit up. He sat up in his chair and addressed Nee in a less stern voice.

"I know you didn't kill the tailor's daughter, but I'll tell you what you did do yesterday afternoon. Just nod your head yes if my statement is correct, and shake your head no if it is wrong. Understand?"

Nee nodded his head.

"When the tailor came to Yang's house to collect the money for the wedding suit, you overheard both the dispute and that the tailor threatened to go to court right away."

Nee nodded his head.

"You were presented with an excellent opportunity. You always lusted for the tailor's daughter, but had never had the chance to be alone with her. Now you could pretend to deliver your master's payment for the wedding suit and coax her to open the door while her father was here at the tribunal. That's why you took along this fake gold nugget," Judge Dee held up a golden nugget in his hand.

The man closed his eyes and nodded reluctantly.

"Your dirty trick worked, and the girl let you in and you forced a kiss on her. As you stuck your tongue into her mouth she became angry and bit off half of it. You ran to the Temple of Confucius to use the ashes of the incense to stop your bleeding. Crouching under the altar, you stayed the rest of the day and all night until he found you this morning." Judge Dee pointed at the night watchman named Koong Ren.

Nee nodded again and touched his forehead to the ground as an expression of submission with respect commonly known as "kowtow," which literally meant "knocking one's forehead". He did that several times, pleading for mercy. The clerk had recorded all the judge's words and Nee's nodding on a piece of paper. He passed it to Nee to put his thumb mark on it as approval. Judge Dee ordered twenty strikes for Nee, to be executed later when the pain from loss of his tongue was gone. That would distinguish the punishment by law from that of nature or providence.

As the constables took Nee away, Ma Joong brought in the young fellow and made him kneel in front of the judge. "Your Honor, I found this lazybones still sleeping at noon," Ma Joong reported. "And I've checked the mark down there, too," he added as he winked to the judge.

Judge Dee nodded approvingly and gave the youngster a stern look.

"Speak up!"

"This insignificant person is Wu Lin. I'm a Candidate of Literature, preparing for the next level of examinations which will take place in the provincial capital next year."

"Shame on you, a student of literature!" Judge Dee admonished him. The young man's eyes were quite closely set, and his eyebrows nearly met. Many believed that as a sign of focus and intelligence. If he could pass his exams next year, he would be appointed a magistrate like the judge himself. For that reason alone, Judge Dee felt sorry for the lad.

"How do you know the merchant named Yang Feng, and how did you get yourself invited to his son's wedding?"

"My late father used to teach at Yang's house. As a scholar, he never passed his exams. That had disappointed *his* father. My grandpa was a merchant and not a learned man. In his will he said that my father could not spend any money until he passed the exams. My father was never able to pass. He brought me with him to Yang's, teaching both Yang Hua and me at the same time. I left Yang's house when my father passed away last year. He left a similar will and I have to pass the exams."

Judge Dee nodded several times as the young man answered. Many questions in the judge's mind had been easily answered. Having lived in the house before, the young man could of course find his way to the bride's room. Being a poor student, he had no chance with girls unless he could pass his exams. When all of a sudden a beauty was within arm's reach, the temptation was just too strong.

"What did you do after dinner?" The judge now conducted his interrogation with much more confidence, and the young man blushed. "As a student and a knowledgeable person, you should know better. A girl should not lose her virginity to anyone but her husband. You are completely responsible for her suicide."

"What? She killed herself?" The young man's face turned ashen.

"Now, tell me how you killed the tailor's daughter."

"That girl died too?" Wu Lin fell to the ground in a dead faint.

A constable came over and poured cold water on him. Another constable held steaming hot vinegar under his nose. Gradually the student came to, and his face was very pale. He looked at the judge in confusion as if in a dream.

"Kill the bastard!" "Revenge!" "Make him confess!" "Use the tortures!" "Why the wait?" The onlookers in the courtyard yelled. Judge Dee rapped the bench with his gavel, and everyone instantly became quiet.

"If you can't remember what you did yesterday, let me remind you," Judge Dee said. "On your way to the wedding, you passed the tailor's house and heard a terrible scream. A wild man ran out, his hands covering his mouth. Curiosity made you enter the house. You saw a girl standing in the hallway, dumbfounded. The front of her robe was soaked with blood. You didn't know what had happened: for she went into shock when she realized she had bitten off someone's tongue. You saw her beauty, and took advantage of her confused mind. You fondled her and rolled up her robe. She remained silent, even when you pulled down her underwear. But when you deflowered her, she spat out the tongue and screamed. You quickly covered her mouth with your hands. Your fear made you violent, and your hands blocked her breath. Cowardly, you ran away not knowing you had killed her. Your first taste of a woman made your lust insatiable. You committed a second crime, sneaking into the bride's room after dinner. As she had never seen her husband before but only heard his voice, you could easily pass as her husband if you kept your mouth shut. That's what you did, isn't it?"

The young man gave Judge Dee a defiant look. "That's the most sensational story I've ever heard. Where is your evidence?"

Judge Dee snapped at him angrily: "Why don't you just pull down your pants and let us look at the big mole on your left butt?"

Huge laughter broke out in the crowd, and Wu Lin dropped his head in embarrassment.

"Confess, and I'll spare you from the torture."

The crowd in the courtyard felt both fury and envy towards the young man. They were furious with him for the deaths he had caused. But the crowd also envied him the extraordinary experience of enjoying himself with two virgins in one day. "Torture him!" "Why wait?" They shouted. A magistrate had only two legal constraints on the use of judicial torture: first, the death of the tortured would require the punishment of the magistrate for such excess; or second, an unusually strong objection from onlookers might also restrain the judge. The young man knew only too well that he had no chance of gaining popular sympathy.

"I confess," Wu Lin whispered. The clerk grabbed his hand and pressed his thumb on the notes to make his confession official and final. In his resonant voice, Judge Dee announced: "The case is closed. The criminal Wu Lin, who has caused the loss of two innocent lives, will be decapitated. He shall be jailed until we receive the approval from our August Throne. All possessions of this young man, including his inheritance, shall be divided between Yang Hua and Bao Yuan as compensation, or smart money, as it is called."

The crowd cheered while only a few old women bothered to weep for the two young victims, the tailor's daughter and Yang Hua's wife. As the spectators began to leave, the tailor kowtowed to thank the judge. When the merchant and his son did the same, Judge Dee suddenly asked the wealthy man: "Why didn't you pay the tailor for the suit?"

The merchant was taken aback. He was just about to argue, but Judge Dee stopped him impatiently. "Your servant, Nee, must have known the truth, otherwise he wouldn't have been so sure that the tailor would go to court."

Yang started to rant, but Judge Dee interrupted him: "I have something else to settle with you."

He pulled from his sleeve the old man's will and held it up in the air. "Do you remember your father-in-law's will?"

"Of course I do."

Judge Dee signaled Sergeant Hoong to bring in Mrs. Woong and her son. The young man looked shy but well brought up. The woman now appeared more confident than at her first meeting with the judge. Pointing to her the judge spoke to Yang Feng: "And you must remember this woman as well."

The merchant looked at her with candid contempt.

"Why did you take this young man's position and everything that belongs to him?" Judge Dee suddenly asked as he pointed at Mrs. Woong's son.

Yang Feng was startled. "Your Honor, my father-in-law bequeathed everything to me!"

"Who said that?" Judge Dee retorted, smiling.

"You have his will in your hand, Your Honor," Yang Feng cried.

"You mean this piece of paper?" Judge Dee waved the old man's will in his hand. It was written in an uninterrupted long line: *This old man is sixty nine his wife has just delivered a son no one believes that it is truly his all of his properties shall be given to his son in law and others shall get none.*

The merchant stared at the judge and spoke up quite aggressively: "Yes!"

"What a pity that you simply don't know how to read!"

From Sergeant Hoong's hand Judge Dee took over a large piece of paper and hung it from his high bench down to the earth. "Read it by yourself, you idiot," Judge Dee said.

Yang Feng saw the old man's will written in Judge Dee's elegant handwriting, with line breaks:

This old man is sixty-nine
His wife has just delivered a son
No one believes that [the old man could still father a son]
It [the son] *is truly his*
All of his properties shall be given to his son
In-law and others shall get none.

The man became speechless. Judge Dee said: "Check it against your own copy at home, and transfer everything you have to this young man here, except the smart money your son will receive from Wu Lin. From now on you shall be a dependent on your son for your wellbeing. And don't forget to pay the tailor!" The judge rapped his bench with the "wood that frightens the hall," an oblong gavel he had constantly used in court to draw absolute attention.

The merchant raved and the constables had to take him away. Mrs. Woong and her son knocked their foreheads on the ground to thank the judge for justice. "Don't thank me. It's my duty. Come here and read it," Judge Dee beckoned to the young man and showed him what had been engraved on the magistrate's oblong gavel as a constant reminder of his solemn duties to the state and the people:

A judge must be a father and mother to the people,
Cherishing the good and loyal, helping the sick and old.
Though meeting out stern punishment to every criminal,
Prevention, not correction, should be his purpose.

Back in his private study, as he took off his official robe of green brocade and his winged judge's cap of black-velvet, Judge Dee asked Sergeant Hoong. "Didn't I tell you I was going to teach these greedy people a lesson?" Sergeant Hoong chuckled as he helped the judge put on his blue house robe and a black skullcap, "Surely you did, Sir."

CHAPTER 2

▼

A SLIP OF THE TONGUE

"Any news about the famine in the north, Sergeant Hoong?" asked Judge Dee on a sunny morning two weeks later.

"The official report hasn't arrived yet, Your Honor, but quite a few bodies have floated down the Grand Canal from the northern district," the gray-bearded sergeant replied.

"You showed me the first body yesterday, Sergeant. What a disgusting sight!"

The sergeant covered his mouth, recalling his shock at seeing the emaciated corpse. Poo-yang was a district with fertile land and there had been neither floods nor droughts. Not only did the farmers prosper, but merchants were also thriving. Located on the Grand Canal that crossed the Empire from north to south, Poo-yang derived much of its profit from the busy traffic. Both government and private ships often harbored outside the western city gate. The constant coming and going of travelers brought good customers to restaurants and shops. The canal and the rivers that flowed into it abounded in fish and provided living for the poor. As the people of this district had been prosperous and content, taxes had been paid on time till last year. The famine in the north came as quite a surprise, and it must have been caused by some unusual circumstances. Sergeant Hoong shook his head as he wondered.

The morning tribunal session had just concluded. Judge Dee spoke to Sergeant Hoong in his office while the former house servant and now confidential advisor served him a cup of his favorite tea. The judge's private study was next to the main hall of the tribunal, separated by a colorful brocade screen. He was relaxing in his black skullcap and blue robe, folding his hands in his spacious sleeves where two large inside pockets hid almost anything less than a foot long.

Before he had time to finish his tea, however, the gong at the gate was struck three times. The rule everywhere in the Empire was that anyone could hit the gong at any time to request an emergency session of a tribunal. Judge Dee had to don his official robe and the magistrate's winged cap again. As he glanced in the mirror to adjust his cap, he reflected on his image in the mirror. Without his official cap, he could be anybody on the street, and anyone wearing that cap could claim to be the magistrate if no one had known him before. In fact, if he and Ma Joong had switched their positions on their first day in Poo-yang as a practical joke, people might never find it out, unless…. His thoughts were interrupted as he heard his name loudly announced in the court-hall.

By the time he ascended the dais and sat behind his high bench in the court, Sergeant Hoong and Ma Joong stood behind his chair, holding signs that read: "Be serious" and "Be silent." Looking toward the entrance of the hall, Judge Dee saw a woman of about thirty with an ordinary face. Reluctantly following her was a man of the same age, and then a lively and enthusiastic young fisherman, bare-footed, wearing rolled up pants and carrying a bamboo hat on his back. Judge Dee ordered two constables to bring them in. The tribunal's courtyard soon swarmed with dozens of curious onlookers. The constables made the woman and men kneel before the bench, and Judge Dee addressed the woman:

"Speak up! Who are you, and what grievous wrong have you suffered, to make you beat the gong before the noon session of the tribunal convenes?"

"This insignificant person," the woman said, referring to herself, "is named Wang *nee* Liang, wife of Wang Deh-san." The woman held her hands loosely clasped beneath the outside of her left breast, moving them up and down, in the customary female gesture of salute.

"We live in the Turnip Village, outside the West Gate of the city. Last year's crops were terrible because of an unknown insect. We don't expect a good harvest this summer either. My husband and his friend, Koong Da, decided to try their luck as peddlers. Early this morning, they were supposed to leave Poo-yang on Fisherman Lee Djao's boat. My husband left home at dawn, with ten pieces of silver in a blue cloth bundle on his back. Half an hour later, I heard Lee Djao's voice outside my house: 'Mrs. Wang, is your husband home?' 'No,' I said, 'He left home half an hour ago. Didn't he go on your boat?' 'We must have taken the different paths,' he mumbled and left. Half an hour later he returned with Koong Da. This time I opened the door and let them in. They said they had been waiting for my husband, but that he had never showed up. 'Impossible!' I said. 'He left home at dawn and carried ten pieces of silver with him, in a bundle just like yours.' I pointed to the one on Koong Da's shoulder. Then Lee Djao exclaimed. 'Your missing husband must have been murdered and it must be Koong Da who murdered him! Count the pieces of silver in his bundle.' Koong Da refused to let us touch his bundle. So I grabbed him, and Lee Djao and I rushed here to report my husband missing. Please, Your Honor, check his bundle and punish this cruel man for the murder of my husband."

Everyone turned to look at the blue cloth bundle on Koong Da's back, and the man looked quite frightened. Judge Dee ordered a constable to take the bundle from Koong Da and pour the contents on the flagstone floor of the court. Ten pieces of silver fell to the ground, and an excited roar arose from the crowd of spectators in the courtyard.

Judge Dee frowned and couldn't believe what was happening. Never had a murder case been so easily solved. The noise from the crowd made him even more reluctant to accept the case at face value. He rapped the bench with his gavel, the "wood that frightens the hall." Everyone in the courtyard immediately fell silent.

"Speak up!" Judge Dee bellowed at Koong Da, who was quivering on the ground in front of the bench. "This insignificant p-person," he tried to speak steadily, "is named Koong Da. Wang Deh-san and I have been best friends since boyhood. We agreed last night to each bring ten pieces of silver and leave Poo-yang on Lee Djao's boat this morning. We planned to do business together. I went to the boat, but no one was there. A few moments later, Lee Djao came. We waited for Wang Deh-san for about a quarter of an hour. Then Lee Djao suggested that we fetch him at his home. Your Honor has heard the rest of the story. Please believe me."

The man's words made sense, and clearly there was not much evidence against him. Judge Dee looked intently at Koong Da, and then at the fisherman. The judge was about to speak, but thought better of it. He stared at the woman, then at Koong Da and Lee Djao again. Based on the little he had heard the judge felt that each of the three might have a motive and opportunity to commit a crime. But since this was not a regular session and as he did not want to drag it out, Judge Dee ordered the jail warden to put Koong Da in a temporary cell and the emergency tribunal to close.

When Judge Dee returned to his private study, followed by Sergeant Hoong and Ma Joong, he signaled them to sit down. "Your Honor," Sergeant Hoong asked, "do you really think we have a murder case on our hands?"

"What do you mean, my sergeant," Judge Dee asked, giving the word a slightly sarcastic tone, for the sergeant usually had some unique and witty observations.

"I'm just wondering, Sir, if it could be possible that Wang Deh-san is merely missing. Maybe he just wanted to leave his plain-looking wife."

"That's a good point, Sergeant!" Ma Joong exclaimed for the first time in the morning. He had been feeling blue because he hadn't set his eyes on a single good-looking woman since waking that morning. When there were no beautiful women, the sessions bored him.

"Sergeant Hoong is right. Mrs. Wang is definitely plain. That could mean," Judge Dee deliberately paused for a second before he went on, "that there is a pretty girl involved." Seeing Ma Joong become more interested, Judge Dee gave Sergeant Hoong a smile. They both knew their colleague was a flirtatious man. Attracted to his own line of argument, Judge Dee caressed his long side-whiskers and continued: "Out of jealousy Mrs. Wang could have murdered her husband. Or, for the same reason, either or both Lee Djao and Koong Da might have killed Wang Deh-san, for either of them might lust after the same pretty girl who loved Wang Deh-san. But we don't have any evidence."

"If greed were the motive," Judge Dee frowned, his knitted eyebrows indicating a very high degree of concentration, "both Koong Da and Lee Djao should be our primary suspects. Of course, Sergeant Hoong's guess that Wang Deh-san might be still alive could also be right. This is a case with too many possibilities! We don't even have enough evidence to use torture against any of the suspects. Our law does require confession. But how can we make the criminal talk?"

The judge fell silent as he pensively stroked his beard. A constable brought in several documents for Judge Dee to review. Sergeant Hoong prepared ink for the judge to write his comments or response. Before he left the room with Ma Joong, the gray-bearded sergeant made a pot of tea for the judge. Recalling how he had made the man confess without his tongue, Judge Dee giggled as he moistened his brush-pen and began writing. The judge was quite satisfied with the way he had solved a few recent cases. In one of the letters he had just received, his boss, the Prefect at the prefecture who supervised six neighboring districts, praised him highly in words and quite admired him for solving three cases on the same day.

Judge Dee left his desk and went across the room to open the window. A pungent smell came in with the fresh air, and he immediately recognized it as a special type of fried bean curd known as the "stinking tofu." Those who love it felt it was the best food on earth. Others hate it and could never understand how anyone could actually eat such a disgusting thing. Judge Dee was a lover of it, but his

Third-wife hated it just as strongly. The judge took a deep breath, enjoying the smell in the air. It came from the main kitchen, and he knew that in about an hour or so he would have it for his lunch.

The gong at the tribunal gate was struck three times to announce the coming of the noon tribunal session. Judge Dee quickly gulped his tea and put on his official dress. Pushing aside the corner of the brocade screen that separated his office from the court-hall he entered the court and sat behind his high bench. Sergeant Hoong and Ma Joong stood behind him, holding the two big signs. Constables and other personnel of the tribunal stood in rank. One of them had proudly announced his arrival before the judge entered. The yard outside the open court-hall was packed with spectators; there was no more standing room. People came to hear more about the murder that Wang *nee* Liang had presented that morning.

Judge Dee rapped the bench sharply with his gavel, formally announcing the beginning of the noon session. To the disappointment of the crowd, he did not address the murder inquiry. Hearing nothing exciting, most of the crowd wandered off. As the judge was just about to finish the session, he heard a commotion at the entrance. He sent one of his constables to see what it was all about.

The constable returned with a middle-aged woman. Her face was not made up, but traces of heavy makeup remained. Although she was no longer young, her full red lips and smooth complexion made her attractive. She wore a long black skirt with a red sash around her waist, and a loosened dark-green jacket that did more to bare rather than cover her still shapely bosom. A little vulgar, thought Judge Dee, but so many men like this kind of woman! He was about to turn and see how Ma Joong reacted, when he overheard the lieutenant whisper to Sergeant Hoong behind him: "That is a woman one could have some fun with!" Judge Dee smiled. "Too old for me though," Ma Joong added a few seconds later, "but she might be good for Chiao Tai, except that he is looking for a serious love and doesn't like vulgar women anymore."

The constable made the woman kneel down in front of the judge's high bench, and she spoke up in a coarse voice: "This insignificant woman," she paused, looking up at the judge to see if he was at all interested in her, "is named Peng *soong* Lan. I live next to the market not far away, on Great Peace Street. My husband passed away two years ago. Last year, bad luck struck again, and my son died. His wife still lives with me. She has no children, so our family name, Peng, won't be carried on." She blinked several times, trying to force some tears.

"As if my misfortune weren't enough, I recently find my house often visited by idle men. My daughter-in-law has apparently enjoyed it, despite our tradition and law forbidding a widow from such contact with men. I've admonished her over and over again, but she just won't listen. Now I have to file a formal complaint against her. Please punish this disgraceful woman and teach her a lesson, Your Honor."

Hearing her statement with all his patience, Judge Dee finally roared out: "Disgusting, if what you've said is true. Where is this imprudent young woman?" He recalled that his predecessor, Magistrate Feng, was also very strict about domestic rules. Any offence to the Confucian doctrines such as children having to obey parents or widows having to remain virtuously isolated inside her house would have been punished ruthlessly.

"At home, Your Honor," the woman quickly replied, apparently pleased that the judge had believed her.

Judge Dee ordered Ma Joong to fetch the young widow right away. His lieutenant happily took the order and went off. Judge Dee waived his hand, and a constable came and held the plaintiff away. The judge took the moment to inform the public about the famine in the north. He knew that his words would quickly spread from mouth to mouth throughout the entire district. Although the official document hadn't yet arrived, he wanted his people to be prepared. He ordered all the corpses collected and brought to the tribunal, ensuring their proper burial.

As a magistrate, Judge Dee wished that all households in his jurisdiction could put food on their tables. People called him a "parent official," as if the magistrate were a parent of everyone in his district. If a famine were to occur, he had to declare it to the Imperial Court. Usually, tax exemption would follow, and perhaps some free food would be allocated from the capital or neighboring districts. A false declaration, however, could cost a magistrate his career and even his life. That was probably why the official announcement of a famine in the northern district hadn't come yet, although several bodies had already been found in the Grand Canal. Judge Dee wondered how and whether he could manage such a balance nicely; he would have liked to take a little risk and proclaim the famine now.

Ma Joong returned with a slender young woman. She knelt down in front of the high bench. After a frightened glance at the magistrate, she cast down her eyes, waiting shyly to be addressed.

"Speak up, and look at me!" Judge Dee growled at her. The woman held up her head. Her large, moist eyes and gracefully curved eyebrows made her very attractive. Her faded blue cloth robe could not conceal her splendid figure.

"This insignificant person is named Peng *wu* Mei. I r-really don't understand why this officer from the tribunal has brought me here." Her timid voice revealed her innocence and bewilderment.

Judge Dee caressed his long side-whiskers and changed to a more friendly tone as he resumed his interrogation. "I've heard that idle young men often visit your house. Isn't that true?"

"Yes, Your Honor, that is quite true."

Such a prompt confession surprised Judge Dee. "Then who are these young fellows, and what do they want?" The judge roared, reverting to his more awe-inspiring voice.

"I have no idea. There are so many of them. They all come to talk to my mother-in-law, and they seem to have a lot of fun."

"Liar!" screamed the elder woman. The younger one was startled, but she controlled herself quickly. "Your Honor, I spoke the truth, and nothing but the truth," she said. "I know it is hard to disagree with my mother-in-law, but believe me, please." After a second thought she added: "One particular young man comes almost every other night. His name is Lee Djao." As soon as she mentioned that name, the few remaining onlookers in the tribunal courtyard murmured among themselves, for they all remembered seeing the young man that morning as a witness in the murder case.

At Judge Dee's order, Ma Joong brought the fisherman back in. The courtyard soon became crowded again. As Lee Djao knelt down in front of the bench he asked: "Your Honor, for what reason, may I ask, am I returned to this tribunal?"

"You should ask yourself that question, if you are a law-abiding citizen. Speak up!" Judge Dee spoke sharply.

"I really don't know," Lee Djao's voice trailed off, as he realized from the judge's voice that something was amiss. Meanwhile, the judge changed his tack and lowered his voice to speak in a more coaxing tone. "Have you heard the rumor that there have been infamous activities at the Peng's residence?"

Lee Djao's eyes opened widely. He was caught by surprise. Looking around he found both the elder and younger Peng standing on the side. Rolling his eyeballs quickly for three seconds he answered decisively: "Yes, Your Honor. I did hear the rumor that the young Mrs. Peng has a couple of lovers."

"Do you know who they are?" Judge Dee asked.

"No.... I mean yes, Your Honor." Lee Djao seemed to have made up his mind, but still hesitated for a moment before he said: "I heard it was Koong Da and Wang Deh-san." An excited roar came from the crowd in the tribunal courtyard. Sergeant Hoong and Ma Joong turned and looked at each other, exchanging a quick look of mutual understanding that only the two of them understood.

Judge Dee sprang up from his chair. He did not like this new development at all. Although it fit his previous theory, it seemed too much of a coincidence. The judge remained silent, letting the noises among the crowd grow louder and louder, as people became more and more impatient. Giving Lee Djao a sharp look, Judge Dee waved his hand and had a constable lead the fisherman away. At his signal, the constables brought back the two Mrs. Pengs and they knelt in front of him. The crowd became quiet again. To the elder one the judge said: "I'm glad you've brought to my attention the unpleasant situation at your home. In due time this magistrate will bring peace back to your home." Having said that, he rapped the bench with his gavel and closed the session.

Hardly had Judge Dee retreated to his private office and changed his clothes with Sergeant Hoong's help, than Ma Joong exclaimed excitedly: "Your Honor, how right you were this morning, when you guessed that a good-looking girl was involved in the case! Why didn't you put screws on that young wench's hands and make her confess?" The "screws" were of five sticks of hardwood about ten inches long, in stringed rows. When the fingers were put between the sticks and the strings tightened, it hurt tremendously.

Judge Dee didn't answer Ma Joong's question. He sat down at his desk and sipped the tea that Sergeant Hoong had poured for him. After a few moments the gray-bearded sergeant cleared his throat and broke the silence. "I don't understand. If the young Mrs. Peng didn't tell us about the fisherman and her mother-in-law, we wouldn't even listen to Lee Djao and his talk about her lovers."

"Exactly!" Judge Dee said. "I no longer believe my previous theory. Now I think the fisherman is slandering the young woman, just as he did Koong Da. The poor man is still in jail. I have to talk with him this afternoon. I don't like this Lee Djao at all. Maybe it's his character, but right now he is my primary suspect. Sergeant Hoong, I want you to talk with Wang *nee* Liang this afternoon and see if she can give us any new information. Meanwhile, Ma Joong should pay a visit to Lee Djao and his boat to check anything suspicious. After that he should visit the Peng's neighbors to see what they have to say about these two women." Judge Dee had heard two knocks on the door. As a servant brought in lunch for the judge, Sergeant Hoong and Ma Joong left to fulfil their respective assignments.

Absentmindedly, Judge Dee ate his lunch. Preoccupied with his deep thoughts, he did not even notice the pungent smell of the "stinking tofu." It came with a small dried salted fish, two dishes of fresh vegetables, and a bowl of rice. Usually he would drink a tiny pot of rice wine to go with his favorite dish, but today he did not even touch his wine pot, a delicate vessel made of porcelain just the size of a man's palm. After the judge had finished his lunch, Sergeant Hoong returned with a big pot of hot water. While making the tea for the judge, he murmured: "Tomorrow is the holiday of Cold Food."

"I nearly forgot!" Judge Dee exclaimed. It was a custom to visit ancestors' graveyard on that day, but his late father was buried outside the wall of the capital. Traveling between Poo-yang and the capital would take weeks if not months. The judge had to set up a ceremony at home to pay the tribute to his late father and ancestors. The most important was to have the ritual of feeding the ancestors with symbolic food. Otherwise, it was believed, they would be hungry and couldn't sleep well under the ground.

"As I passed the women's quarters," the gray-bearded sergeant continued, "your First Lady asked me to check with you on your plans for the family tomorrow. Do you want to pay tribute in the morning or in the afternoon?" As an old servant of Judge Dee's late father, Hoong was the only male beside the judge who was allowed to see Judge Dee's three wives, and he felt honored by this privilege.

"Tell her that we will do it in the morning," Judge Dee said. His First Lady was the eldest daughter of a high official in the capital who had been his father's best friend through his life. The couple had married at their parents' arrangement twenty years before when the judge was twenty and she was nineteen. The deep understanding established between them after the marriage had always been a great comfort to the judge, especially in time of stress. Having received an excellent classical education and being a woman of strong personality, she fairly supervised the entire domestic affairs with a firm hand. Judge Dee never heard a complaint against her from either a housemaid or servant, or his other two wives.

Judge Dee picked up a bound volume of classic poetry from his large bookshelf and lay down on his couch. Reading poems often excited other officials, but not Judge Dee. He found poetry useful only in putting himself to sleep. Like most men, it was his habit to take a nap every day. But today even reading poetry couldn't put him to sleep. He decided to skip his nap and walked through the quiet corridors to the tribunal jail. When the warden saw the magistrate coming he jumped up from his seat and bowed low respectfully. "Lead me to Koong Da," the judge ordered.

*   *   *   *

None of Judge Dee's several inquiries brought any results. His conversation with Koong Da yielded no new information. Sergeant Hoong visited Wang Deh-san's wife and learned nothing. Ma Joong located Lee Djao's boat and took a good look at it in Lee's absence, but found nothing suspicious. However, his visit to Peng's neighborhood did confirm one thing; his neighbors had noticed frequent visitors, particularly the fisherman Lee Djao, but they couldn't tell whether it was the elder or the younger Mrs. Peng who received these men.

When the afternoon session opened, two men brought in a new case. Kneeling on the floor in front of the high bench, they spoke simultaneously. "This insignificant person…." Judge Dee raised his hand and interrupted them. "One at a time! You first." The judge pointed at the one kneeling on the left, a tall, large man clad in costly silk robe. He had a broad, florid face and a neatly trimmed black beard.

"Your Honor, this insignificant person's name is Tian Han, and I own over 200 acres of land outside the West Gate. Tomorrow is the Cold Food Day. To prepare for the ancestor worshipping, I sent my servants to the grave hill where my ancestors' graves are located. But this scoundrel interrupted their work, claiming the land to be his."

"Your Honor," the high-pitched voice came from the other man kneeling on the floor. "This insignificant person is named Chu Moo. Poor as I am as a pawnshop assistant, I did own the land where my ancestors are buried."

"Did you say you *did*? Have you sold the land to someone recently?"

"The truth is, Your Honor, I never sold it to anybody. It's just that thirty years ago I misplaced the deed, and have been unable to find it."

"Your Honor, for the past thirty years, this scoundrel has always disturbed my worshipping ceremony on the holiday of Cold Food Day. This year is worse than ever for Cold Food Day is not until tomorrow and he's already bothering me."

"Can you prove that the land belongs to you?" Judge Dee interrupted Tian Han and asked. "Eh…" Tian Han hesitated for a few seconds, and answered with downcast eyes, "I can't prove it either, for I lost my deed." He looked the judge in the eye and said: "But I swear it's mine. I know my father and grandfather are both buried there. I just can't find the damned deed!"

"Keep a civil tongue!" Judge Dee scolded, "I find this a most incredible case!" Judge Dee stood up abruptly. The two wings sticking out from the sides of his judge's cap flapped. "Can't we find some record in the registry of the tribunal,

Sergeant Hoong?" As the gray-bearded sergeant was about to leave the court to check the record, a senior clerk knelt down in front of the high bench. "Your Honor, the tribunal's record is missing. For the past thirty years, these two gentlemen always came to the tribunal on the day of Cold Food, asking for justice. But none of the magistrates had the wisdom to..."

Judge Dee raised his hand, stopping the man from saying anything disrespectful of his predecessors. He looked pensively at Chu Moo, who had a thin face with a gray goatee. Standing still and caressing his long side-whiskers, Judge Dee thought for a while, and then he rapped the bench decisively with his gavel. "Tomorrow, this tribunal will have its morning session at the grave hill. Both Chu Moo and Tian Han will have their ancestor worshipping ceremonies there for the last time. The tribunal will take over the land as public property, because neither of them can prove ownership of the land. This session is closed."

Both Tian Han and Chu Moo complained that was not fair and raved about how the land had belonged to them for generations. But when Judge Dee rapped his bench again with his gavel, Chu Moo shut his mouth and kowtowed for the last time before he left the court. Tian Han, on the other hand, kept raving, and the constables had to take him away and kick him out of the court.

The next morning, hundreds of people came to the grave hill. A huge rectangular reed mat was laid on the ground. The judge's high bench was set up on the end of the mat just as it was set up in the court-hall. The bench was covered with the same piece of red brocade, which looked much brighter in the early morning sunlight. Judge Dee sat behind his bench, wearing his green shimmering brocade ceremonial robe and his black winged judge's cap. He surveyed the crowd, and his silence soon had the effect of making the crowd quiet. Sergeant Hoong and Ma Joong stood behind him. Six constables took their place, standing before the bench in two rows, three on either side.

A hardwood table stood on the mat. Four large plates of food and fruit were arranged neatly as a symbolic service for the ancestors. A pair of long, red candles was lighted as were a bundle of thin green sticks of incense in a bronze altar. Constables brought Chu Moo and Tian Han to the judge. They both knelt to kowtow, until the judge stopped them momentarily. "The session hasn't begun yet. You may stand up. We don't need such formality," Judge Dee said cheerfully. The morning breeze obviously made him more vivacious. "As I promised you yesterday, each of you will have one last chance to worship your ancestors. Now proceed. Who will be the first?"

Chu Moo stood up quickly and lighted a bundle of green sticks of incense and held it in his hand. Judge Dee observed him carefully. The burning incense sent heat waves into the air and made the man's gaunt face look a little distorted. The man knelt down again, this time in front of the hardwood table, and kowtowed. But his forehead barely touched the mat and only for a brief moment. Then he quickly rose and walked to the table. He held the thin green sticks up in the air for a few more seconds, put them down in the bronze altar, bowed slightly, and retreated.

Now it was Tian Han's turn. The food and fruit on the table had been taken away. In their place, the Tian family had put twice as much food and fruit, to show that they were more affluent and loyal to their ancestors. Tian Han lighted a bundle of thin purple sticks of incense, of better quality, imported from India. He knelt down in front of the table, just as Chu Moo had done. As he kowtowed three times, tears came to his eyes. He rose and shuffled to the table, and held up the purple sticks in the air for a long time before putting them in the altar. As he bowed he couldn't control himself, and began to rave. "Please forgive me, my dear ancestors. Next year you'll be hungry. All's my fault. How can I face you when I join you under the ground?" He collapsed in tears and refused to be moved by his servants. Judge Dee had to order the constables to intervene.

The judge rapped his bench with his gavel, although it did not sound so loud and "frightening" as in the court-hall. But even the most distant spectators could see that a scared Chu Moo had been brought back to the angry judge. "How dare you try to fool this magistrate? I checked all the tribunal files. None of my predecessors could close the case, obviously for lack of evidence. Most of them favored you, though, believing you were a poor underdog bullied for years by this rich landowner. For the same reason, I also favored you at first. But you failed me just now. This land can't be possibly yours. How do I know that? People do not worship others' ancestors, for that was an insult. When you were forced to do that, we all saw how briefly you had touched your forehead on the ground. And that's because you were uncomfortable. Now confess." Chu Moo was speechless. He did not know that his body language could have betrayed him so ruthlessly.

Turning towards the constables, the judge suddenly spoke in an unpredictably dramatic tone: "Constables!"

"Yes, Your Honor!"

"Are you there?"

"Yes, we are!" The six constables rattled their tools of torture. They seemed to understand their magistrate quite well, and their actions symbolically presented all the majestic power of a tribunal.

Chu Moo, quivering all over, confessed his crime. "Yes, I invented the scheme after I've heard from his servant that he couldn't find his deed. I even bribed a clerk to destroy the tribunal's copy. I know I deserve a thousand deaths, but please have mercy, Your Honor, for I have a ninety-year-old mother to support." He knocked his forehead on the ground, hoping to get some last-minute sympathy from the judge.

"You deserve fifty strikes." Judge Dee picked up five short rulers from his bench and threw them on the ground. Each represented ten strikes. As soon as the judge gave the order, two constables came over and pulled up Chu Moo's robe to leave his buttocks bare. In turn they struck his bare buttocks with a bamboo club that was five feet long. While the two constables were executing the punishment, Judge Dee ordered the other constables to collect rocks and stones, leaving the puzzled spectators murmuring excitedly among themselves.

When Judge Dee had decided to have the morning session in the open space instead of at the tribunal building he also had another plan, bringing both Mrs. Pengs and Lee Djao to the session as well. As soon as they knelt down in front of his bench, Judge Dee addressed the elder Peng. "This tribunal has confirmed your report. Indeed vagabonds have paid unwanted visits to your house recently. A young man named Lee Djao was identified going there the most often. I'm sure you want to teach him a lesson and stop him bothering you. As your Magistrate, I allow you to hit him with these rocks and stones. Don't worry about the consequence. Even if you killed him by accident, this tribunal would take the full responsibility. Now proceed."

The woman was startled and couldn't believe her ears. Seeing that the judge was serious, she moved reluctantly towards the rocks and stones. By the time she reached them, her mind had changed. She looked around, spat on her palms, and pretended to be angry, as if she were determined to punish the young fisherman. After a few weak tries and inevitable failures with large rocks, she picked up a handful smaller ones and threw them at Lee Djao's shoulders.

Judge Dee beckoned Ma Joong and whispered to him. Then he addressed the younger Peng. "Now it's your turn, young woman." The slender girl walked to the center of the mat. With her maximum strength she picked up the largest rock and moved to Lee Djao. Raising the heavy rock with both hands she threw it at his head. Kneeling as he was, Lee Djao had no way to dodge. In his terror, he screamed desperately: "No, Mrs. Wang!" At that very moment, Ma Joong sprang from his place behind the judge and threw himself at Lee Djao. With his left foot he kicked Lee Djao on the shoulder to push him aside. The next moment Ma Joong was squatting where the fisherman had been, holding the heavy rock above his head.

The whole crowd exclaimed with excitement. Some recognized Ma Joong's quick action as a skilled boxer's trick called "the golden cicada sneaked out of its shell." Others argued that it was "replacing the pearl with a fish eye." Most argued that it was "replacing the roof beam without notice." The argument went on, as this was part of the fun at a public gathering. People loved it.

Judge Dee had to silence the crowd with his gavel. "Enough," he said. "Lee Djao must be the paramour of the elder Peng, not the younger one. As you have all seen, the elder Peng tried not to hurt him but the younger one did just the opposite. She must have been a hindrance to the elder one at home. If I had been a little careless or lazy, and listened to her lies, the elder Peng could have sent her daughter-in-law back to her parents, and had more fun at home with Lee Djao and other vagabonds. Now everything is clear. The case of Peng vs. Peng is closed. Fifty strikes for Lee Djao and fifty for elder Peng." Judge Dee picked up the rulers from the bench as a measurement of the punishment. "This session of the Poo-yang tribunal is...." Before the word "over" came out from his mouth, his voice suddenly trailed off.

"Wait a minute! A moment ago we heard Lee Djao say 'No, Mrs. Wang,' instead of 'No, Mrs. Peng.' Now I know who killed Wang Deh-san. Bring Wang *nee* Liang and Koong Da here." A huge roar broke out from the onlookers, and Sergeant Hoong and Ma Joong stared at each other in astonishment.

Judge Dee paced around his high bench impatiently. When constables brought in Koong Da and Wang *nee* Liang, the judge resumed his seat. He rapped the bench with his gavel to quiet the crowd. "Tell us again what happened yesterday after your husband had left home at dawn."

"Yes, Your Honor. After he had left I tried to sleep, but I couldn't. About half an hour later, I heard Lee Djao's voice outside my house: 'Mrs. Wang,'"

"Wait!" the judge stopped her.

"Did he say 'Mrs. Wang' instead of 'Mr. Wang'?"

"Yes, Your Honor."

"Was that true?" Judge Dee asked Lee Djao."

"Y-yes, possibly. So what?"

"So, it is you who have murdered Wang Deh-san!"

Lee Djao's face turned ashen. The whole audience had been listening with bursting excitement. Now they could no longer hold their surprise. A big roar arose from the crowd.

Judge Dee had to use his gavel again. "You pretended that you hadn't seen Wang Deh-san that morning, but your tongue betrayed you. Knowing that only his wife was at home, you called out 'Mrs. Wang' instead of 'Mr. Wang.' How could you possibly know that he wasn't at home if you didn't murder him? You were actually pretending to fetch him at home. You should have called for 'Mr. Wang.'"

The fisherman was dumbfounded and collapsed. A constable held him up by his collar.

"Speak up!" Judge Dee roared.

The fisherman remained silent, and the judge roared again: "Constables!"

"Yes, Your Honor!"

"Are you ready?"

"Yes, we are!" Six voices responded simultaneously, and twelve feet stamped on the ground twice in turn.

"Oh, no! Please, Your Honor. I confess. Yesterday Wang Deh-san came to my boat early in the morning. While waiting for Koong Da, I saw a floating body from the north. No one pays much attention to these bodies now since there are so many of them because of the famine. I turned around and saw the heavy bundle on his back. I knew there must be silver pieces there, for he had told me that he and Koong Da were going to travel as peddlers. It suddenly occurred to me that if I killed him and pushed his body into the water, it would just float down the canal like the other one. No one would ever notice it. So I pointed behind him and said, 'Here comes Koong Da.' When he turned I hit him on the back of his head with my oar. Then I took his bundle, and pushed him off the boat."

Lee Djao finished his narrative, realizing this was probably his last public speech, and perhaps the longest in his short life. He twisted his lips and gave Judge Dee a blank stare.

"That's why you had a slip of the tongue when young Mrs. Peng threatened your life. In that frightened moment, you were confused and thought it was Wang *nee* Liang who was taking revenge on you. So, you cried: 'No, Mrs. Wang!'"

As Judge Dee concluded his deduction, the spectators all nodded in agreement. At that moment, six fishermen rushed in with three bodies. One of the fishermen panted excitedly: "Your Honor, this insignificant person is Chiao Yoo. Yesterday you ordered us to bring in bodies floating from the north. Look what we've found on the western bank of the canal!"

Wang *nee* Liang screamed hysterically as she threw herself on one of the bodies. "My husband! Take revenge for me, Your Honor."

Judge Dee stood up. "I, the magistrate of Poo-yang, now announce the conclusion of the murder case of Wang Deh-san. The murderer, Lee Djao, shall be held in jail, until our August Throne approves the death sentence. This session of the Poo-yang tribunal is closed."

The crowd cheered, but Judge Dee stood silent amidst all the noises around him, for he suddenly realized something he had never thought about before. The reed mat his high bench stood on looked very small and his high bench seemed low in the open space. This was contrary to their appearance in the magnificent tribunal building with its blue tiled roof and surrounding courtyard. The judge rubbed his eyes and looked again. Sure. All human powers seemed trivial when overshadowed by nature's magnificence. The judge inclined his head and smiled.

CHAPTER 3

▼

MAGISTRATE PAN'S
PREDICAMENT

Judge Dee's office was crowded and noisy tonight. Even the constables on duty outside the tribunal wall could hear their jovial voices inside. Two of his lieutenants, Chiao Tai and Tao Gan, had just returned from the Chin-hwa district. Judge Dee had sent them to assist its magistrate in dealing with a recent disturbance at the market place caused by a gang of pickpockets. Judge Dee's Poo-yang district was bordered on one side by the Chin-hwa district and on the other by the district of Woo-yee. While a jubilant Magistrate Lo held sway in Chin-hwa, a very strait-laced and austere Magistrate Pan administered Woo-yee. On previous occasions the two magistrates had often asked Judge Dee for his help.

The judge sat at his desk, sipping his favorite tea, "Hairy Tiptop," the product of the neighboring Anhui Province. Tao Gan, clad in a long robe of faded brown cotton and a high square cap of black gauze, described what he had done at the market in Chin-hwa. He had a long, melancholy lean face with a drooping moustache and a wispy chin beard. A mole on his left cheek sprouted three long black hairs. He walked around the room quickly and then slowly, and suddenly stopped. He crossed his arms, pretending to be a thief, and snapped his fingers under his forearm, indicating how he had just successfully picked someone's pocket. Everyone in the room laughed. Chiao Tai added that Tao Gan had actually picked the pocket of a pickpocket and let the thief apprehend him. In revenge, the angry thief had taken Tao Gan to the headquarters of the thief network nicknamed the "Mice Club." Chiao Tai had followed them and arrested all the members of the gang.

"Bravo!" Judge Dee congratulated them on a job well done. His lieutenants had both lived up to his highest expectations. Before Judge Dee met and reformed him, Tao Gan had been a swindler, thoroughly familiar with picking locks and pockets, loading dice, and forging seals. Chiao Tai and Ma Joong had been in "the green woods" and once attacked the judge and his entourage on the road outside of the nation's capital. Judge Dee had used his treasured sword to defend himself vigorously against the two highwaymen. His intrepid personality and impressive persuasion had induced them to give up their other profession then and there and volunteer to serve the judge as his devoted servants.

Sergeant Hoong served another round of tea to everyone in the room. Tea drinking had just come into fashion, and to serve the tea, people had the choice of two colored porcelain pots and cups: dark brown or light blue. Tonight, the sergeant was using the light blue pot. He poured the tea into each blue teacup, which sat on a saucer of the same color. The current fashion required a drinker to hold both the cup and the saucer. Ma Joong was not yet used to it. By the time he remembered to pick up the saucer he had already drained more than half of his tea. The sergeant looked at him in admonishment, almost as a father looking at his son. Ma Joong stuck out his tongue and made a face, to which the gray-bearded man shook his head, smiling in rebuke.

Judge Dee remained relaxed at his seat for another minute. Then, suddenly putting down his cup and saucer, he sat up in his chair, and from his spacious sleeve pocket he pulled out a folding white silk fan on a bamboo framework. He put it down on his desk and searched for something else in his sleeve pocket. This turned out to be a note in a big brown envelope.

"Magistrate Pan of the Woo-yee district sent me an urgent message this evening, requesting that I visit him immediately. I'll put Ma Joong and Chiao Tai in charge of the tribunal and go to Woo-yee tomorrow morning with Sergeant Hoong and Tao Gan. I'll be away for three days."

To Ma Joong and Chiao Tai, he added, "You may both leave now. It's very late, and you'll have an early session tomorrow." The deep friendship between the two swordsmen made them as close as blood brothers. Though not as formidable a boxer as Ma Joong, Chiao Tai was an expert archer. He had once been a loyal soldier and lieutenant in the Imperial Army, and possessed a dogged patience that was a great asset in the detection of crimes. The combination of the two made Judge Dee feel confident in putting the tribunal temporarily in their charge.

Turning to Tao Gan, the judge said, "You may leave, too. You've had a long journey today, and you need a good sleep tonight." After the three lieutenants left the office, Sergeant Hoong prepared another pot of tea for the judge, noticing that the judge was on his fifth refill. Judge Dee had become a fan of tea shortly after tea drinking came into fashion. He had recently decided upon "Hairy Tip-top" as his favorite, which had a strong flavor even after the third refill. Sergeant Hoong sat down, quietly waiting for the judge to reveal something of a more confidential nature. Experience told him that was why the judge had kept him in his office at this late hour.

"My colleague Pan is in trouble," Judge Dee said. "Three days ago, his wife found a woman's slipper in his office. It was tiny and made of reed. Later, she matched it with another one in their daughter-in-law's room. The jealous lady charged her husband with adultery, and the embarrassed young woman killed herself. Magistrate Pan hasn't been able to oversee his tribunal sessions for three days. His wife badly scratched his face and pulled off nearly half his whiskers."

"She may have jumped to conclusions too soon, but I am also wondering how the slipper of his daughter-in-law could possibly have ended up in his office," said Sergeant Hoong.

"Let's not worry about his domestic affairs for the moment. During his absence his tribunal received two cases. Three days ago, a pawnshop owner charged his widowed daughter-in-law with adultery with a young man named Lee Kuen, his next-door neighbor and a student of literature. The pawnbroker's evidence was a pair of jade plummets, usually used as decorations for folding fans. His wife had given the plummets to his son and daughter-in-law as their engagement gifts. Recently the neighboring student brought one of the plummets to the pawnshop, asking how much he could sell it for. The pawnbroker was outraged to see his family gift in the wrong hands. On the first day of Magistrate Pan's absence, the pawnbroker brought in a written complaint."

Judge Dee picked up his cup and saucer for more tea, only to find it was all gone. "Being a strait-laced man," the judge cleared his throat by making a light cough, "Magistrate Pan is usually very harsh on such a crime. Now that he himself is under the same charge, he feels disqualified to oversee such an investigation," the judge added.

Sergeant Hoong refilled the cup as Judge Dee continued his narrative. "On the second day, the wife of a traveling merchant was found dead at home. She was a pretty woman, and was holding her own kitchen knife when she had died. The vein in her left wrist had been cut, and there was lots of blood. It looked like a suicide, except that a folding fan was found on the floor with a poem on it dedicated to Lee Kuen, the student charged with adultery by the pawnbroker. This is the fan of that murder suspect." He handed over the folding fan to Sergeant Hoong.

"Ah, it's *this* Kuen, which means a giant fish that has, the legend states, turned into a bird," said Sergeant Hoong, pointing at the Chinese character that is pronounced "Kuen." "I thought it would be *another* Kuen, which means elder brother." The sergeant was referring to the student's name written on the folding fan. A cultured man carried such a folding fan throughout most of the year. The fan would be beautifully painted and drawn with handsome calligraphy, intended both as decoration and a display of the possessor's classical literary taste. Often a jade plummet was attached at the end as decoration, but not on this fan!

Sergeant Hoong stared for a while at the poem in black ink on the white silk, but was unable to make sense of the strange connection between the two cases. He returned the delicate fan of silk and bamboo, asking, "Magistrate Pan wants you to investigate the murder, doesn't he?"

"If it *is* a murder," Judge Dee said. "And the plummet theft or adultery case as well, in addition to the mystery that has led to his daughter-in-law's suicide, I must presume," the judge added, in an obvious smile of self-congratulation. "If the cases we've recently solved have taught me anything, I'd say that murder is often easier to solve than domestic cases. As the proverb says, 'Even a wise judge can hardly understand domestic affairs.' What a mess at Magistrate Pan's house now! I do believe in his innocence, for otherwise he wouldn't let me touch the case at all." Judge Dee grinned, as he reflected on his reputation as an excellent detective.

Putting his teacup and saucer on his desk, Judge Dee went into more details in the pawnbroker's case. To start with, Magistrate Pan seemed to have lost the paper upon which the case was written. He had searched everywhere, but to no avail. He remembered, however, the name of the student was Lee Kuen and the pawnbroker lived in the third house on the Third Street inside the South Gate, heading east.

"Is it possible that this is because that the pawnbroker now wants to withdraw the case? He may have either stolen the record or bribed a constable to do it for him," Sergeant Hoong suggested, as he recalled a recent case where the criminal had destroyed a tribunal file thirty years before.

"For what reason?"

"Well, let's just say that he did have an affair with his widowed daughter-in-law. He may have discovered that she also had a relationship with this neighboring student. Out of jealousy he brought the case to the tribunal. On second thought, he began to fear that a court investigation might bring his own crime to light. What do you think of that possibility, Your Honor?"

Judge Dee didn't answer. A few seconds later, he murmured to himself: "I've been wondering why everything was misplaced. First it was the slipper, then the jade plummet, and finally the folding fan was found without the plummet on it."

The night was getting late. Sergeant Hoong left the office and Judge Dee slept on his couch. When he had to work late on a case, he would sleep alone, for he hated to disturb any of his three wives. Each of them had her own apartment with her kitchen and maid. The judge would usually join them one at a time. Unless they were traveling in areas with poor accommodations, Judge Dee never slept with all three together. As a Confucian scholar and official, he thought it proper to keep things in rank and order.

Lying on his couch, Judge Dee reflected on the very different life style of his colleague. Magistrate Pan had only one wife, a daughter of a retired Prefect, whose power used to be several times stronger than that of a district magistrate. She had never allowed her husband to take a second wife. Ten years older than Judge Dee, Magistrate Pan had a twenty-year-old son who could neither read nor write. Last year his parents had married him to a dwarf about four feet tall. Unlike Judge Dee's office, Pan's was connected to the family quarters rather than the court-hall. Pan's wife did not want to give him the opportunity of being alone with another woman. She was entering menopause and easily became upset. If she was irritated, she was also quite irritating, making the life of others around her very unpleasant and miserable. Judge Dee certainly did not look forward to the day when his three wives would reach that age!

The next morning, Judge Dee set off early with Sergeant Hoong and Tao Gan. When they arrived at the city of Woo-yee, dusk was falling. Having nothing helpful to offer yet, Judge Dee did not want to meet with Magistrate Pan. Instead of staying in the guest quarters of the tribunal, the judge decided to spend the night at an inn.

A banner of blue brocade was hung outside the inn's front door. "Best Home, Not at Home," was the name of the inn. As they checked in, Judge Dee noticed it was a tidy, cozy place with but a few guests at the moment. Breakfast would be served in the dining room and was included in the price. The innkeeper, a middle-aged man with a round face, bowed low and politely to the judge, even though Judge Dee had deliberately concealed his identity. He ordered a room with double bed for himself and Sergeant Hoong, and a room with single bed for Tao Gan, which surprised not only the innkeeper but also the sergeant and Tao

Gan. "This fellow snores terribly at night," the judge explained to the innkeeper. They all laughed.

Judge Dee and his two associates settled down in the room with the double bed. As soon as the servant who had brought in a pot of hot tea left the room, the judge said: "I'm afraid you won't be able to put your room to good use tonight, Tao Gan. I want you to pay a secret visit to the pawnbroker's house after midnight. See how it is connected with that of his neighbor, the student. I'm particularly interested in the structure of the building and any possible hidden access between the two houses. Also, find out how far away the dead woman's house is."

Tao Gan smiled, playfully twisting the long drooping hairs on his cheek. Having been a swindler before, he really enjoyed this type of spying. As he stood up to leave for his own room to take a nap in anticipation of a long night of work, he took a large bronze coin with a square hole in the middle out of his pocket, and casually tossed up in the air. As it fell, he raised his head and caught the coin securely on the tip of his nose. Judge Dee laughed with Sergeant Hoong. The deftness of the reformed swindler was truly amazing, and entertained both of them enormously.

After Tao Gan left the room, Judge Dee took out the folding fan from his sleeve pocket. Slowly he unfolded it, carefully studying the poem on it. There was little doubt it was about Taoism:

You can't say that Tao exists
And you can't say that Tao does not exist
But you can find it in the silence
When you no longer bother with important deeds.

As a Confucian scholar and official, Judge Dee didn't think very highly of either Taoism or Buddhism, more especially the latter. He thought that most people who believed in these religions were either lazy or simply stupid. But even the most intelligent scholars sometimes felt attracted to the wisdom in these religions. For example, the poem on the fan seemed to excuse those readers who had not troubled to study Taoism while their careers took so much of their time; yet, the poem seemed also to imply that they would enjoy it more later on. How clever! The dialectical wisdom in the poem was typical of Taoism, and Judge Dee admired that aspect of Taoism very much.

Comforted by the hope of finding Tao eventually, Judge Dee quickly fell sound asleep. When he woke early next morning, sunlight was already streaming into his bedroom, warming him. He awoke to yet another bit of Taoist wisdom, embedded in the name of the inn, "Best Home, Not at Home." How accurate! Judge Dee thought. Indeed, the more he appreciated Taoist wisdom, the less comfortable he was with the assumption that the poem on the fan could have been dedicated to a young student, whose shallow experience and low status hardly matched the sophistication of the writing. To advance in such a professional career, the student had to pass many exams in literature. The more exams he passed the higher the office he would gain. Yet, he had just begun such "important deeds." Why would the poet dedicate such writing to Lee Kuen?

Judge Dee and Sergeant Hoong had a casual breakfast in the dining room. The judge's favorite was a deep-fried, slightly salted rice cake with no sugar, crunchy outside and soft inside. A man of about thirty was setting up a small table at the other end of the room. A placard hanging from the table read "Mr. Wang with the Magic Pen," indicating that he was a scribe and accountant. The man had a pale and rather reserved face. His old cotton robe had rectangular patches on the elbows to cover the holes. He's probably even too poor to have a wife, who would have made the patches oval and more attractive, thought Judge Dee. Just then, Tao Gan returned to the inn. His face appeared pale under the sunlight of the early morning. As soon as he sat down at the table, Sergeant Hoong served him a cup of tea. Tao Gan swallowed the tea in a few quick gulps and wiped his lips with the back of his hand.

"The houses are attached and share the same beams. I think they were built as one but later split into two. I didn't find any hidden access connecting them. Each has two bedrooms, one in the front, and one in the back. Both the young man and the widow live in the two front rooms."

"Isn't that odd?" Judge Dee asked. "Most thoughtful parents would put their widowed daughter-in-law in the back and take the front one themselves. Similarly, Lee Kuen should have slept in the back and made use of the front one as a study or a sitting room." Judge Dee fell silent as he reflected on his own question.

All of a sudden, an exclamation by Sergeant Hoong burst forth. The gray-bearded man pointed at the wall behind the judge, speechless. The poem on the fan was copied on the dining room wall! Judge Dee understood that scholars loved to leave their poems behind as they traveled and stayed at inns. He quickly opened the folding fan from his capacious sleeve pocket. One glance was enough: although the poem was indeed the same, the handwriting was not. Just as he was about to question the innkeeper, he thought better of it. He turned to Tao Gan and whispered: "Let's go to the other place first, and we'll visit the pawnbroker's house later."

As they were checking out, the innkeeper gave them a great smile, wishing them good luck and prosperity. "I wish," remarked Judge Dee casually, "that I no longer have need to bother with important deeds." Seeing the perplexed face of the innkeeper, he quickly added, "so that I could find Tao, of course." He pointed his finger to the dining room wall where the Taoist poem was written.

"I see," the innkeeper said cheerfully, the professional smile working its way back up his face. "I too wish I could retire early, so that I could join him traveling. That Taoist priest has left many poems in my inn. He wrote that one last week. A truly remarkable man! He looks fifty, but people say he is already over seventy. He stops by once a year, and no one knows much more about him."

"What an enviable life, indeed!" Judge Dee caressed his long side-whiskers and fell into deep thought.

✳   ✳   ✳   ✳

The traveling merchant's house was at the northeast corner of the city. Two constables stood guard at the front. Sergeant Hoong showed them Judge Dee's official card. "On behalf of your Magistrate Pan, I am now in charge of the murder investigation," the judge added quickly and presented Magistrate Pan's letter. The constables bowed low, and respectfully opened the door.

Judge Dee was shown into the kitchen where the woman's body had been found. A chilly breeze was blowing in through a small opened window. Judge Dee glanced at the window and heard a constable's voice behind his shoulder: "We let in the air to blow away the smell, Your Honor." Judge Dee nodded, with a smile. He liked this young constable who seemed smart enough to anticipate his questions. The judge turned around and asked: "When was the murder reported, and by whom?"

"The warden of the northeast quarter reported the murder three days ago. Our magistrate was absent during the morning session. The clerk wrote down the case and later passed it on to him. He sent us here with the coroner. The victim held a knife in her hand. Her vein was cut open, and we saw lots of blood on her evening robe and on the kitchen floor. The coroner tried to lift her arm, but it had completely stiffened and he said she must have died before midnight. I found a knife missing in the kitchen, and her neighbors all agreed that it was the knife in her hand. They said her husband had left on a business trip two weeks ago, and before leaving he had asked them to look after her. Each morning, she and the neighboring women went grocery shopping together. They discovered her body when they came to her door. Oh, I nearly forgot. The door was open when they came. I checked behind it and found a folding fan."

Judge Dee paced around in the room, his hands behind his back. The report from the young constable was admirably succinct. For a brief moment, the judge did not know what questions he wanted to ask. There seemed no more information to be collected. As he stopped at the window and looked out, a gust of chilly wind hit him full in the face. "How could I have overlooked *that* detail!" he exclaimed. Momentarily, his face lit up, but quickly he fell into somber contemplation.

As the judge left the house, Sergeant Hoong and Tao Gan quietly followed. The somber face of the judge made the two remain in utter silence. They both knew that the judge hated to be disturbed while he was trying to work out his theories. He only briefly emerged from his deep thought to hire a palanquin, and instructed the bearers to carry him across the city to the pawnbroker's house.

Sergeant Hoong knocked on the door and presented the judge's official card. Only a glimpse of it made the man at the door fall onto his knees and kowtow on the floor. "We're not in the tribunal and I'm not your magistrate. There's no need for formality," Judge Dee said. "I came on behalf of Magistrate Pan. Tell me about the case against your neighbor."

"My neighbor! I wish I had never taken him as a tenant."

"Isn't it odd that he sleeps in the front bedroom?" asked the judge casually.

"You must be a god from Heaven who knows everything everywhere on this earth!" The pawnbroker exclaimed. "Three months ago, my daughter-in-law mentioned that the young student next door often stayed up late. She could hear him recite from his books at midnight. They were both using the bedrooms at the back then. My wife suggested that we move our daughter-in-law to the front, in case something brewing between them. You know how difficult it is to ensure that a widow remains a widow. Too many temptations! I'm not a Confucian, but I would like to see her follow his teachings and remain faithful to my late son. We moved her, but that bastard followed!"

Having heard her husband mention her, the pawnbroker's wife appeared at the door with a pot of tea in her hand. It was just in time, for the judge had found himself quite thirsty. The woman, clad in a plain brown robe, was evidently quite thoughtful; she refrained from meeting with other males, even visiting officials. As Judge Dee returned the empty teacup with the saucer, his impression of the woman was positive.

"How could you be so sure that Lee Kuen had *your* jade plummet, not someone else's?" Judge Dee said, resuming his interrogation of the pawnbroker.

"Believe me, Your Honor. As you probably know, these plummets are not very expensive, but each pair is unique. You have to keep the pair together. Once you lose a piece, you'll never be able to match it. That's why parents use them as love symbols for their sons and daughter-in-laws. The infamous woman in our house must have given a piece to Lee Kuen, and the bastard had the nerve trying to sell it back in my own shop! When my wife asked about the plummets, the bitch said she couldn't find them. That's just a lie; she must still have the other one. Your Honor should search her room and her body, if I may suggest. I'm sure you'll find it somewhere." The man licked his lips as he imagined the sensation of searching her body. From the adjacent bedroom came a young woman's weeping. "There you go. She is going to make a scene again," the wife complained.

The hostility of the couple towards their daughter-in-law made Judge Dee feel quite sorry for the young widow. His instinct told him that she must be beautiful and that her in-laws had perceived her beauty as a threat. If the strait-laced Magistrate Pan should oversee the investigation, he would quite likely believe her to be guilty. On the other hand, if this had been a case tried by Magistrate Lo, who loved every beautiful woman he met, he would give her all the latitude possible! While Judge Dee was thus reflecting upon the potential unfairness in the law and its enforcement, he noticed a smile on Sergeant Hoong's face, indicating that the gray-bearded man appeared to be thinking on the same lines and knew what the judge was contemplating. Tao Gan, to the contrary, didn't seem to have a clue what was going on in the judge's mind. It was amazing how differently human minds worked.

"Can we ask her to join us here?" Judge Dee asked politely, as he knew this was not a tribunal session.

"Certainly," the pawnbroker eagerly nodded, wiping the corner of his mouth with his right thumb. He hadn't seen her for a while. Following Confucian rules, they had been avoiding seeing each other, even though they were living under the same roof. His wife left the room and returned shortly with a plainly clad woman of about twenty years old. Judge Dee overheard Tao Gan whisper to Sergeant Hoong behind his back: "Look what Ma Joong missed today. That's the price he pays for being in charge of our Poo-yang tribunal!" The judge had to agree that she was extraordinarily beautiful: her skin exceptionally white and delicate.

"When was the last time you saw your jade plummets?" Judge Dee asked the young woman.

"I can't remember," she wiped her tears on her cheeks with her sleeves. "I always put them above the beam in the roof so that no one else can touch them. They are the only things I have to connect me with my late husband. When my mother-in-law asked, they were not there."

"Is anything else missing in your room?"

"Not really." Glancing at the elder woman, she added: "But recently I noticed that things had been moved around quite a bit."

"What do you mean? I've never touched any of your stuff," the pawnbroker's wife snapped.

The young woman kept her head down, not looking at anyone in the room.

Judge Dee began to have a theory. He had always wondered why and how so many things had been misplaced. The young woman's words reinforced his suspicion. In a casual and friendly tone, he spoke to the pawnbroker, "I'm going to suggest that my lieutenant Tao Gan help you move your daughter-in-law to the back of the house."

"Meanwhile, young lady," he turned to the beautiful young widow, "don't forget to show my lieutenant what has been moved around. He has a special talent, and may help you find the plummets. By the way, do you often hear the neighboring student recite from his books late at night?"

"Yes, Your Honor. Every night."

"Really? Let's see. Today is the fifth. How late was he studying on the night of the first moon?"

The young woman counted her fingers and thought for a while. "That night he was reciting an essay by Confucius on the importance of being moderate. I remember this clearly because at the same moment I heard our night watchman knock his stick on the street to announce midnight."

"I see," Judge Dee nodded, and turned to Tao Gan. "Sergeant Hoong and I will be back soon. Hopefully you will be finished by then."

To the pawnbroker the judge said, "We'll now visit your neighbor, or tenant, which you call him. By the way, why didn't you call him your tenant when you brought the case to the tribunal?"

"It's Mr. Wang's idea, Your Honor. You know, there is a scribe at the inn named 'Best Home, Not a Home.'"

Judge Dee and Sergeant Hoong glanced at each other.

"I had asked him to write out the case for me, for I heard the magistrate was ill and would only have the clerk to write the case. I didn't trust the clerk," the pawnbroker hesitated a second, "because once I didn't give him a square deal, and he may still remember that."

"You said it's Wang's idea to put in the word 'neighbor' instead of 'tenant'?" Judge Dee asked.

"Yes. He said that sounded better, for I might have to share certain responsibility if I had taken in a bad tenant."

"True. For Heaven's sake, you've been well advised." Judge Dee abruptly finished his interrogation and went to see the student next door. When he was no longer interested in something or somebody, the judge began the next task.

Although his late father had often admonished him for such impoliteness, his behavior never changed.

As they walked to the next door Judge Dee whispered to Sergeant Hoong: "Now that we know the pawnbroker took the trouble to ask a scribe to write the case for him, your earlier speculation seems less plausible. Our stay at the inn has fortunately advanced our inquiry. But sooner or later I would have gotten that scribe's name from the pawnbroker. I hate to think that I could solve this case by depending on luck!"

Before Sergeant Hoong could ask any further questions they were at Lee Kuen's door. Judge Dee's visit took the young man completely by surprise. He appeared at the front door, wearing a square black cap and a plain house robe. The young student barely had any furniture in his room, and apparently had not expected any visitors. The judge looked at him for a moment and thought that in the eyes of the prudish Magistrate Pan, this handsome young man could easily qualify as a suspect in adultery. Judge Dee introduced himself, telling the student that he was a suspect of both adultery and murder. The young man was dumbfounded. "You charge me with adultery, *and* murder? I've been studying hard, and don't have the time! In three months, I'll take the exam."

Judge Dee ignored his naïve defense and asked, "Why do you live in the front bedroom instead of the back one?"

The young man blushed. "I often stay up late. I have a feeling that someone is listening from the other side of the wall when I'm reciting from my books. The old couple living next door might think I'm seducing their daughter-in-law. I don't want to get into trouble. So I recently moved. But she seems to have followed me."

"Can you explain why you had her jade plummet?" Judge Dee asked.

"So that *is* hers? Wait a minute. You mentioned a murder a moment ago. You don't mean she is dead, do you?" the young man asked anxiously, searching for something in his sleeve pocket.

Judge Dee ignored his question and shouted: "How did you get it? I'm asking you."

"I found it in my bedroom. I have no idea where it came from," the young man muttered, producing a jade plummet from his sleeve pocket and handing it over to the judge. Judge Dee took a good long look at it and returned it to Lee Kuen.

"Show me where you found it."

The young man led the judge into his bedroom and pointed at a spot on the floor. Judge Dee looked up and found it was right below the wooden beam that extended into the pawnbroker's house. He nodded and smiled.

"When did you receive this gift from the old Taoist priest?" He took out the fan from his sleeve pocket and unfolded it to show the young man his name on it.

"I've never seen that before!" the young man exclaimed. "Who put my name on it? Why?"

Judge Dee smiled again. Enough was enough.

"Forget about everything I've said. Pretend we have never met. Go back to your studies and prepare for your exams." Once again, Judge Dee abruptly finished his interrogation and left the house. Sergeant Hoong gave the young man a bitter smile, as if to apologize for the judge's brusque behavior.

"I'm famished!" Judge Dee exclaimed. "Me too," the sergeant said as he followed the judge to the street. It was nearly three o'clock, and lunch hour was almost over. They quickly went to the nearest restaurant where they had to settle for six deep-fried scallion-pancakes, the only entrees still available.

"Please save two for our friend Tao Gan," the judge instructed before he devoured his first pancake. After finishing his own first one, the sergeant asked: "What's our next step?"

"Our next step?" the judge raised his eyebrows.

"What shall we do about the mystery of the murder?"

"There is no mystery anymore." Looking at Sergeant Hoong from under his bushy eyebrows, the judge blinked with a smile. "Don't you see that all our problems have been solved?"

Sergeant Hoong stared at the judge, disbelieving his own ears. The judge went on quickly, "The murder was an accident. The intruder only intended rape. With the darkness of the night of the first moon he thought he would hide his own identity. He knew she wouldn't tell anybody about it, not even her husband. But he knew she would take revenge if she knew who did it. To fool her, he brought a folding fan and deliberately left it behind the door after he had made his way inside her house. He had copied the poem on the fan as if it were dedicated to the student. He thought this was a perfect setup, and that the woman would think a man named Lee Kuen had raped her. He overlooked one thing. Spring has just arrived, and it is still much too cool and too early for a man to carry a folding fan. I have to admit that I myself overlooked this fact until a chilly gust of wind blew while I was standing behind the window at the woman's kitchen." Sergeant Hoong nodded vigorously as the judge unveiled his theory. "Then why the murder?" the sergeant still had his doubt.

"Having detected a stranger inside her own house, she bravely tried to defend herself, and ran to her kitchen for her knife. Unfortunately, the man grabbed her from behind. He struggled to take her knife from her right hand by stretching her right arm in front. As she desperately tried to hold her knife and used all of her strength to move backward, she exceeded his grasp for a brief moment, and accidentally cut the vein on her left wrist. The cut was much too deep, and made her bleed to death. He immediately ran away, and forgot about the folding fan he had brought to fool her and set up the student. With her dead he shouldn't have left any trace behind. But he didn't have the time to think things through, and therefore betrayed himself."

"Who is the man then?"

"It can't be the student, for he was reciting Confucius at home till midnight, if we can trust the young widow. And he lives far away from the victim's house. For the same reason, it can't be the pawnbroker. He didn't have time to be away from home without his wife taking notice. The fact that it is still too cool to carry a folding fan excludes the possibility of a long-standing adultery. I once suspected that she might have killed herself after her lover had broken her heart. That's why at first I wasn't sure there was a murder at all. After I heard that the pawnbroker had asked the scribe to write the case for him, I began to have a new theory. The poem on the fan is a convenient setup. The criminal knows that she, as a married woman, will never stay at the local inn to see the poem. But sooner or later she would likely hear that Lee Kuen was involved in a current tribunal investigation. It's quite easy to blame the same person for more than one crime, and she would believe Lee Kuen was the man who came to rape her. So the question to me became quite simple and straightforward: Who set the student up? Only one man has enough information to do so, and that is…"

"The scribe?" asked the sergeant, holding his hand on his chest to calm his palpitation.

"Exactly. Only he knows how to write Lee Kuen's name correctly. When the pawnbroker asked for his help, others might have overheard the name. But to know how to write his name is a completely different matter. Just as you said before, it could be the character that means a fish or the one that means a brother."

"So, it *is* him," murmured the sergeant. "How long ago did you figure *that* out?"

"I'd almost completed my theory as we knocked at Lee Kuen's door. I just needed to verify a few minor points," the judge concluded, quite satisfied. He then set things quickly in motion. "Go to see Magistrate Pan with my visiting card. Tell him to hold the scribe for interrogation. I'm going back to the pawn-broker's house to see how our friend Tao Gan is doing. You may stay in the tribunal and wait for me there. We'll stay in its guest quarters tonight."

"Your Honor," Sergeant Hoong felt he could no longer withhold his question, "why haven't you started any work on Magistrate Pan's domestic case yet?"

"How could I?" Judge Dee retorted somewhat bitterly. "I can hardly interrogate either the magistrate or his wife. She is the daughter of a retired Prefect. I bet she has been at her parents' house since the reed slipper was found in her husband's office."

"Then how are you going to solve the case?" Sergeant Hoong asked.

"Maybe I won't. But I have a feeling that the two adultery cases are quite similar. If I can solve the jade plummet case, the reed slipper case may get solved as well," Judge Dee winked, caressing his long side-whiskers.

*   *   *   *

Judge Dee returned to the pawnbroker's house with the scallion pancakes for Tao Gan. The latter quickly reported his findings while devouring his food. He had found a plummet in a spider web at a corner of a wall. The dust made it hard to notice, although the dangling web was right beneath the wooden beam that extended to Lee Kuen's house. Judge Dee exclaimed. "Ah ha! I got you." Three tiny black balls of mice dung lay mutely in his palm. "Mice moved the plummets over to Lee Kuen's house and into this corner as well."

Turning to the pawnbroker, Judge Dee said: "I suppose that you'll withdraw your case, won't you?" The man licked his dry lips and nodded reluctantly. Judge Dee wished he could see the happy face of the young widow, but she wasn't in the room. With a triumphant mood, the judge left the house with Tao Gan and headed for the tribunal.

Magistrate Pan stood up promptly as he saw the tall figure of Judge Dee. He bade him to sit down in a large chair opposite his desk. "Ah, ha! At last I have the pleasure of receiving you as my honored guest." His exaggerated tone made his welcome sound a bit artificial. Sergeant Hoong was already in the room. Now he stood with Tao Gan behind their master. "You helped me solve the death puzzle already. Please let me hear your wisdom on these other two cases as well," Magistrate Pan said.

"Well," Judge Dee said, "as far as I know, the pawnbroker will soon withdraw his case against Lee Kuen. I spoke with him before I came here."

"What?" Magistrate Pan couldn't withhold his surprise. "You've persuaded him to drop the case? How did you do that?"

Instead of answering the question, Judge Dee asked his own: "Where exactly did your wife find the reed slipper?"

"My humble woman never told me," Pan sighed, crestfallen.

That was exactly the effect Judge Dee had wanted to achieve. He let the silence linger in the room. Suddenly, in a deliberately loud voice, he began to talk about the other case. "The sole evidence of the pawnbroker was that the young widow had lost her plummets. Here is what we found. Mice have moved them. One was pushed over to Lee Kuen's house, and we found the other one dangling in a spider web. The only criminals are the mice."

"The mice!" exclaimed Magistrate Pan, putting a hand on his forehead, carefully avoiding the side of his face where his skin was still burned from his torn whiskers. "Of course. That must be it. I've had mice since I moved in this house. The whole town must have mice."

"In that case, I suggest you permit my lieutenant Tao Gan to search your place, if you don't mind," Judge Dee said.

"Of course not, but why…. Oh! My…." Magistrate Pan's voice trailed off as he realized what Judge Dee was up to.

Tao Gan took action promptly. He squatted down at a corner of a wall but soon stood up again. He beckoned to the judge to come over. Judge Dee rose and invited Magistrate Pan to come with him. Standing behind Tao Gan they could see a hole in the wall, just big enough for the sleeper of a short woman.

"May I?" Judge Dee asked.

"Go ahead, please," said Magistrate Pan.

Judge Dee kicked the hole with his boots and enlarged it by two inches. "Proceed until you have reached the other end of the tunnel," he ordered. Tao Gan took out a special knife from his pocket and began to work.

"Let us know when you find something interesting," Judge Dee said cheerfully.

Both he and Magistrate Pan sat down, waiting for the result. "Please forgive me for being a bad host." Magistrate Pan clapped his hands and spoke to the servant who came to the door. "Tell the kitchen staff to send in dinner for our distinguished guests."

Tao Gan came and placed a piece of paper on the desk, and then poured a handful of tiny black balls of mice dung on top.

"My goodness! Where did you find that?" asked Magistrate Pan.

"The tunnel led me to a room that your servant said belonged to your son and daughter-in-law. I would say it was the mice that had moved her slipper here," said Tao Gan, twisting the few long black hairs that sprouted from the mole on his cheek.

"He is right. A reed slipper is light enough for mice to move, and people only wear such footwear in the summer, giving many opportunities for the 'crime'. As for motivation," Judge Dee smiled, "I really don't know, but presumably a reed slipper could serve some purpose for the mice to build their house."

"For Heaven's sake! I'm saved, both for my career and marriage!" Magistrate Pan exclaimed, "I can't care less for the motivation of mice."

He stared at the mice dung and then at the paper, which had many holes in it. "Why," he exclaimed again. "Isn't this what the pawnbroker brought in? I've looked everywhere, but just couldn't find it.",

Judge Dee picked up the paper and waved it at Magistrate Pan. "I believe this is written in the same handwriting as that on this fan." He pulled the fan out from his sleeve pocket and unfolded it. "Now you can see for yourself. Time for me to return it anyway."

Turning to Sergeant Hoong, Judge Dee pointed at the student's given name, Kuen, written both on the paper and the folding fan. "What did I tell you? Only the scribe knew how to set up the student, correctly writing the *character*." Judge Dee tapped on "Kuen" that meant a fish, not a brother.

The door opened as servants began to bring in dinner dishes. Magistrate Pan said to Judge Dee: "You must let me prepare a formal banquet for you tomorrow, celebrating your quick solutions of all the cases that have brought you here."

Judge Dee smiled, "I'm afraid I'll have to leave in early morning, for I've promised my other lieutenants that I would be home by tomorrow night. But I'll leave Sergeant Hoong and Tao Gan behind, if you want. They may enjoy your hospitality on my behalf and help you write up the cases for the tribunal file. When you write to the Honorable Prefect to send for your wife, feel free to use me as a witness of what we have discovered here today." Magistrate Pan sighed, "My poor children! They've been married for only a year."

On his way home alone the following morning, Judge Dee couldn't help but think of the young beautiful widow and the handsome student. The two seemed a perfect match. But the sacred social order based on Confucian doctrines made it very difficult, if not impossible, for a widow to remarry. The young man would do just fine. As long as he passed his exams and got appointed to an office, he would easily find another beautiful young woman for a wife. The widow, however, would have a long way to go. Especially with her exceptional beauty, her life would be full of temptations, perhaps particularly from her father-in-law, who was obviously a weak, if not wicked, character.

Judge Dee sighed and shook his head. Beauty might not be a good thing, either to the individual who had it, or to the society at large. No wonder it was a Taoist warning that "when everyone saw beauty in the beautiful, it was already ugly." Maybe the Confucian way of controlling the temptation of such beauty within a household was the best way to handle it. Or, was it really?

It was Magistrate Pan's predicament that had brought Judge Dee to Woo-yee. Now, on his way back to Poo-yang, the judge found himself in yet another predicament. Reflecting upon the large social and moral dilemma, he found that he had lost quite a substantial part of the satisfaction he would otherwise take in solving three such puzzling cases all in one day.

CHAPTER 4

▼

THE MAGIC POT

After a simple dinner of rice and sweet soup, Judge Dee and his three wives started a game of dominoes in the dining room. The four of them sat around a square table, engrossed in the game, while the candle light on the table silhouetted their figures on the walls. Beyond the warmly lighted room, everything had turned pitch black.

The First Lady sat opposite the judge. She had an oval, regular face. A well-tailored robe of blue and white embroidered silk showed off her figure, still well formed for a woman of thirty-nine. Her hair was done elegantly, drawn up in three heavy coils, and fixed by a thin gold hairpin. She looked at her dominoes quite pensively, much absorbed in the game.

The Second Lady sat to Judge Dee's right. Hers was a pleasant, homely face; her hair was done up in much simpler coil to the back of her head. She wore a jacket of violet silk over a white robe. Although not well educated, she was shrewd enough, and supervised the household accounts. Both she and the First Lady had been married to Judge Dee at the same time twenty years before. Judge Dee's father had arranged the two marriages to help improve the prospect of having at least a son to carry the family name Dee. The judge had had no children for seven years when his Second Lady gave birth to a girl. He had almost given up hope when his First Lady finally delivered him a son eleven years after their marriage.

The judge had been married to his Third Lady for just six years. At the time, he was serving as the Magistrate of Peng-lai, his first appointment by the Emperor. She and the judge now had a three years old son. The judge had put her in charge of teaching all his children, for she had had an excellent education in classics. Her own personal interests were mainly in art and calligraphy. She had her hair done in an elaborate high chignon, which gave profile to her tender, finely chiseled face. She sat to Judge Dee's left, wearing a long-sleeved gown of blue silk with a red sash under the bosom.

It was pleasant and convenient to have four people always ready to play dominoes. Judge Dee and his three wives particularly enjoyed the especially complicated form of the dominoes that they were playing, and they took it very seriously. Half an hour had passed while the four were immersed in the game. Several maids brought in fresh tea, watermelon seeds, and various dried fruits, but the four players had paid little attention, as they approached the final and decisive phase of their first round.

Slowly stroking his black beard, Judge Dee calculated his chances, which appeared meager; in his hand, he held a three and a blank. He did remember clearly that all the other threes had already been played, and that one double blank remained. One of his wives must be holding it back. If he could force it out, he might take the win.

"Make your move!" Judge Dee said impatiently to his Second Lady, who was prolonging her hesitation with distracting questions while patting her glossy black coiffure. She put a double four on the table.

"Pass!" said the judge, inclining his head, much disappointed.

"I pass, too," the Third Lady said, winking at the judge.

"I win!" The First Lady called out excitedly. She threw out her dominoes, a four and a five, and rapped on the table triumphantly with her knuckles.

"Congratulations!" the judge exclaimed, somewhat thinly, as he was packing up his own pieces. "Who's been holding that double blank? I've been looking for it for a while."

"Not I!" His Second Lady announced as she uncovered her last domino. Judge Dee turned to stare at his Third Lady, who then quietly uncovered hers. It was the double blank. She smiled mischievously, having deliberately kept what she knew Judge Dee had so badly needed in order to ensure a win by his First Lady. Such clever subterfuge helped make the game more fun; it kept his First Lady happy, and yet would not irritate the Second Lady. His Third Lady was not only the youngest and the most beautiful of his wives, but also the most talented and best educated. And most importantly, both as a woman and wife, she was lively and deft.

The game having ended, everyone started eating the snacks and drinking the fresh pots of tea that had been ignored during the game. The quiet atmosphere in the room was interrupted when Sergeant Hoong arrived saying a constable was waiting outside at the doorway to report the presence of Magistrate Lo of the neighboring Chin-hwa district. This was indeed quite a surprise, as visitors were hardly to be expected at such a late hour.

"Show him into my office as soon as you see the lamps are on," Judge Dee said, and the constable returned to the visitor at the entrance of the tribunal.

"And he is not alone," Sergeant Hoong added quickly in the corridor after the constable had left. "Magistrate Lo has brought two men with him, but he said he doesn't know them. One of them had robbed him on his way here. But since it was so dark, he couldn't tell which one was the robber and which one had helped him to catch the robber, and now the two men are accusing each other of the crime."

As Sergeant Hoong followed the judge along the roofed corridor, he whispered that Magistrate Lo was incognito, that is, not in his official dress. Judge Dee shook his head, smiling. He felt quite sure why his colleague would visit his district in the evening under disguise. Poo-yang was a flourishing town of about twelve thousand people, and there were many young, attractive courtesans.

Soon after Sergeant Hoong had lighted the oil lamp on the desk in Judge Dee's private office, the constable escorted the plainly dressed guest into the room. The magistrate from Chin-hwa was portly; his hands were pudgy and his pointed moustache and wispy short beard made his face look even rounder than it actually was. Once settled in Judge Dee's office, Magistrate Lo spoke in a contrite tone, "I do apologize for interrupting your evening like this, Elder Brother."

"No. Not at all! It's I who should apologize that you've suffered such a robbery in *my* territory. Could you please elaborate on it to help me solve the case?" Judge Dee asked, looking at Magistrate Lo directly in the eye.

"I was walking near your Drum Tower in the northeast corner, looking for a restaurant, although there didn't seem to be one in that neighborhood and I wasn't really that hungry. Anyway, it was dinnertime and getting dark outside. Someone from behind surprised me and took all my money. At that moment, another man passed by and saw what was happening. The robber ran off and the other chased him. When I caught up with them a few minutes later, they were accusing each other of the robbery. My money lay on the ground between them. I couldn't see the features of the men very well because of the dark. So I couldn't identify which was the robber, and who had helped me catch him! But I'm sure one of them is the thief. I suggested that we see the magistrate, and they dared not to refuse. Both men are here, and surely you will figure out who is the thief."

"Where are they now?" Judge Dee asked, excited by both the challenge and the fact that his colleague had so much confidence in him.

"Our constables are holding them," Sergeant Hoong answered.

"I shall interrogate them publicly in the morning session tomorrow," Judge Dee said to Magistrate Lo. "As you know, the Imperial law requires that such investigation be kept public." Turning to Sergeant Hoong, the judge ordered, "Put them both temporarily in the jail for tonight." Then to the constable, he said: "Go to the nearest restaurant, order the best food, and bring it here as quickly as you can. Magistrate Lo must be quite hungry."

"Not really," Magistrate Lo waved his hand with a troubled sigh, but the constable had already left. Glancing at Sergeant Hoong, the portly man hesitated, opening his mouth but failed to speak. "Sergeant Hoong is my most confidential advisor. You can trust him as you trust me," said Judge Dee. "Elder Brother! I'm in trouble, bi-big trouble!" Magistrate Lo spoke in a broken voice. He covered his face with his sleeves and bowed deeply to Judge Dee. When the rotund fellow removed his sleeves, Judge Dee noticed that his eyes were full of tears. "Come on. You're always a joyous fellow. What is this all about?" Judge Dee asked.

"Two days a ago, a farmer reported to my tribunal that he had discovered a big pot full of gold buried in his cotton field. He also found a note with a royal seal on it. And it says whoever finds the treasure must return it immediately to the royal coffers. I asked him to bring me the gold and sent a constable to go with him. I instructed the constable to secure the gold in my office. In fact, I saw the farmer and his brother carry the pot in, using a bamboo shoulder-pole."

In a few quick gulps Magistrate Lo drank down the cup of tea that Sergeant Hoong had served him, and then continued: "I was much too busy yesterday, and nearly forgot about the gold. This morning, looking at the pot I thought of bringing it to our Prefect. But I was dumbfounded. All the gold has turned into dirt! The clods were each molded in the shape of horseshoes and painted just like real gold, but I could break them easily with my hands. And the royal note was still there, mocking me. How can I bring the pot to our Prefect? It is a capital crime to tamper with royal gold. And how many heads do I have? Not more than one, for sure." Absorbed in the recounting of his troubles, the portly magistrate somehow found his usual sense of humor returned.

"The whole tribunal was quite excited when the farmer reported the gold, and a large crowd witnessed it as he and his brother carried the pot to my office.

Rumors will soon spread if I do not pass the gold along to our Prefect. I desperately need to solve this case before the rumors reach his ears. Luckily no one yet knows that the gold has turned into dirt. And I certainly do not want anyone to know! I come here because you're my only hope." Magistrate Lo sobbed as he bowed again, nervously moving his rotund body.

Judge Dee felt terribly sorry for his colleague, who had the reputation for enjoying life with beautiful women. Probably no one had even noticed his nocturnal absence from Chin-hwa, for everyone just assumed he was somewhere enjoying the company of another courtesan.

"Who has access to your office?" Judge Dee asked.

"No one," Magistrate Lo answered. "I put a new lock on the door after the gold was stored there, and I have the only key."

The constable returned with a large bucket in his right hand, keeping the dinner ordered for Magistrate Lo warm. In his left hand, he held a small round folding table. He put the bucket on the floor before he could unfold the table, and then he began to move the plates from the bucket onto the table. There were four delicious dishes: a smoked fish, honey short ribs, "beggar's chicken," and red glutinous rice with dates and beans wrapped in fresh green lotus leaves. The constable quietly helped his over-weighted guest sit down at the table. Judge Dee also sat at the table, intending no more than to be polite, as he had already had his dinner. The delicious smell however, made him hungry again. Without hesitation, he started to eat and soon consumed nearly half of the food. His guest, to the contrary, ate almost nothing. The royal decree had terrified him as a sword hanging over his head, and had ruined his appetite.

Stroking his long side-whiskers, Judge Dee murmured to Magistrate Lo: "I must assume you've brought the royal note with you."

"Yes," Magistrate Lo produced a piece of paper from his sleeve pocket and gave it to the judge. Judge Dee lit a second oil lamp on his desk, to better examine the note. The vermilion seal argued for its authenticity; a field of scattered flecks of gold glittering on it underlined its value. The writing itself was done in thick, glossy black ink. The quality of the ink further underscored the royal status of the note. There was no doubt that it was genuine. Judge Dee comprehended the gravity of the matter now. He drank the tea in his cup in one long gulp, draining it to its very last drop.

As he collected himself, Judge Dee decided upon the following arrangement. Sergeant Hoong should accompany Magistrate Lo to the guest quarters at the tribunal for the night. The next morning, Chiao Tai and Tao Gan would go to the Chin-hwa district with Magistrate Lo and bring back the pot with all the horseshoe-shaped clods in it. Judge Dee wanted to have a careful look at this allegedly magical pot that had turned the real gold into plain dirt. He would also instruct Tao Gan privately, asking him to search Magistrate Lo's office looking for any secret or unknown entrance.

After he had sent Sergeant Hoong away with Magistrate Lo, Judge Dee closed his office door from inside and was about to pass the rest of the night quietly and alone. Before he put out his oil lamps he again examined the royal note, but found the glow from the ink and gold dots on the paper difficult to look at in the lamplight. He rubbed his eyes and gave up his plan for further study.

*   *   *   *

As soon as the morning session began, Judge Dee called in the two men temporarily jailed in the tribunal's prison. They had accused each other of the robbery of Magistrate Lo, although neither knew the portly man's actual identity. Judge Dee introduced the case as having been brought by a traveling merchant who had had an emergency errand and who had already left the district of Poo-yang.

The constables prodded both of the men to a kneeling position in front of the judge, and one of them spoke up immediately. "Your Honor, this insignificant person is named Ta Chien, and it is a terrible mistake to detain me. Yesterday evening I was kind enough to help a stranger on the street catch a runaway thief. Who would have thought that the robber would turn around and accuse me of the crime? Please correct this terrible wrong, Your Honor. Otherwise, no one will ever try to stop a robbery again." The man kowtowed on the floor three times, begging the judge for justice.

The other man followed with his own version of what had happened the previous evening. "Your Honor, this insignificant person is named Tong Pan. I was on my way home from the drugstore where I work as a clerk. My boss was late in returning to the store to collect the money that came in that day. As I passed by the Drum Tower I saw a fat man being robbed on the street. I ran after the robber and caught him. When the fatty arrived, the robber dropped his booty and accused me of the robbery. I was terribly wronged, Your Honor." The man knocked his forehead on the floor, also three times, just as Ta Chien had done.

Judge Dee gave a penetrating look at Ta Chien and Tong Pan. Both were medium height, average-sized men in their early twenties, and neither had any distinguishing marks or features. They both wore cheap blue cloth robes and casual black caps. In neither man's narrative could the judge find any fault. Each man seemed to have been much wronged by a clever and cunning man. But who was it? Judge Dee caressed his long black beard and stared at the two men one more time. Suddenly he spoke loudly at Ta Chien. "Why were you roaming that part of town during evening?"

The man was taken aback. "I,...I was just wandering in the street," he hesitated and his voice trailed off.

"Speak the truth! A law-abiding citizen wouldn't be wandering in that part of the town at that hour, unless he had a good reason." Judge Dee pressed the point home as he leaned forward, his long black beard nearly touching the high bench covered with wide red brocade.

The man sighed, "Well, here is the truth. I was fired yesterday. My parents had sent me to a goldsmith in Chin-hwa to be his apprentice. They thought I could learn more there because Chin-hwa is a richer district and the demand for gold products is greater. Five days ago, my master wanted to instruct someone else how to make gold into horseshoe shapes. I was jealous because the other apprentice had started only the week before while I have been his apprentice for five weeks and he never showed me how to do it. So I grumbled, whispering behind his back: 'Why haven't I been taught the skill first?' My master must have overheard me. Yesterday when he couldn't find his mold for horseshoe-shaped gold he suspected that I had stolen it from him. I argued my innocence, and he became irritated and fired me. With no place to stay in Chin-hwa, I had to come back to Poo-yang. That's why I was passing by the Drum Tower in the dark of the evening." The young man finished his sad tale, rubbing his nose with the sleeve of his robe.

Judge Dee sat back in his chair, stroking his long side-whiskers. The interrogation had gone a full circle. His first suspect now seemed more likely to have told the truth. Judge Dee tried to visualize what had happened the night before. He could imagine one of the men chasing the other, and finally catching him, both still panting. Then, as the portly Magistrate Lo caught up with them at the corner of the street, the one that had been caught had suddenly dropped his booty on the ground to accuse the other of the theft. Quick thinking!

Suddenly, Judge Dee smiled, unconsciously glancing at his own legs. Then he stared at the two men and shouted:

"Stand up! Both of you."

Neither man could quite believe his ears. They both looked at the judge, hesitating and confused.

"Yes. I said you both may stand up now."

Both men stood up. Staring at their legs, Judge Dee commanded: "I want you to race each other. Whoever gets to the South Gate first must be the innocent man. Now run!"

Both men were puzzled, and neither could follow Judge Dee's logic, but they quickly began running. Turning his head to Ma Joong, who stood behind him as usual, Judge Dee told him to follow the two men and arrest the slower one.

Shortly afterwards, Ma Joong returned with Tong Pan in tow, followed by Ta Chien. "Your Honor," Ma Joong said. "This man, Tong Pan, is the loser in the race."

"You must be the robber then," Judge Dee said. "Now, confess."

"I'm truly innocent, Your Honor. I just can't run that fast," the man defended himself, still panting.

"Nonsense. That's exactly why you are not as innocent as you have claimed. Don't you realize that you have already been caught twice? Because you couldn't run fast, Ta Chien caught you last night. For the same reason, you are a loser today. If he were the robber, how could you catch him? You're a slow runner but a fast liar! Even a child can see that you are the robber."

As soon as Judge Dee explained the case, the man looked pathetically silly. The entire court-hall echoed in laughter. He kowtowed frantically, begging for mercy. Judge Dee ordered him to be clubbed twenty times on the shins, to make him an even slower runner. That gave rise to a big hurray, as the crowd of onlookers in the courtyard loved the apt punishment. Turning toward Ta Chien, Judge Dee said: "Give me the name of the goldsmith who fired you yesterday. I'll write him a letter in your behalf, telling him that you helped to catch a robber in this district. He may want to reconsider his decision and take you back as an apprentice." The young man knocked his forehead on the floor to show his gratitude. The morning session was over.

✷   ✷   ✷   ✷

The next day, Judge Dee couldn't rest well during his afternoon nap. He was so anxiously await the return of Chiao Tai and Tao Gan to see the mysterious pot. He didn't believe in any such 'magical' power, of course. But nevertheless he was reminded of a legend that his late father had told him many times before when he was a boy. He called in Sergeant Hoong, for the latter had often heard the story, too, as a servant in his father's mansion.

"Do you remember the story about a magic vat?"

"You mean what the Old Master often told you when you were young?"

"Yes. Isn't that a fascinating story? You know, we're going to have a magic pot to inspect today when Chiao Tai and Tao Gan return from Chin-hwa," the judge said with a smile.

"I see. I certainly do remember how the Old Master used to tell the story. Once upon a time, there was a poor peasant. He rented a small rice patch from a landlord who was rich and greedy. Most of the crops went to the landlord to pay for the rent, and the poor peasant didn't even have enough to fill his own stomach. One day the poor peasant discovered a vat underground in the rice field where he was working. It was a huge ceramic vat covered by a wooden lid. When he removed the lid, the vat seemed empty. But the vat was huge, and the poor peasant wondered what could be at its bottom. He put his head inside to look. His hat fell in. He picked it up, but found another one inside, exactly like his own. He picked that one up. There was another hat, and another. He picked them up again and again, until he had a hundred hats! The honest peasant told his story to his poor friends and gave away all of his hats."

"His rich landlord soon heard of it," Judge Dee interrupted the sergeant and took over the storytelling. "He demanded that the poor peasant give him the vat for the land was his and therefore so was the vat. As soon as the peasant gave him the vat, the landlord dropped a piece of gold in it, hoping it would make him a hundred more. To his surprise and disappointment, the gold disappeared instantly! He dropped in another piece, and it disappeared too. He kept on dropping gold into the vat until he had lost a hundred pieces of gold! Desperate, he went to fetch a candle to search for the missing gold," Judge Dee couldn't go on with the story, for he was laughing so hard now.

Sergeant Hoong continued the story in his own words. "At that moment, his aged father came over to take a look at the magic vat. The man was too old to stand steadily at its edge, and he slipped and fell into it. When the landlord came back with a lighted candle, he found his father upside down inside the vat. He pulled his father out, and another one appeared in the vat. He pulled the second one out, and a third one appeared inside. He pulled a hundred times and got a hundred old Papas to take care of for the rest of their days!" Now both the judge and sergeant were laughing as loudly as young children. The remembrance of the folk tale had entertained them tremendously.

Sergeant Hoong finally controlled himself and finished the story. "Now the landlord was more desperate than ever, and he was determined to make the magic vat work and create more wealth for him. He held the candle inside the vat to see if any gold remained at the bottom. Alas, the candle slipped out of his nervous and sweating hand. It dropped to the bottom and turned into a hundred lighted candles. The flames set his entire house on fire and cost the greedy landlord a huge fortune."

The moral of the story was obvious: the rich landlord was punished for his greed, and the poor peasant was rewarded for his honesty. What about Magistrate Lo's character, Judge Dee wondered. He had seen a big change in the mood of his colleague, who used to be an easy-going person and had seemed only interested in indulging himself with beautiful women. Almost every visit to Poo-yang that portly magistrate had made previously was for the single purpose of enjoying the company of a beautiful courtesan.

The judge shook his head slowly as he spoke to Sergeant Hoong, "You know, as a boy I was always fascinated by how justice was told in the story. I often wondered why my father had told me the story so many times. Now I begin to see something else: the power to reproduce. Isn't it fascinating that one thing can be reproduced over a hundred times? Truly amazing, isn't it?"

"I see what you mean," the gray-bearded sergeant understood immediately what the judge was referring to.

From his desk Judge Dee picked up the royal note left by Magistrate Lo and stared at it for a long while. Something made it seem suspicious to him now. Why would the royal family, which owned so much gold upon earth, store just a relatively small amount in an isolated place and go to all the trouble of issuing a special proclamation to protect it? Judge Dee frowned, as it didn't make much sense to him.

At that moment, a constable announced that Chiao Tai and Tao Gan had returned from the Chin-hwa district. They brought in the pot and placed it on the judge's desk. The size of the pot was much larger than the judge had expected, nearly as large as a tub. Judge Dee ordered all its contents taken out and counted. There were almost two hundred and fifty clods shaped like horseshoes. Only a few were broken into crumbs. All the clods looked alike, a result of quite an accurate method of reproduction. Judge Dee winked at Sergeant Hoong, and both smiled.

Tao Gan began to tell of his discoveries in the Chin-hwa district. "When we arrived at his office, Magistrate Lo took out his key to open the new lock on the door, only to find that it wasn't locked at all. Then he recalled that he didn't use the new lock when he had left for Poo-yang, because the gold had already turned into dirt. I doubt if that's the only reason he didn't use the new lock."

"What do you mean?" Judge Dee asked.

"Obviously he was a careless person, and he would likely have forgotten to use the lock, even if the pot were still holding gold," Tao Gan explained.

"The magistrate also had a busy schedule with beautiful women," Chiao Tai added. "As we stood in his office, three courtesans came to visit, individually of course. He wasn't in the mood, and sent each right away."

"His casual relation with these beautiful women may have given any of them the opportunity to steal his key and have it reproduced by a locksmith," said Tao Gan. "Heaven knows how many women have his keys!"

"I also found it disturbing that he really didn't care about the pot until the gold had become dirt. He didn't even know how many pieces he had received until we counted them in front of him," Chiao Tai added.

While his two lieutenants excitedly reported their findings in Chin-hwa, something else distracted the judge. When he glanced at the royal note on his desk, he noticed some crumbs of dry dirt on it. They must have been left there when the pot was emptied. Casually he blew them away. Then he frowned. He had been looking at the paper from the side when he blew off the crumbs. From that particular angle he could see clearly that the writing in black ink was written on *top* of the vermilion royal seal. That proved the note to be a forgery. The royal seal had already been set there before anything was written over it! Someone must have stolen a piece of blank paper with a royal seal on it. Maybe the paper had been used to test the quality of the vermilion ink or that of the seal itself. For whatever reason, the writing requiring a prompt return of the gold to the royal coffers was nothing but a hoax. But why? Judge Dee fell into somber contemplation again.

After a while, his prolonged preoccupation began to embarrass his lieutenants. Tao Gan and Chiao Tai looked at each other, together deciding to retreat and leave the judge alone. Sergeant Hoong followed them to the door and was also about to disappear, but then he thought better of it. He returned to his desk to begin putting the horseshoes back in the pot. While the sergeant was working on the clods, Judge Dee remained absorbed in his thoughts. Having replaced the very last piece, the gray-bearded man tried to lift the pot to place it on the floor but he found it heavier than he had expected. "What a fool I am! I should have placed the pot empty on the ground first. Well, it just reminds me of how old I am. I can't even carry a pot of dirt, not to mention a pot filled with real gold."

"What about real gold?" Judge Dee was aroused from his deep thoughts, looking blankly at the exhausted sergeant.

"Just ignore me. I was talking to myself, Your Honor. I was such a fool to put back all the clods before I moved the pot to the floor. Give me a hand, please, will you?"

"You are absolutely right, Sergeant Hoong!" exclaimed Judge Dee. "Of course the real gold would be much heavier! Too heavy, I would say." The judge jumped up from his chair. Ignoring the perplexed face of the sergeant, the judge said: "Call back Chiao Tai and Tao Gan, and ask them how they carried the pot here."

The two lieutenants returned in a hurry and told the judge exactly what they had done. They had had to borrow a cart from Magistrate Lo. Once they arrived at the Poo-yang tribunal they used a bamboo pole to carry the pot on their shoulders, just as the farmer and his brother had done when they had carried the pot into Magistrate Lo's office.

Judge Dee asked Tao Gan: "Was it a heavy load for you to carry?"

"Not too heavy, but by no means light. I'm not Ma Joong, you know," Tao Gan said.

Judge Dee smiled. "I should have thought of this before." Turning to Sergeant Hoong, the judge said: "Go to the First Lady and tell her I want to borrow a gold bar. Then take it to a goldsmith and ask him to make one gold piece in the shape of a horseshoe, exactly the same size as one of these." Judge Dee picked up a clod from the pot. "We'll soon find out how much two hundred and fifty pieces of real gold of this size weigh. My guess is that they would be too heavy for two people to carry."

"So the pot carried to Magistrate Lo's office was never filled with real gold!" Tao Gan cried. The daring scheme amazed him.

"And the pot wasn't magic at all, for it didn't turn gold into dirt after all," Chiao Tai nodded, feeling satisfied that things were making sense now.

"And the farmer didn't need to turn in the gold either," Judge Dee added.

"What?" Both lieutenants and Sergeant Hoong asked simultaneously.

"That royal note is a fake. The royal vermilion seal was printed onto the paper before, *not after*, the note was written, and therefore it does not pertain to the inscription at all! The whole thing is a hoax. Think about it. Why should the royal family stash the gold there in the first place? Why should it issue a special note to protect it? The note does not even inventory the number of gold pieces in the pot. There's only one likely explanation. The note was invented by someone who, for some reason, wanted to bury the gold underground but was afraid that others might turn it up by accident. By claiming it belonged to the royal coffers, the person was hoping to scare off anyone who might discover the gold. Think about how its finder might respond. If he took the gold, he was committing a capital crime. And he would be afraid there might be even special marks on the gold to give him away. On the other hand, if he turned the gold in, a magistrate might suspect he had kept some of it. He could never prove his innocence. To spare himself, he'd better of leaving the gold where it was."

"That makes excellent sense," Chiao Tai applauded.

"The trick has worked, but only to a certain point," Judge Dee continued in his deduction. "The farmer truly believed it was royal gold. But he didn't want to turn it in, or to put it back underground either. Knowing that his magistrate was careless, the farmer thought he could outwit him. It is my guess that five days ago the farmer sent his brother as an apprentice to the goldsmith whom Ta Chien had worked for. The new apprentice then stole the mold and the brothers had made the fakes before the farmer reported to the tribunal. The fact that Magistrate Lo had sent only one constable to his home convinced the farmer that the magistrate had no idea how heavy the gold would be and that gave him much more confidence. Even if he was caught as he brought in the pot, he could pretend to be a fool and blame his own stupidity. Everyone would laugh, and Magistrate Lo would let him go. The cunning farmer would get to keep the real gold when he got home, unless the magistrate still believed in the faked royal note."

"What a daring hoax!" Tao Gan exclaimed. "I would never have thought of that myself." The lieutenant had been quite a swindler himself before Judge Dee reformed him. He still envied anyone who aimed at being an even more daring swindler.

"Now," Judge Dee said, "we can tell our friend Magistrate Lo to use some cheap tin or lead or any such mixture to make horseshoes and paint them gold and put them in the pot. In a tribunal session he should tell the farmer to carry the pot of "gold" home. Just tell him that the royal note is a fake and he can keep all the gold. Then everyone will see how the farmer fails to carry the pot. At that moment, Magistrate Lo can reveal the swindle and confiscate the real gold for the crime of setting up a district magistrate. Under a threat of torture, it shouldn't be difficult to make the farmer confess where he is hiding the real gold."

Judge Dee pulled out a piece of paper from his drawer. Sergeant Hoong prepared some ink for him. The judge quickly wrote down all the points in his theory, and added that it really didn't matter whether the farmer's brother had actually apprenticed to the goldsmith or not. That could be speculation based on the coincidence of Ta Chien's story. The mere fact that two people couldn't carry that much gold would suffice to convict the farmer.

Judge Dee folded the paper, put it inside an envelope, and handed over to Chiao Tai. "Take this letter to Magistrate Lo, and return that common pot." He pointed to the pot that Chiao Tai and Tao Gan had brought from Chin-hwa. What a waste, the judge sighed. To cheer up his lieutenant, the judge teased

Chiao Tai: "Our light-hearted magistrate will likely reward you with one of his beautiful women." Chiao Tai's face blushed. He was seeking serious love in a mature, sophisticated woman of beauty, but had had no luck so far.

Before dinnertime, Sergeant Hoong returned from the goldsmith with the newly minted horseshoe-shaped gold. It weighed one and a half catties (—*a Chinese weight unit that was a little more than a pound*). Two hundred and fifty pieces would weigh more than four hundred pounds! Even Ma Joong couldn't carry that much weight. Sergeant Hoong passed the gold to the judge, who weighed it in his hand, smiling.

Judge Dee left his office to return the gold to his First Lady. Each of his wives had a separate apartment. Although the Second and Third Ladies freely went in and out of hers, the First Lady never set her foot in theirs. She deemed that a way of demonstrating her dignity. Judge Dee approved and adhered to this Confucian custom, as he believed that such reverence for order and rank would best guarantee peace and harmony within a household.

On his way, Judge Dee stopped by the Third Lady's rooms. He found her sitting at her desk, practicing calligraphy. From the way she was pursuing her delicate artistic interests, the judge knew she was happy in his household in harmony with his other two wives. He nodded at her beautiful handwriting, approving her exquisite taste. Then he noticed something new: a bundle of colorful flowers were gracefully arranged in a porcelain pot on her tea table. Each time he came he found something fresh and cool. The judge smiled contentedly.

"Tonight, we'll play dominoes again," said the judge. "But no tricks this time!" he warned.

CHAPTER 5

▼

THE DRAGON AND THE TIGERS

Judge Dee had been quite moody for nearly two weeks now, because few cases had arrived at his Poo-yang tribunal. The tranquility was most unusual, and seemed almost unreal. Even dust was collecting on his high bench around the brown wood of oblong moldings that was supposed to "frighten the hall." Without spectators gathering there, his tribunal courtyard had a bleak and abandoned look. The prolonged quiet had become almost unbearable to the judge, a forty-year-old energetic magistrate and a devout Confucian scholar, who was always ready for action.

Today was Sergeant Hoong's birthday. Judge Dee and his three lieutenants had given him a lunchtime celebration at a restaurant named "Four Springs a Year." The judge would have invited them to the restaurant for dinner, but his First Lady had already suggested a family style banquet be held in the evening. Seeing that the tribunal routines had become so dull for her husband, she wanted this opportunity for a party to cheer him up. Indeed, such boring routines had nearly caused a crisis at home. During the past week, the judge had become increasingly irritable, often blaming the maids or even his wives for trivial matters with little or no reason at all. For her own sake and the family's as well, his First Lady dearly wanted this birthday banquet to change her husband's mood.

Judge Dee's other colleagues could not join the party at the house. Sergeant Hoong was his only male colleague who was allowed to see his three wives. The gray-bearded man enjoyed such privilege because he had been a house servant at Judge Dee's father's mansion when the judge had been a boy. The judge had also decided to have an additional luncheon party at a restaurant in order to include his lieutenants Ma Joong, Chiao Tai and Tao Gan.

The previous night, Chiao Tai had ordered a smoked roast piglet, the house special at "Four Springs a Year." The noon session at the tribunal had been very short, and they arrived at the restaurant fairly early. Everything was fine until Ma Joong began about to eat the tongue of the piglet, his favorite part. As soon as he had opened its mouth, a terrible smell came out, quickly spoiling everyone's appetite. Some scraps of the piglet's food remained in its mouth! The party finished up in a rush, and Judge Dee returned to the tribunal, even more morose than ever.

In his private office adjacent to the court-hall, he drank a cup of "Hairy Tiptop," his favorite tea, and also tried his usual nap. But it appeared he was stuck in a rut; his short sleep was soon interrupted, when he was awakened to find Sergeant Hoong standing at the side of his couch.

"What is it?" Judge Dee asked.

"Your Honor, I'm afraid you'll have to oversee an emergency tribunal session," Sergeant Hoong said.

"How could I have missed the sound of the gong?" The judge was referring to a huge bronze gong hanging on an ornate wooden frame at the entrance of the tribunal. Anyone could hit the gong at anytime to bring an emergency case. Judge Dee was amazed that he could have slept so deeply and have completely missed its loud bang.

"No one hit the gong, Sir."

"What do you mean? Why do we need an emergency session if no one hit the gong?"

"Your Honor," the sergeant explained, "two families were fighting each other over the drumstick and no one could hit the gong. The fight grew fiercer, and more and more relatives were called to join. Many had blood on their faces. It scared the hell out of me. Luckily, Chiao Tai returned. He quickly brought them all into the court-hall, and sent me to wake you up. I'm sorry to interrupt your nap."

"Never mind that!" Judge Dee said. He donned his official cap and robe in front of his silver mirror. The emergency actually made him feel much better. It reminded him of his prestige and power. Stepping inside the court-hall, he saw two rows of people kneeling in front of his high bench. While waiting for him, these people had been quarreling again. A huge crowd had gathered in the tribunal courtyard. Their gossip joined the noise of the quarrel. Judge Dee silenced them by pounding his gavel, the "wood that frightens the hall." Picking the first person in line on the left, the judge grunted: "You. Speak up!"

"This insignificant person is named Hua Tao," a man of about fifty said. Judge Dee could tell from his shabby clothes that he was a poor peasant. "I live in the Hua's Village outside the South Gate. My daughter used to help me with farming, although she should have been married long ago. As I'm so poor, no one would marry my son, Hua Liang. Last year I finally found him a wife in the neighboring Lin's Village when he was thirty-one. But..."

The man turned towards the people kneeling on his left and shot an angry look at them. "I never thought this woman would kill my son!" The man cried, wiping his nose with his finger. "This morning she put poison in his food, and he died instantly after he ate the lunch she had brought to his field."

"Were you present when he died?" Judge Dee asked.

"No, I wasn't."

"Who told you about his death then?"

"My daughter," the man turned around and pointed to a woman in her mid-twenties. She glanced at the judge, buried her head in her chest, and humbly answered:

"This insignificant woman is named Lin *hua* Pin. I was visiting my parents this morning. They left home after lunch and I was washing the dishes, when my sister-in-law ran in the door and cried: 'Your brother died in the cotton field!' I went with her and brought back his body. Under my questioning she admitted that he had died soon after eating the food she brought him for lunch."

"Where is the woman now? I want to question her myself." Judge Dee said.

"Here is she, Hua *lin* Li-mei," a woman kneeling on the right responded nervously. When she held up her face, Judge Dee saw that she was plain looking and about the same age as her sister-in-law.

Before Judge Dee could ask her any questions, the man kneeling ahead of her spoke: "Your Honor, this insignificant person is named Lin Yu-shen, father of Li-mei and her twin brother, Li-ben. Today is definitely not my day. I came home for lunch, only to find my house burned down and my son dead inside. It must be arson; his wife killed him."

"What made you say that?" The report of another death and the blunt accusation surprised the judge.

"If Your Honor will kindly lend me your ear I'll tell you all the details," said the man. "It's my fault that I didn't make myself clear in the first place." From the man's tone of voice Judge Dee realized that this man was a street ballad singer.

"My son," the man continued, "was not exactly a normal lad. Mentally challenged, so to speak. Since he's my only son, I really worried about how to carry on our family name. Last year I found him a wife. She's two years younger, and is now twenty-six. I was damned wrong, and shouldn't have her as my daughter-in-law. They were not born for each other. He was born in the year of tiger and water, and she was born in the year of dragon and wood. As dragons and tigers often fight each other, wood always stays on top of water. I really shouldn't have allowed this marriage. The first day she came to my house I could tell how bitterly she hated us. She hates my son because of his silly head. She hates me for arranging the marriage, and she hates my daughter because of the swapping."

"Swapping?" Judge Dee sat up in his chair and raised his hand to interrupt.

"Excuse me, Your Honor. It's my fault again that I haven't made myself clear." The ballad singer knocked his forehead on the floor. "First things first. It's *her* parents who asked me for my daughter's hand for their son. When Lady Wang, the professional go-between, came to my house and suggested the marriage, I checked the Feng Shui zodiac fortune book. It should be a perfect match. He was born in the year of dog and earth. My daughter is four years younger, born in the year of tiger and water. While water and earth get along well, tigers and dogs never fight each other. I may have kept my daughter at home for too long, and I have raised her as a boy. She could even climb trees. None of my neighbors likes her. It became as difficult to find her a husband as it was to find my son a wife. Lady Wang came just in time. But I was too greedy, and wanted an even better deal. I told her I would only agree if their daughter also married my son. I totally forgot to consult my fortune book. That's how my son-in-law's sister became my daughter-in-law. Look what has happened. She killed my son, and her father is now accusing my daughter for murdering his son. My daughter is innocent. Please punish the other woman."

"Yes!" people kneeling behind him echoed. They were all relatives of the Lins. Those kneeling next to them shouted back, "Shame on you! Your daughter is the murderer." These were the relatives of the Huas. Judge Dee pounded his gavel on his bench. Overwhelmed by what he had heard, the judge closed his eyes and shook his head. He wished he could have some tea, but that was not allowed in the court-hall. Swallowing as he caressed his beard, he asked the woman named Hua *lin* Li-mei: "What did you cook for your husband?"

"Nothing exotic, just fish and rice," the woman sobbed.

"What did you do after you finished cooking?" asked the judge.

"I took the food to him."

"To the field?"

The woman nodded.

"How far is it from your home?"

"Only a quarter of an hour's walk, for I took a short cut through a wood of the chaste trees.[1] Otherwise it would take me twice or three times as long."

"Can you be more precise?" Judge Dee frowned.

"Well, three times longer. But today I relaxed in the woods a little while. I climbed a tree to pick up a beautiful flower. It's blue and white. I tried to wear it on my head, but it slipped away from my hand and dropped to the ground. I played with the petals. They were too pretty to let go."

"Do you have any of the food left?"

"Not a single bite. My husband ate it all. He was so hungry that he blamed me for cooking too little rice. He asked me to help him take out the fish bones so that he could eat faster."

"I assume you did, didn't you?"

"Yes, of course."

"Then what happened?"

"Well," the woman's voice trailed off.

"Speak up!"

"After he finished eating, he stared at me and smiled, and wanted to do what we only do at night. He was trying to take off my clothes but suddenly collapsed and died," the woman began to weep. Onlookers in the courtyard broke out laughing as they heard the vulgar scene, but then turned quiet again as the woman's tale of the sudden death sent a chill down their spines.

Judge Dee caressed his beard and thought for a while. Then he announced: "This session is over. Put both women in the temporary cells in the jail while we're waiting for the coroner's report."

As the judge was about to leave his seat, the woman named Lin *hua* Pin shouted: "Don't be fooled by her tears. I'm sure my brother died of the food she had brought him. No mercy, please."

Judge Dee stared at her while the crowd in the courtyard was dispersing. He was about to ask something, but thought better of it. Quietly he turned around and retreated to his private office, followed by Sergeant Hoong and Chiao Tai.

---

1. Chaste tree: the *agnus castus*, a willow-like tree.

His two other lieutenants, Ma Joong and Tao Gan, had not returned to the tribunal yet and missed the entire emergency session.

"So, what do you think?" asked the judge, after he had changed into his usual dress of a casual robe and a skullcap.

"Lin Yu-shen was quite a character. His narrating was peculiar but articulate. His daughter, on the other hand, was dull and plain looking. Our friend Ma Joong didn't miss anything this afternoon," Sergeant Hoong smiled.

"I can't believe that woman poisoned her husband with food. She would have tried to disguise herself a little better," Chiao Tai commented.

"You've got a good point, Chiao Tai," Judge Dee said approvingly. "Using poison to kill is a serious and meditated murder. One would expect the criminal to be at least a little more sophisticated and careful. The fact that she didn't even try to create any alibi for herself made me suspicious. Besides, we don't learn of any motives at all."

"Lin's story about matched or mismatched marriages is fascinating. Do you believe in that?" asked Sergeant Hoong.

"That stuff comes from a sect of Taoism that emphasizes rituals and formalities. Most other Taoists care much less about it. As a Confucian scholar, I certainly do not believe in any of that nonsense. But it sounds clever and helps me understand people better, for they do behave according to their beliefs, don't they? The retarded Lin's marriage couldn't work, because it had never been expected to work. I personally sympathize with his wife, Lin *hua* Pin. But that just proves she has a motive to kill her husband, doesn't it?"

"My head gets dizzy when I try to distinguish the two women," Chiao Tai said. "They are of the same age and look quite alike. The more I think about them, the more I get confused. I don't know if I can ever possibly see one as guilty and the other as innocent. I'm lost, Your Honor."

Judge Dee smiled and said: "I won't blame you, Chiao Tai. It *is* confusing. The two families brought their cases to the tribunal at exactly the same time. Both husbands are dead and their wives have each been accused. And they are brother-in-laws and sister-in-laws. But let's stick to the facts. The only facts we have now are the following. Both men died unnatural deaths. Hua Liang died soon after he had eaten the food his wife had cooked and brought to him through a wood of the chaste trees. Lin Li-ben was dead after the fire, but we don't know if he was alive before the fire. And we do know that his wife had good reasons not to love him. On the other hand, Hua Liang's wife has no apparent motive to kill her husband. These are all the facts, and we need to collect more."

As he was speaking, the judge began to search in his bookshelves for a medicine book. He had a complete bookshelf devoted to medicine books. The judge had a fairly wide knowledge of medicine, and in order to do his detective work he had disguised himself as a physician more than once. He searched five of his books before he found what he was looking for. The judge then smiled and put back the books on the shelf.

At that moment, Tao Gan and Ma Joong returned for the afternoon tribunal session. "I heard about the case of brothers-and-sisters-in-law. Did I miss anything?" Ma Joong asked excitedly, cracking the knuckles in his hands.

"No, you didn't. Both women are much too plain for you, my brother." Chiao Tai's answer made everyone laugh, as they all knew how Ma Joong was only interested in pretty women. Seeing that all of his colleagues were present, Chiao Tai began to apologize for the dirty piglet he had ordered at the restaurant. "I know Your Honor didn't want to make a big fuss at the restaurant. People may hear all kinds of rumors, hurting the reputation of the restaurant and ours as well. They may say we're arrogant because we're from the tribunal," said Chiao Tai. As a loyal subordinate and former soldier, he felt protective of Judge Dee's reputation.

"But I was curious and wanted to know how it could have happened," he said. "So I went back and pulled the chef aside, questioning him but telling him not to disturb the restaurant owner. The chef was quite surprised, and said this had never happened before. Then he remembered that today's piglets were prepared by one of his assistant chefs who didn't look too well when he came to work in the morning. The chef now believes that something must have happened to the young man that made him forget to clean the piglet's mouth. If he did, the chef laughed, nothing would remain inside the mouth, unless the piglet had been roasted alive. He apologized to me, and gave me our money back."

Just at that moment a constable knocked at the door and announced the arrival of the owner of the "Four Springs a Year."

"Show him in," Judge Dee said.

A man in his fifties with a round face was led in, followed by two other men. They all knelt down in front of the judge and knocked their foreheads on the floor respectfully.

"This insignificant person is named Ruan Tan, the owner of 'Four Springs a Year.' Here are my chef and his assistant," he pointed to the men on his right and left. "We deserve a thousand deaths," the man said. "We had the honor of having you in our restaurant this morning. I should have served Your Honor in person, but they failed to inform me of your presence. The damned fool dared to screw up your order, and I fired him after I learned of it. I brought him here for you to punish. I know I'm beyond forgiveness, but please have mercy."

The man kowtowed half a dozen times until Judge Dee interrupted him. "Stop! We're not in a tribunal session, and you don't need to be so humble. You didn't do anything terribly wrong, and that's why I didn't summon you for questioning at the restaurant." The judge had long before run out of patience, and he didn't like people who had little dignity and submitted to power too easily.

After a second thought, the judge said, "But it doesn't hurt for you to learn a lesson and make sure this won't happen again."

"Surely. May I never forget this lesson for the rest of my life! Even in my next life!" the restaurant owner vowed, still very nervous.

Just then, they heard the gong at the gate announce the regular afternoon session. Judge Dee gave a last appraising look at the three men kneeling in front of him. The assistant chef's face was quite ashen, and the judge began to feel sorry for him. Waving his hand impatiently, Judge Dee dismissed his three unsolicited visitors.

A new case was presented at the afternoon tribunal session. The constables brought in two men to kneel in front of the judge.

"This insignificant person is named Wang Second," the plaintiff said. "I'm an antique dealer, and my shop is in the market place right behind the tribunal compound. This morning I was running to my shop in a hurry because I had overslept. By accident I knocked over a vendor selling twisted fried rings made of salty dough. His hamper overturned and all his rings were broken in pieces and jumbled together. I apologized and offered to compensate him for fifty rings. He said that I had ruined at least two hundred rings! We couldn't agree and have quarreled the whole day."

"Don't you have better things to do with your life," the judge scolded as he looked him over. The man's face was full of pockmarks, and his sweaty, bumpy skin glistened. Judge Dee quickly averted his eyes to look at the other person, a man with a thin face and shrewd eyes, who was twisting his fingers while listening. "And what do you have to say?" the judge asked him, hardly expecting a story any less pathetic.

"This insignificant person is named Chang Third," the fried ring vendor answered in a quiet voice. "I have nothing to add, for he has said it all. I got up early, and made over two hundred rings. They are now all ruined. He must pay for them." He knocked on the side of the hamper and showed the judge what was left inside.

"That's all the remains of the two hundred rings?" Judge Dee asked.

"Yes."

"Do any other vendors sell fried rings in the marketplace?"

"Sure. Across the street a man named Lee Fourth sells fried rings too."

"The same type?" Judge Dee asked.

"Yes."

"The same size?"

"Yes."

"Then what's your problem?"

The ring vendor blinked his eyes. Obviously he couldn't understand Judge Dee.

The judge smiled. Then he laughed. He laughed whole-heartedly for two full minutes. Everyone in the court-hall looked at him, completely confused. Giving the ring vendor and the antique dealer each a stern look, Judge Dee sighed and smiled again. He caressed his long side-whiskers with his left hand, and rapped the bench with the gavel in his right hand.

"What a waste of my time! I was trying to solve two murder cases, and you came here just to tell me of your silly dispute. That should have been solved right away quite easily in the marketplace, for that's where the answer is to be found." The perplexed face of everyone in the court-hall indicated that no one understood him. "Well," he added, "in a few minutes I can tell you exactly how many rings you had in your hamper." He pointed at the ring vendor.

Judge Dee ordered a constable to go and buy a stale ring from Lee Fourth. When the constable returned, Judge Dee asked him to weigh it and then weigh what was left in the hamper. The constable reported the weight, and Judge Dee rapped his bench with his gavel, very angrily: "Chang Third, you only had forty-seven fried rings in your hamper. How dare you ask him to pay for two hundred rings? How do I know it's forty-seven? That's really simple. Here is a ring made by Lee Fourth, and you acknowledged that's the same as yours. What is left in your hamper only weighs forty-seven times more. I asked the constable not to buy a fresh ring, because that might have too much oil in it and thus weigh much more. Wang Second has been indeed quite generous when he offered to compensate you for fifty rings. You, a greedy pig, dare to demand two hundred rings from him! Here is your punishment: slap your face two hundred times, right here and now. That's exactly what you deserve, not money for the rings, but slaps on your face."

The crowd cheered for the judge's simple and fair solution. As Chang Third slapped his face and counted to about one hundred, his cheeks became swollen and that suddenly reminded the judge of the piglet at lunch. He recalled what the chef at "Four Springs a Year" had told Chao Tai. Nothing would remain inside the piglet's mouth, unless the piglet were roasted alive. That's exactly what the chief had said. Interesting, Judge Dee thought. That gave him a new idea, and he couldn't wait to explore it.

That evening, the family banquet for Sergeant Hoong's birthday went quite well, except for the fact that the judge's mood had already changed. The easy irritation and upsetting feeling that had plagued the house for weeks had completely gone. His First Lady soon realized that she had actually no need to hold such a party; her husband wouldn't be annoyed by domestic matters anymore. He often strayed into his own thoughts and was noticeably quiet at the table, giving only an abstracted stare if spoken to.

The first thing the judge did the following morning was to ask Chiao Tai to make Hua *lin* Li-mei prepare three helpings of the same food as she had cooked for her husband the previous day. "I want her to bring one serving of the food to the field through the woods of the chaste trees. Have her take another there by the other path, and leave the last serving at home," Judge Dee ordered. He then added a few words in Chiao Tai's ear. The lieutenant nodded, clicking his heels; his face had rarely been so serious.

As the noon session began, over a hundred onlookers crowded in the tribunal courtyard, eager to see how their astute judge would resolve the murder cases of the two brothers-in-law. Judge Dee ascended the dais and sat behind his high bench, wearing his official robe of green brocade and the judge's cap of black velvet that had two wings sticking out on each side. Silently, Sergeant Hoong and Tao Gan stood behind the judge, holding the big posters that read: "Be Silent" and "Be Serious." Their slender figures made spectators wonder where Ma Joong and Chiao Tai were today. Judge Dee rapped the bench with his gavel, and all the spectators stood still, just as "silent" and "serious" as the court had required.

Judge Dee's resonant voice echoed in the court-hall with its usual power that represented all the authority of a tribunal. The shining eyes of a large unicorn embroidered in a dark-violet curtain hung on the wall behind him seemed to be staring at any onlookers who dared to look around while the judge was talking. "As you all know, two murder charges are currently pending, and this magistrate is determined to solve both today." The judge then softened his tone and smiled. "Now watch. I have a lively show for you to enjoy." He raised his hand. At his signal, Ma Joong and a constable brought in a pair of piglets. The white little animals ran around, screaming here and there from time to time, while some constables set to work in the center of the court-hall. Only gradually did the spectators in the courtyard begin to realize what the constables were doing. They were set-

·ting up an oven for smoking roast piglets! The astounded crowd had no clues what their judge was up to.

Other constables led in the two accused women and made them kneel in front of the Judge. "Now," Judge Dee spoke in his resonant voice to the entire court, "let me start with Hua *lin* Li-mei. She has been charged with murdering her husband with poisoned food. This morning, under my instructions, she prepared three servings of food exactly the same way as she cooked yesterday for her husband. I told her to bring one serving of the food to the place he had died, walking through the woods of chaste trees just as she had done before. I also asked her to take another serving there by the path, which is three times longer. The last serving of the food was left at home. I asked my lieutenant Chiao Tai to collect all the three servings and bring them here. Now watch."

Chiao Tai brought in a black-and-red lacquered tray with three dishes on it. He placed the tray on the judge's high bench. Each plate had a tag of white silk hanging under it, labeling each serving of the food. A constable brought in a stray dog from the street and fed it with the food that had been left at home. The dog swallowed the food and waggled its tail. The constable led it away. Another constable brought in a second stray dog, and fed it with the food that had been sent along the path. The dog ate the food and sat down waiting for more. The constable led the dog away. A third dog was brought in. It barked hungrily at the last dish, the food that had been sent through the woods of chaste trees. Chiao Tai fed half of the food to the dog. It swallowed it in a few quick gulps and barked for more. Chiao Tai raised his hand, and a constable handed him a paper bag. Using a pair of bamboo chopsticks, the lieutenant took a blue and white flower out of the bag. Judge Dee explained that it was a flower from a chaste tree. Chiao Tai stirred the rest of the food with the flower and fed the dog. It waggled its tail and ran briefly around, barking anxiously, as if looking for a mate. All of a sudden, it collapsed on the ground and died.

A commotion broke out among the spectators. Judge Dee rapped the bench with his gavel to quiet the crowd. "You've all witnessed how the dog died. Let me explain what happened. It turns out that chaste tree flowers can be extremely dangerous at this time of the year, because when the flower begins to bear its fruit, it is a strong and instant sexual stimulant. This morning I asked Chiao Tai to follow Hua *lin* Li-mei through the woods. As you all know, Chiao Tai is an excellent archer. He spotted a chaste tree in blossom and brought down a flower with a single shot. You may remember the woman said yesterday at this court that she had played with the petals of a flower. She also said she had helped her husband take out the fish bones. That's how the poor man was poisoned. The innocent woman has no motive to kill her husband. The case is closed, and she is free to go."

Members of the Lin family cheered. "Now watch this," the judge pointed at the two piglets in the constables' hands and ordered one piglet killed with a nail driven into its neck. Both piglets were put in the oven and roasted with the aromatic smoke from burning wood. The piglet roasted alive made a large sound of screaming before it was suffocated. Soon, a delicious smell floated in the air and made the mouths of many onlookers in the courtyard water. The judge ordered the piglets taken out to check the inside of their mouth. A constable reported that the piglet with the nail in the neck had nothing inside its mouth, but that the mouth of the other piglet was full of muddy ash.

Judge Dee summoned the coroner. "Didn't you say that there was nothing inside Lin Li-ben's mouth?"

"That is true, Your Honor," the coroner attested.

With a triumphant smile, Judge Dee turned slowly to the woman named Lin *hua* Pin. "Your husband was already dead when you set the house on fire, wasn't he? Otherwise his mouth would have been full of muddy ash, just as the piglet that was roasted alive." Judge Dee grinned as he vividly remembered what the chef at the "Four Seasons a Year" had told Chiao Tai.

The woman named Lin *hua* Pin remained silent.

"Speak up, young woman!" Judge Dee demanded.

The woman bit her lips and kept her silence.

"Bring in her accomplice," ordered the judge.

Ma Joong brought in the former assistant chef at the "Four Springs a Year" and pushed him to kneel in front of the judge. The young man shivered all over, as he saw the instruments of torture in the hands of six constables: the long clubs of bamboo, the thick whips made of snakeskin, and the innocent-looking hand screws. He closed his eyes and spoke with all he had remaining of his own voice.

"This insignificant person is named Hua Yong. I worked as an assistant chef in the 'Four Springs a Year.' Lin *hua* Pin and I grew up in the same village, and we've been lovers since we were teenagers. As an orphan, I have never had enough money to give her father as betrothal. After her father married her to that mental retard, we kept on seeing each other at her parents' house. It was getting more and more difficult to do so. Recently, I saw a beautiful flower on a chaste tree near her parents' home. I tried to get it for her, but the flower slipped from my hand. My dog picked it up for me. To thank him I let him lick the flower. But then suddenly he jumped around and collapsed. The day before, I told my girl how my dog had died. She said she would try the flower on her husband, and if it worked she would set the house on fire so that no one would find out. Knowing what she was going to do, I was nervous at my job and forgot to clean the mouth of the piglet that Your Honor had ordered. Please forgive me. I'm still young, having just turned twenty-four toady." The young man knocked his head on the floor and held out two fingers of his right hand and then four fingers of his left.

"Traitor!" the woman clenched her teeth.

"You betrayed yourself, young woman," Judge Dee said. "Yesterday when I began interrogating you, you weren't even sure it was the food that had poisoned your brother. But later you became absolutely certain, and even yelled at me when I called the session to a close. That made me wonder. After I consulted my medicine book and learned about the poisonous nature of the flower, everything became clear. While your sister-in-law has never intended to kill her husband, you murdered yours and tried to cover it up by burning the house down. When you heard she had played with the flower before feeding her husband, you knew the inevitable consequences only too well. That's why you shouted 'No Mercy' as I was about to leave my seat," the judge pointed at the chair he was sitting on. Then he suddenly realized that his cap was tilted, and he quickly raised his hands to adjust it. It was a serious offence to the Imperial rule for a magistrate not to wear his cap properly. While holding his hands on his cap to help it stand upright on his head, the judge glanced at the young man and asked the woman, "He has confessed already. Shall we hear yours as well?"

Lin *hua* Pin closed her eyes. "It's all over, and it's all fate," she muttered. Putting her thumb mark on the court recording as her verbal confession, she saved herself all the torture. Hua Yong glanced at her with some feeling. As she shot him back an angry look, he looked away and dared not return her look.

Judge Dee picked up five short rulers from his bench and threw them on the floor. That symbolized the measure of punishment for Hua Yong: fifty strikes with bamboo clubs on the bare buttocks, for adultery and not informing the authority of an intended murder. The judge picked up a longer and wider ruler from the bench and marked it with a vermilion brush-pen and wrote the name Lin *hua* Pin on it, indicating she would be decapitated as a murderer. A constable took her away to jail where she would be kept until the Emperor himself approved the sentence.

After Judge Dee retreated to his private office, Sergeant Hoong served him a fresh cup of tea. "Your Honor," the gray-bearded man said cheerfully, "I must admit that I now believe even more than ever in the Feng Shui zodiac predictions. The assistant chef is turning twenty-four. He must be born in the year of horse and fire. His lover is two years older, born in the year of dragon and wood."

While dragon and horse may race together, eventually the wood will be burned by fire. On the other hand, you found Hua *lin* Li-mei innocent, and she was born in the year of tiger and water. Your Honor is also a tiger, but twelve years older. You were born in the year of tiger and gold. After all, it's a younger tiger that you have saved. It makes sense."

Judge Dee sipped his tea and smiled. "Come on! You don't expect me to set a criminal free simply because we are both tigers, do you? The so-called perfect marriage between Hua Liang and Hua *lin* Li-mei didn't work either. What can you say about that? The tiger ate the dog, or the water flooded the earth?" The gray-bearded sergeant chuckled, as he helped the judge change from his official dress back into a casual robe and a small skullcap.

When the judge sat down again he caressed his long side-whiskers and said, "But you do remind me of my age, Sergeant. As a golden tiger, I'm already forty. According to our great master, Confucius, a man should establish himself by thirty and understand everything by forty. By fifty, he should even know the will of heaven. Sadly I don't understand much, and have to learn a lot more and much faster!"

CHAPTER 6

▼

A TALE OF WATERMELONS

It was a hot summer day and exceptionally humid. Judge Dee's Second Lady had asked a servant to send some fresh-cut watermelon slices to the judge's private office, where he had just awakened from his afternoon nap. The judge looked out the window. He remembered that he had seen a lot of clouds before his nap. It now seemed that heavy showers were likely. Both his black cap and his blue house robe were soaked with perspiration, and a moist sheen glistened on his black beard and long side-whiskers.

He also remembered that he had had a dream, which had something to do with the Water Palace, a residence of the Third Princess, the favorite daughter of the Emperor. During his previous vacation trip to the town adjacent to her palace, Judege Dee had been secretly summoned to investigate a mysterious case in which the Princess's life was at risk. At the very first meeting, she had stitched an Imperial warrant into the judge's robe and appointed him an Imperial Envoy. He was thus invested with power superior to anyone but the Emperor himself! She had obtained the warrant from her Imperial father, pre-signed but left without any appointee's name, so that in case of just such an emergency she could appoint someone to help protect her. Judge Dee had soon successfully exposed a conspiracy on the part of her chief eunuch and had saved her life.[1] After that, he had returned the warrant to her as requested.

To relinquish such power had presented little difficulty for him, as the judge had no ambition to serve at the Imperial court at this time. He understood there were many steps to climb before he could reach such a position. The temporary status as an envoy was just an unusual episode and surprise. His life style hardly felt the same after he had returned to his modest post as the Magistrate of Poo-yang, though. It had been difficult to slow down and readjust to the routines of ordinary life. Daily business at the tribunal seemed dull. Even the long-standing rivalry at dominoes with his three wives had become tedious in the quiet summer evenings. The fact was that he no longer felt content with his life anymore. He wanted very badly to do something more important, but wasn't quite sure what that might be.

He bent forward, and picked up a slice of watermelon to quench his thirst. In the humid summer heat, the melon tasted delicious. The judge reflected on this fact for a moment, and then smiled. His late father had wanted him to know that it took some difficulty and often even suffering to fully enjoy all the pleasures in life, and now he truly believed his father's words.

"Where is Sergeant Hoong?" the judge asked his servant.

"He is learning piri with Tao Gan," the servant answered. Piri, a windpipe musical instrument of Persian origin, had recently become fashionable throughout the entire country, and Tao Gan was the first in the Poo-yang tribunal to learn how to play.

"Send him in. I want to play some chess with him," said Judge Dee, who had developed an interest in a new type of chess recently introduced from India. After his glimpse of life inside the palace, Judge Dee felt he understood better why his late father had often said: "It's lonely at the top, and chilly too." His father had served as a cabinet member for the previous Emperor, the father of the present one. Judge Dee had always believed in his father's perspicacity, but his most recent first-hand experience at the Water Palace helped him to understand this shrewd observation much more deeply. Of all those in her employment, the Third Princess could only trust her nanny! And just as strangely, those whom she could most easily hurt were likely to be those she held most dear, particularly her secret lover, the handsome young general who was assigned to protect her. Inside that highly isolated upper strata of society, life had become very narrow; holding onto power had become its only purpose.

Judge Dee picked up another slice of watermelon to savor its flavor. Sweat, rolling from his forehead to his cheeks and nose, dripped onto the melon. The

---

1. For more adventures of Judge Dee at the Water Palace with the Third Princess, please read *Necklace and Calabash* by Robert van Gulik, Charles Scribner's Sons, New York, 1967.

few grains of salt that had added to the melon made it taste even sweeter. That helped him reflect on life. A little pain could make one's life feel sweeter. Happiness did not necessarily require staying on 'top.' Indeed, possessing everything desired was almost guaranteed to spoil much of the fun. Reflecting on such a paradox, Judge Dee nodded and felt his heart closer to Taoism than ever before. All scholarly officials entered their career as disciples of Confucius, but as they grew older, many became believers of Taoism, privately at least. Judge Dee wondered if that was happening to him too.

While he was playing chess against Sergeant Hoong, with Tao Gan as an onlooker, Judge Dee's attention wandered off to the two recent cases pending at the tribunal. "So, what do you think we should do about the frogs, Sergeant Hoong?" the judge asked.

Three days before, a farmer had come to the tribunal to file a charge against a neighboring youth. The farmer had called him a vagabond, for the young man did not do any farming, but caught frogs in the field and sold them in the market as gourmet food. Because frogs were natural predators of the various insects that ate rice grains, the loss of the frogs from the rice ponds had resulted in an invasion of swarms of insects. For the past two days, quite a few farmers had come to the tribunal with similar complaint, except that they did not know whom to blame, for they had failed to find a frog catcher. Even had they found one, Judge Dee could not have punished him, because catching and selling frogs was perfectly legal.

Stroking his beard, Sergeant Hoong talked and blinked at the same time, a habit of his whenever he found he had much to say and had to say it fast. "Your Honor, I think it is time to put out a ban on frog hunting. At least through the summer season, until the rice is ripe for harvest. Gourmet appetites have to be held in check, and the farmers' interests must be protected. After all, farming is the principal occupation in our land."

"I understand and quite agree with Sergeant Hoong on the importance of farming to our district," Tao Gan said, expressing his disagreement with Sergeant Hoong as politely as possible. "But I doubt the useful effect of a ban on frog sales. It may create a stronger demand in the black market. As long as the rich have deep pockets, they will easily find suppliers." Tao Gan was speaking from his own experience. He used to be a swindler and knew well how a black market worked.

"That's exactly what a Taoist master would argue," Judge Dee said, stroking his long black beard. "In the long run, a government ban may only create a greater demand and make things even worse. So, the Taoists advocate the principle of doing less or nothing, and they are against pretty much of any reform or innovation."

Judge Dee raised his hand in a gesture quickly understood by Sergeant Hoong, who had served him for many years. The sergeant prepared the judge another cup of hot tea. As he was sipping, the judge soon realized how grateful he should be to have benefited from yet another morsel of Taoist wisdom. This time it was the "contrary" logic of tea drinking. On a summer day like this, hot tea could make its drinkers feel cooler. By contrast, cold tea would only stimulate thirst. As a Confucian-trained scholar, he was alarmed at how fascinated he had recently become with Taoist observations. "I wish everyone were a Buddhist," the judge suddenly spoke loudly, "so that no one would bother with frogs. Buddhists are all vegetarians, aren't they?" He laughed as he saw the perplexed faces of his two associates. Neither of them could believe that their magistrate would actually become a believer in Buddhism.

Decidedly, Judge Dee put down his teacup and saucer as he made up his mind. "In the next tribunal session I'm going to announce a ban on frog-trapping and selling. Anyone caught in frog trading will be jailed for thirty days. That should guarantee a good rice harvest. As a Confucian scholar and official, I just can't sit here and do nothing but wait for the Tao to work its way through. We'd better do something. Have to do it *now*, and do it as *fast* as we can." Judge Dee banged his desk with his right hand so heavily that he almost sent his light porcelain teacup flying into the air.

Sergeant Hoong and Tao Gan glanced at each other. They did not say a word, but in the bottom of their hearts they both fully agreed that once again this was the judge they had known. Ever since that unusual vacation trip to the town near the Water Palace, the judge had behaved strangely. Neither of them knew anything about his adventure in saving the life of the Third Princess; he would keep that a deep secret till his very last day on earth for the sake of the privacy of the royal family.

"Now," turning to Tao Gan, Judge Dee asked, "did you make any progress in your investigation?"

The day before, a wealthy merchant had reported a house burglary to the tribunal. According to him, someone had secretly dug through the outside wall of his house at night and taken all the silver coins he kept at home.

"I did find that some of the earth had recently been removed and put back again," Tao Gan said.

"That proves nothing," the judge interrupted him impatiently, twirling his teacup on his desk, "unless you're sure he didn't do it himself!" He stopped the cup by tapping it quickly with his palm. Picking up a third slice of watermelon from a blue and white porcelain tray on his desk, Judge Dee went on: "It is an old trick for a rich man to falsely report a burglary in order to avoid taxes. Many have even tried to bribe officials to accept their claims." He took a big bite of his watermelon slice, wiping its sweet juice off his mouth. Trying to eat and to talk at the same time nearly caused him to bite his tongue.

"The merchant didn't seem to me to be a cheat," Sergeant Hoong asserted, caressing his beard.

"I also have a favorable impression of him," Judge Dee said, returning the watermelon rind to the porcelain tray. Only one more slice remained. "But we can't just rely on our own instinct." He tapped the porcelain tray with his long fingers, gazing at the last slice of watermelon as if debating whether to eat it or not, while in fact he was trying to sort out quite a different problem. The judge feared that many more false claims might come up if he accepted this one too easily.

Next morning, his concern proved to be well founded. As soon as the morning session began, another merchant came to report a burglary, which had allegedly occurred that previous night when everyone in the household had been soundly asleep. Fifty silver pieces were missing, and traces of earth indicated some dirt had been removed and later replaced.

As much as he disliked seeing such cases accumulate, the judge had to wait for the results of further investigations. A hasty decision could make a bad situation much worse. Just as the proverb says, "Rash, rash, nothing is achieved but trash."

"This tribunal will conduct a thorough investigation, and you have my personal guarantee of a fair adjustment to your taxes if your report turns out to be true," Judge Dee said, caressing his long side-whiskers. "With all due respect, however, I have to warn you that justice will run its own course, and you will be punished without mercy if it proves to be a hoax. It's not too late to withdraw your case if you wish." Judge Dee released his long side-whiskers with a flick of his fingers, as a hint that he would let the man go without asking further questions.

After a moment of silence the man cleared his throat with some effort and spoke with a quiet but clear voice and in a firm tone. "Your Honor, everything I've said this morning in the court is true. I have faith in you and the heaven above us all. I'm sure you'll find all the evidence you need in due time." He knocked his forehead on the flagstone floor to show his respect, leaving the court with an air of an injured pride.

Yet another case was awaiting Judge Dee's attention. A constable had ushered in two other men and had them wait aside while the merchant was still in court. Now they were brought to kneel before the judge. The constable apparently knew one of them, and treated him with some respect. The man introduced himself: "This insignificant person is named Chang Shen, a gatekeeper at the North Gate." Judge Dee felt surprised that he had failed to recognize the gatekeeper, whom he met so often. Maybe that is a sign of getting old, Judge Dee thought. He wasn't happy that he was already forty years old.

The gatekeeper continued. "Your Honor, yesterday afternoon you announced a ban on frog trading at this tribunal, and we put out dozens of posters at the city gate. What do you think has happened? This morning I caught a man red-handed smuggling frogs."

The man kneeling next to the gatekeeper knocked his forehead on the floor and started to introduce himself in a most abject manner. "This insignificant person is named Woo Foo." Judge Dee frowned, as he couldn't clearly hear the man's name.

"Speak louder!"

"My name is Woo Foo! I know I'm guilty, and I deserve to be punished." After that curt statement he knocked his forehead again and remained in silence.

Judge Dee looked at both men pensively, stroking his black beard. It seemed to be a straightforward case. Chang Shen charged Woo Foo with smuggling frogs, and Woo Foo had confessed his crime. Nothing could be simpler. But when things seemed too obvious, Judge Dee became a little suspicious. "How did you find the frogs?" he asked the gatekeeper.

"Your Honor, he put them inside emptied watermelons." The gatekeeper held up a watermelon and showed the judge that a small triangle piece of its skin had been cut off and put back after the pulp had been all removed. He took out the triangle, and showed the judge the inside. He pulled out live frogs, one by one, six altogether. The free frogs began to jump around on the floor.

"Good job!" the amazed judge exclaimed. It wasn't clear to whom he had applied that comment, though. He sat up in his chair, his eyes following the jumping frogs in all directions. One of the frogs even reached Ma Joong, who was standing with Chiao Tai behind the judge as they usually did in tribunal sessions. As the frog sneaked into the inside leg of his pants, Ma Joong giggled and started to jump about, trying to get rid of the annoying little creature. Gusts of laughter broke out in the court, and even Chiao Tai couldn't help laughing. "Brother! You'd better watch out. Now that a frog is inside your pants, your luck may change at any moment, for better or worse."

Ma Joong was hypersensitive to anything appearing to be the least inauspicious. This comment made him turn pale. "Help me, Brother! I don't want to die yet." Such naïve alarm triggered yet more guffaws; even Judge Dee found he had to cover his face with his large sleeve to keep others from seeing him laugh. Ma Joong reached into his pants where the frog had taken refuge, and then squeezed; the poor little creature died instantly and its body dropped to the floor.

When the judge eventually stopped laughing, he rapped his high bench with the gavel to silence the court. The six constables stood up straight, with various tools of torture in hand. Ma Joong and Chiao Tai stood upright too, stiffly behind the judge. Judge Dee asked Woo Foo, the frog smuggler: "What do you have to say for yourself now?"

Woo Foo knocked his forehead on the floor once again and answered: "This insignificant person has nothing to say," and then added, "I had bad luck today."

"What do you mean you had bad luck?" The passive demeanor of the smuggler annoyed the judge. "Didn't you know that I announced a ban on frog trading yesterday afternoon right here at this tribunal? You can't deny that, can you?" Judge Dee asked. He would not tolerate his authority being ignored like that.

"I heard it," the man answered curtly.

"Who told you about it?"

"My wife. She also said that the price for frogs would be very high from now on and we could make some quick money by capturing and selling them," the smuggler began to talk more freely.

"Where were you going to find a buyer?"

"I was about to try my luck at one of those expensive restaurants. The 'Four Springs a Year,' to begin with."

"Whose idea was it to stuff the watermelons?" Judge Dee asked.

"Again, that was *her* idea, Your Honor. Her name is Ching Bai," Woo Foo pronounced his wife's name with a subtle pride in his tone.

"Did she tell anyone else about the idea?"

"Not a soul. She assured me that it was an original idea and no one else would have thought about it. 'Pretty soon we'll be rich enough to own our own rice pond,' she said," Woo Foo imitated his wife's tone as she had said those exact words.

"How did the gatekeeper detect your smuggling?"

Woo Foo sighed, crestfallen, "He stopped me and searched my basket. He picked up a melon and turned it around, until he found the removable triangle on the skin." Woo Foo smiled bitterly as he finished his story. The court-hall became dead silent. The man's evident want of any enthusiasm in defending himself annoyed Judge Dee. The case had been resolved before he could start investigating! Suddenly, Judge Dee thought about something. He asked Chang Shen, the gatekeeper, "Where do you live? How far is it from his house?" Judge Dee pointed at the frog smuggler, Woo Foo.

Taken aback, the gatekeeper mumbled: "I live outside of the North Gate. Only a mile from his village."

"Did you know him before?"

"No," Chang Shen shook his head.

Judge Dee shouted to the constables: "Arrest Woo Foo's wife for adultery with Chang Shen!"

Ignoring the flabbergasted smuggler, Woo Foo, the judge proceeded to interrogate Chang Shen with a series of questions. "How could you possibly know to stop him at the gate? No one but he and his wife knew of the ingenious smuggling plan. You haven't bothered to check every melon peddler for smuggling, have you? And why did you turn his watermelon around and search for the removable triangle in the skin? You must already have known the secret. Isn't that right? You said you didn't know him. But you also said you live only a mile from his house. How could you possibly know that if you didn't know him?"

Each of these questions reverberated like thunder in the ear of Chang Shen. His whole face and neck reddened as he realized his foolishness. He knocked his forehead on the floor for mercy. "Your Honor, I confess everything." The man knew only too well what kind of torture was awaiting him if he did not confess. "I'm having an affair with his wife. Yesterday when I heard the ban that a frog smuggler would be jailed for thirty days I saw a great opportunity. I told her to encourage her husband to smuggle frogs. She convinced him that in this season no one would think watermelons suspect. I was on duty this morning and just waited for him to show up. I'm lucky that he was the first watermelon peddler I had to stop."

Judge Dee ordered fifty strikes as the punishment for Chang Shen. And the same punishment awaited Woo Foo's wife in the next session when she would be called to confess. Woo Foo would be jailed for thirty days. Before the constables took him to the jail, he thanked the judge for the detection of his wife's adultery. He had always admired his wife for her cleverness, but he never thought that she would use it to cheat on him.

The man was so embarrassed that he dared not to look at anyone in the court as he left. The spectators in the courtyard jeered him mercilessly. When he had banned frog sales the day before, Judge Dee had not expected that it would help him detect adultery today. Feeling a little sorry for the ashamed man, the judge silenced the spectators with his oblong gavel and closed the tribunal.

*   *   *   *

The morning became hotter as it went on. Not a single patch of cloud floated in the sky to offer shade from the burning sun. As the noon session began, the heat inside the tribunal was almost unbearable. The annoying clamor of the cicadas singing on the trees in the courtyard outside made it even worse. And then a baby's cry suddenly rose to exceed all the other noises. A constable brought in a woman in her twenties, her wailing baby in her arms. A man twice her age followed, hauling a basket with three watermelons in it. He had a florid round face and was naked from his waist up, and his black pants shone under the bright sun.

"This insignificant person is named Hoo Nao. I'm a farmer and grow watermelons. All those melons you see outside the North Gate on both sides of the avenue are mine. They are the best, you can be sure." The man kept on talking like a huckster, nearly forgetting that he was in the court-hall. Yet Judge Dee could barely hear what the man said, as the baby cried loudly. The judge, frowning, turned to the woman and asked: "Can't you do something to stop his awful crying?" The woman looked around, hesitated, and then opened her robe to bare her left breast. The baby sucked her nipple only briefly, and resumed his outcry. The woman had to resort to a simpler but more effective ways: she just jammed her breast into his mouth!

"Proceed!" Judge Dee said, turning again to the watermelon farmer, Hoo Nao.

"I caught her stealing my watermelons, Your Honor. I often lose watermelons to thieves, but I've never caught one red-handed before. Please punish this shameless woman mercilessly, so that others will learn a lesson, and no one will try to steal my melons again."

Judge Dee looked quietly at the woman, as if asking: "Is that true?"

"It's so hot this morning, and my baby wouldn't stop crying. My mother is ill and I was on my way to visit her. When I saw the watermelons I wanted to feed my baby some cool juice. I looked around, but couldn't find the owner of the field. I decided to simply take a melon. As I walked away and didn't have a chance to break open the melon, he seemed to appear all of a sudden from nowhere. I would have offered to pay if I had seen him. I didn't mean to steal. I swear." The woman broke into tears.

"Liar!" the man snapped at her. He pointed at the basket that had three watermelons in it.

"I'm not a liar," the woman shook her head indignantly. "I was telling the truth, Your Honor," she said.

"No, no, no," the man pouted his lips and shook his head. "She stole them all. And she would have stolen more, if I hadn't stopped her."

The baby cried again. The woman held him up to burp him. She put her breast back inside her robe and held the baby tightly against her chest. The baby wouldn't stop crying, and kicked at her stomach.

Judge Dee inclined his head and stroked his long side-whiskers. Although he had three young children, his patience for babies was quite limited. While waiting for the woman to quiet her baby, his eyes fell on the basket that held three watermelons, each a little bigger than a toddler's head. An idea suddenly occurred to him. "Is that yours or hers?" the judge pointed at the basket and asked Hoo Nao casually.

"Of course it is mine! I brought it to the field this morning," the man answered resolutely.

Judge Dee smiled. And then he laughed.

"Give him your baby," he ordered the woman.

The woman was startled, and the man looked at the judge, perplexed too.

"Did you hear me? Just do what I said," Judge Dee repeated testily.

The man awkwardly put his hands out for the baby, while the woman handed it to him, looking quite suspicious. The baby screamed even louder, and his little feet kicked in the air.

"Now, you pick up those three melons for me, please," Judge Dee said.

The man shifted the baby to the left side of his chest, held it with his left hand, and used his right hand to pick up a melon. He put the melon in his left hand, which now had both the baby and a melon. He squatted down to pick up the second melon. Then he tried to put it into his left hand again, but the hand was too full. Holding both the baby and the melon with one hand was not easy. To add another melon was simply impossible. With a melon in it, the man moved his right hand this way and that way. Finally, he put the melon underneath his right arm. Now his right hand was free, but he could barely reach out for another melon. After several clumsy tries, he picked up the third melon, but held it only for a few seconds. The melon under his arm slipped. It dropped to the ground and smashed into pieces. Then the other melon slipped from his right hand and fell back to the basket and cracked. The man lost his balance and sat down on the ground. Holding tight to the baby and the only melon left unbroken, the man sighed and gave a wry smile. The entire court broke out laughing. The woman quickly took back her baby, and patted him on his buttocks. She smiled too. The baby, glad to return safely to his mother's arms, stopped crying.

The man was left holding the last watermelon in his hands, looking very silly. He righted himself and knelt down in front of the judge: "Well, I wasn't exactly telling the truth when I said she had stolen three watermelons. She only took one. I was afraid that Your Honor wouldn't bother with such a small matter. So I picked up two more melons and put them all in the basket and dragged her here. But I wasn't lying when I said I have lost many watermelons to thieves, Your Honor." The man waved his hands in the air to help illustrate his testimony.

Judge Dee shook his head while stroking his beard, listening. "Nothing is too trivial for this tribunal, as long as justice is concerned. Remember, a district magistrate is often referred to as a 'parent official.' That means it's his duty to take care of each of you just as parents take care of their children. A judge must be a father and mother to the people, cherishing the good and loyal, helping the sick and old. A district is just like a large family, and a magistrate treats each citizen fairly. You don't need to come here to resolve every dispute. And indeed you are encouraged not to come here too often. Only when you cannot resolve disputes among yourselves shall you come to the tribunal. But once you are here, you should have absolute faith in me. Never try to outsmart your magistrate in order to cover your dirty deeds. As you've all seen today, that just doesn't work. It's impossible." Judge Dee spoke with such confidence in his tone that few who heard it had any doubts about the justice that he was representing. He had personified it.

Hoo Nao knocked his forehead on the flagstone floor to show his respect. "This insignificant person will never try to fool the tribunal again. I swear to Heaven!"

The baby suddenly cried again. Judge Dee frowned and yelled: "Please give it some watermelon juice. I don't see how anyone could object. Do you?" he asked Hoo Nao.

The man quickly picked up a piece of melon and handed it to the woman. She smiled and said she would pay him for it. The man shook his head, smiling. Turning to the judge, he said, "Your Honor, this insignificant person deeply regrets his selfishness and feels terribly ashamed. Please allow me to make it up. She can borrow my basket and take a few melons to her mother if she wants. For a sick person in summer, no gift is better than a fresh melon. I shouldn't have bothered you at all. To make up for my trouble, let me offer you some of my best melons." The man wiped the sweat off his naked chest with his both hands, and dried his wet hands on the sides of his black pants.

Judge Dee smiled and glanced at his lieutenants and constables. "How could I possibly refuse such a generous offer? When this session is over, we shall all go to your field to pick up the best melons we can find. But I guarantee you that we won't take more than ten. Is that fair?"

The judge was particularly delighted that the case not only had a happy ending but also restored a sense of the higher good to each person. The whole event proved the Confucian teaching that humans were born with goodness in their hearts. Judge Dee decided to use this opportunity to teach the public a lesson in Confucianism. He addressed the court loudly:

"Before we close this session of the tribunal, let me remind you of something with greater importance than the value of a few melons. What we have witnessed today has once again proved how right our great master, Confucius, was. More than a thousand years ago he began to advocate the 'Benevolent Rule.' 'Let humanity be your highest standard,' our master said, 'and completely forget about yourself.' Our August Throne has great respect for Confucianism. Under his benevolent rule, each law-abiding citizen may enjoy the freedom of doing whatever he wants to do, as long as he doesn't hurt the interest of others who are also law-abiding. The whole country is like a big family, and all members are to live in harmony with each other."

Speaking to the woman and Hoo Nao, Judge Dee added: "In the spirit of 'Benevolent Rule,' I won't punish either of you today for your imprudent conduct. Each of you has received enough rebukes. Though my job is to mete out stern punishment to every criminal, it is prevention, not correction, that is my primary aim. Just remember: justice in heaven is everywhere, even if you don't see it. It works like a net. It seems to leak but always catches what it is supposed to catch."

The entire court seemed to be uplifted by the judge's philosophical comments. Everyone was in a better mood and felt ready to share in almost anything. With commendable teamwork, the constables had the official palanquin set up to await the judge at the entrance of the tribunal. They were eager to join him and to enjoy the prospect of fresh melons at the watermelon field outside the North Gate. Judge Dee sat inside the palanquin, leaving the curtains on all sides open to the breeze. The only drawback was that flies could also come in and fly about. They bothered the judge terribly, because these noisome insects might alight on ordure and in the next minute alight upon *him*. The judge frowned on such a thought, covering his mouth unconsciously as the entourage left the tribunal and turned to go north. Two constables carried the judge; two held up a big banner that read: "Magistrate of Poo-yang," and another two walked ahead of the train, each striking a small gong and shouting at intervals: "Make way, Make way," which was how a magistrate and his escort usually proceeded through his district. Ma Joong and Chiao Tai walked on each side of the palanquin, and Hoo Nao followed behind. He was much gratified to have such publicity, calculating that it might well help keep future thieves away from his watermelons.

The avenue was fairly wide and flat. The constables carried the palanquin skillfully, keeping its swinging to a minimum. But before the judge and his entourage got very far, a couple of sleeping drifters partially blocked their passage. The men were lying on their backs facing the bright midday sun. Their arms and legs were askew and akimbo, and they seemed to have been enjoying the breeze.

Judge Dee raised his hand to halt the queue. He looked down at the sleepers, who were both young men in their early twenties. Their evident physical fatigue stirred his sympathy, and he ordered the constables who had already ceased their gong striking and warning cries to make a detour. As they passed along, they could hear the loud snoring of the sleepers. The constables covered their mouths and laughed. Judge Dee smiled too.

He also noticed a couple of smashed watermelons that lay at the foot of both sleepers. The fresh red color of the melons contrasted strongly to the blue and brown colors of the sleepers' dusty clothes. Yet strangely enough, none of the melons had been eaten! Instead, a crowd of flies swarmed around. "What a waste!" Judge Dee thought. The palanquin passed on and the judge and his entourage proceeded along another hundred feet or so.

"Halt!" Judge Dee suddenly shouted. Turning to Ma Joong and Chiao Tai on his left and right, the judge ordered: "Arrest those two sleepers!"

Ma Joong and Chiao Tai could hardly believe what they had heard. Neither could the six constables. The very word "arrest" scared Hoo Nao so much that his knees knocked, and he almost wet his pants.

"Go! Quick! Chances are that those two are the burglars who robbed the merchants' houses at night."

As Ma Joong and Chiao Tai brought the two to the judge, both of them still rubbing sleep from their eyes.

"Let's move on to our melon party! We'll deal with these two thugs later in the afternoon tribunal session," Judge Dee ordered.

During that session, both men confessed their crimes. Afterwards, at his private office, the judge revealed how he had deduced that they were the burglars. Both had looked so poor and so exhausted that they seemed not even to have time to enjoy their melons before falling asleep. But something odd had caught the judge's attention. The watermelons had been at their feet, instead of at their heads!

It turned out that the impression of the swarming flies around the melons kept bothering him as the judge was carried down the road. What a luxury! He thought. But hold on a minute! How could two poor young men afford to squander melons like that? Even he and his constables had to walk a long way in order to enjoy the gift of a few fresh melons. These two young men, so desperate to get a good sleep, had deliberately placed the exposed melons at their feet to attract flies so they would not disturb their sleep. They must have worked quite hard overnight to be so tired at midday, and they didn't care about squandering the melons. Ah, yes, they must have been the nocturnal burglars he was looking for! The judge had just solved a case that morning where watermelons had been destroyed for a more profitable purpose in the frog smuggling. Now these bits and pieces helped him to solve yet another case. He had thus solved three cases in one day, all related to watermelons.

Judge Dee felt thirsty again after he had finished his report. Before he gave even the slightest hint, Sergeant Hoong was ready to stand up and make tea for him. But before the sergeant could make his move, Tao Gan had produced a watermelon in his hand. It happened so quickly and the melon seemed to have appeared from nowhere. Everyone laughed, and the judge knew that the former swindler must have hidden it somewhere and brought the melon all the way from the field they had been in. As the sergeant was cutting and serving the melon, Tao Gan began to play piri, a windpipe musical instrument of Persian origin that had recently become fashionable. The judge hummed and smiled, and inclined his head to the left and right, until he was suddenly choked with a watermelon seed.

CHAPTER 7

▼

FAKE FOR FAKE

Judge Dee had been enjoying the exhilaration of a brisk ride into the countryside for the past half an hour. Although it was a routine early morning exercise, his horse had run a little faster today in the cooler air and had carried him a couple of miles further than usual. As he reached a small Buddhist abbey named Sweet Dew Monastery he thought it was time to return. The bright golden yellow walls reminded him of his first case in Poo-yang. In the previous year, he had investigated numerous rapes at the Temple of Boundless Mercy. Ever since the conviction of dozens of the monks, the popularity of Buddhism had dramatically dropped in this small but flourishing district of about twelve thousand people. Less than a handful of temples had survived, and the Sweet Dew Monastery was one of them. Its walls had recently been painted; the monks appeared to do quite well. Judge Dee observed as he rode comfortably on the back of his favorite horse, whose black and white coat sometimes gave it the appearance of a very tall cow.

A young monk from the abbey was sweeping the floor on the three marble entrance steps. "Isn't it a nice day, Young Master?" the judge addressed the monk politely. "We finally have some cool weather after a long summer. Why, you don't look happy. Can you tell me what's on your mind? Maybe I can help you."

The young man looked up, staring at the judge blankly. Most likely he had not recognized Judge Dee as the magistrate. He must be new and from another town, thought the judge. The young man discerned the tone of paternal concern in the judge's deep voice. So he said, "I just became a monk three days ago! And I didn't want to." Seeing surprise in the eyes of the judge, the young man explained, "My parents died when I was young, before I turned nine. My uncle took everything and kicked me out of the house. Now I'm eighteen and I want to get back everything that should belong to me. My depraved uncle denies that I'm his nephew. Isn't it outrageous? I joined the temple just to forget it all. If I had the choice, I would rather be studying. Someday I may pass all the exams, and the Emperor will appoint me magistrate!" The young man waved the broom in his hand as if it were his brush-pen, writing passionately in the air to demonstrate his skills in calligraphy. The public exams in classic Confucian literature were carefully designed to give every man an equal opportunity to advance in society while serving both the state and the people. The monk's story touched the judge's heart. Feeling pity for this poor lad, he scowled, drawing his bushy eyebrows together, and dismounted.

"Does your uncle live in Poo-yang?" Judge Dee asked to confirm his doubt.

The young man shook his head. Too bad, Judge Dee thought, otherwise I would look into the case. He quickly thought of all the possible ways he could help, and when he spoke again his calm voice had a tone of authority. "Surely there's a way to get back your property, if only you take a bit of risk. However, you must be prepared for some castigation at your district tribunal. It won't be too bad, though. Twenty strikes at the most."

"That is nothing," the young monk responded, waving the broom in his hand energetically, as he hoped to find a way out of his difficult situation. "Please tell me what to do. My uncle is the one who deserves punishment. Twenty strikes aren't enough for him. I don't mind taking a risk, if that's the only way to have justice."

"Well, in that case," asked the judge, "why don't you just threaten to kick his butt?"

The young man could hardly believe his ears, and looked totally confused. Why would this seemingly benign father figure suggest that he do what Confucius had always considered to be an act of the worst ingratitude? Wasn't it the law that, unlike giving offence to a stranger, any offence to parents or any senior relative should be severely punished? He was appalled and leaned his chin on the end of his broom, to stare up at the judge, who was much taller than he. Patting the young man on the shoulder, Judge Dee smiled. "Relax, Young Master. As soon as you threaten to beat him, I'll bet he will haul you to the tribunal and charge you with an offense to your own uncle! With that, he will proclaim officially that you are his nephew. That should help reclaim your father's property, shouldn't it?"

The young man's face instantly lit up. Throwing down his broom, he bowed low to thank the judge for his devious suggestion. "Whatever I have, you'll get one tenth of it," he promised, grinning broadly.

"Remember, your magistrate may still order twenty strikes on your bare buttocks for the offence to your uncle," Judge Dee warned him again.

"I don't care," said the monk as he picked up his broom. He waved it to say good-bye and retreated into the abbey.

Watching the young man disappear, Judge Dee smiled. What would that huge statue of Buddha standing behind the iron front gate think of this? Judge Dee put his hands in front of his chest, with the palms facing each other, bent forward slightly, and murmured with closed eyes, just like a Buddhist in prayer. "Forgive me for taking your recent recruit. However, this healthy young man should really serve his country in a more constructive way!"

With a good feeling in his heart, Judge Dee returned to the tribunal. On his way, he passed five monks. Seeing them reminded him how quickly he had solved the young man's problem. A smile was on his face, until he saw Sergeant Hoong standing at the tribunal entrance waiting for him. Something must have gone badly awry. His triumphant mood disappeared quickly as he dismounted his horse. "Your Honor, we're in tr...trouble," Sergeant Hoong stammered, "Ma...many silver pieces in our public storage vault are found f...fake. Fan Tong, the man in char...charge, told me just an hour ago. Someone must have swindled them, and Fan Tong didn't notice, taking them as g...genuine. Now, we owe a great deal to this scoundrel. Wh...what shall we do?"

Judge Dee stared at his confidential advisor, disbelieving what he had heard. Shortly after he solved several burglary cases in the beginning of the previous month, he had set up a public storage vault in the tribunal compound for private citizens to store their valuables. It was quite the popular move. The merchants had been grateful to him for reducing their worries of burglary. In fact, only a day before, he had received many compliments as he visited the marketplace in the afternoon with his Second Lady. A florist had even given her a bunch of chrysanthemums as a gift. Now, overnight, his innovation had been turned into mockery, making him, the Magistrate of Poo-yang, look more like a fool.

The judge walked quietly to his office, his hands behind his back, signaling a much-troubled mind. In contrast, having relayed bad news to the judge, Sergeant Hoong now felt much relieved. He wiped the sweat off his forehead and followed the judge into his office. The sergeant knew exactly how to help the judge concentrate and sharpen his mind. He served him a cup of his favorite tea, "Hairy Tiptop." A strong tea, its best flavor came after the pot was refilled. Before the judge could get to his second cup, the boom of the huge gong at the entrance of the tribunal announced that the morning session was due to begin. Judge Dee quickly donned his ceremonial robe and his winged cap. Sitting behind his high bench on the dais, he could hardly concentrate on the matter at hand. All he could think of was the storage of fake silver.

Five monks kneeled in front of him. Their shaved heads glowed in the light of the early morning sun. For a moment, the judge almost took them as the ghosts of those guilty monks at the Temple of Boundless Mercy. "Your Honor," a lean man of about sixty spoke hastily while twisting the beads in his long neck-string, a typical adornment of a Buddhist monk. "This humble monk is known by his Buddhist name as Hui Jin. We're from the Sweet Dew Monastery. Last month our old abbot Hui Poo passed away at the age of seventy. A new abbot was appointed in the capital, and he arrived a week ago. Yesterday he told us that he couldn't find our treasure: ten large gold ingots. That's quite impossible! This is a legacy that each abbot saved and passed on. No one has ever squandered it. Our new abbot must have embezzled it. Please interrogate him and punish the thief!" Exhausted by his own speech, the elderly monk licked his dry lips and tried to catch his breath. His chest heaved noticeably, as his palpitations pushed the beads on his belly back and forth.

Judge Dee frowned. To interfere with an internal affair in a Buddhist temple was perhaps the last thing he wanted to do at this moment in his career. His first case in Poo-yang was a notorious series of rapes at the Temple of Boundless Mercy. Unable to get pregnant at home, hundreds of women had visited the temple to beg for the aid of the deities, only to be seduced or raped by the monks! After the conviction, the angry men whose wives or daughters had been victims had rioted and broken into the jail. All the guilty monks had been ruthlessly mobbed and killed on the street. The news had shocked the Buddhist authorities in the capital. Ever since they had been trying to find fault in the judge's handling of the case. An investigation into yet another Buddhist abbey would reopen the old wounds in his relationship with the powerful and well-connected Buddhist authorities.

The hesitant judge remained silent, caressing his long black beard. Looking sharply at each of the five monks one by one, he suddenly asked, "Did all of you see the gold before the new abbot arrived? Are you absolutely sure it was in the temple when he took over?"

The five monks each nodded his head.

"Where and when did you last see the gold in the temple?"

The monks looked at each other; no one gave an answer, until their leader spoke up on behalf of them all. "Our former abbot used to show us the gold in his room on New Year's Eve as we prayed for another peaceful and prosperous year. Just as during the rest of the year, we were told to work harder to polish and make the gold shine in our hearts. Na-mo-o-mi-to-fuo," the elderly man intoned.

Judge Dee couldn't help but frown again. He didn't like what he heard, for he never understood this kind of Buddhist talk. "Well, if that is the case, I'm going to visit your new abbot and see what he has to say. No matter what he says, I guarantee that this tribunal will conduct a thorough investigation and that justice will take its own course." The judge did not want to summon the new abbot to the tribunal quite yet. This roundabout method would offer him more room to maneuver.

Having knocked their foreheads on the flagstone floor one more time to show their due respect, the five monks filed out one by one. The onlookers in the courtyard started to argue with each other. Many were quite astonished, as they had never before heard that the abbey possessed so much gold. How could the monks have kept such a secret so well?

Back at his private office, Judge Dee changed from his ceremonial dress to his casual blue robe and black skullcap. Sergeant Hoong served him a cup of tea. Each of his three lieutenants, Ma Joong, Chiao Tai and Tao Gan, gathered in the office. They had all heard about the trouble at the public storage vault, and knew how serious the problem was. If they couldn't resolve the case and get the silver back, their judge might be charged with embezzlement of public money. This could cost him his office, and even his life. If that happened, surely they would all lose their positions in the tribunal, for all of them were its appointed personnel and the next magistrate would want his own team. Thus the stakes were high for everyone.

The atmosphere in the room kept sober and gloomy. No one talked yet. Ma Joong had little interest in the monk's case, because apparently no woman was involved. Tao Gan was curious about the faked silver, for he had been a swindler himself before the judge had reformed him. He really wanted to know who had the skill and nerve to cheat the tribunal on such a grand scale. Having been a loyal soldier, the faithful Chiao Tai was most concerned about the possible impact of the faked silver on the judge's career. Only the more experienced sergeant had a sense about how much more important the case in the abbey was. At this moment, powerful political enemies were the last things the judge needed. Local opinion had strongly supported his idea of setting up a public storage vault. His personal popularity and motives of public altruism would certainly encourage the Prefect to argue in his favor. But incurring the further enmity of powerful Buddhist authorities in the capital could easily tip the balance. The Prefect might have to punish Judge Dee for his "apparent dereliction of duty."

The silence in the room lingered. Judge Dee looked out the open window into the courtyard. A gusty autumn wind blew dead leaves off the trees; one of the leaves fell on his forehead and remained there. He ignored it for a short while, and then suddenly brushed it aside, breaking the deep silence in the room. "Listen, I wish you were all Buddhists, for they believe that good is rewarded with good and evil with evil, and that life is also part of such a cycle. Even life and death are a cycle, so that the good in this life will be rewarded in the next one, if not in the current life. As long as we are performing good deeds, there is nothing to worry about." He was talking philosophy again. That is where he distinguished himself from other magistrates, understanding each of the major philosophies: Confucianism, Taoism, and Buddhism.

Judge Dee's jesting tone cheered up his colleagues. Chiao Tai began to report his findings at the public storage vault. The swindler had brought in faked silver: ten pieces in the shape of a boat and twenty coins in the size of the palm of a hand. It was a standardized custom that boat-shaped silver weighed half a pound each, and palm-sized coin weighed a quarter pound. Since only the weight of the silver mattered in trading, the clerk at the public storage vault had made a note to the swindler, acknowledging storing ten pounds of silver for him. The clerk also only kept the information on weight but no other details in his dossier, although people who deposited did not know that. The swindler could come back at any moment to get ten pounds of silver all at once or withdraw them in several times.

"Fan Tong hasn't recalled anyone withdrawing that much silver recently. The record shows that two dozen people have each stored ten pounds of silver or more," said Chiao Tai, "and no one has recently withdrawn a large amount. But without knowing the size, shape and amount of each piece, it is impossible to tell who deposited the counterfeits." Chiao Tai concluded his report. Judge Dee nodded his approval of his lieutenant's careful briefing and sound reasoning.

Tao Gan wondered how soon and how much the swindler might begin to withdraw. The criminal had already demonstrated considerable shrewdness by not recouping too soon. Judge Dee knew that he had to resolve the case quickly, for the swindler might take action soon. Bang! Judge Dee punched his desk with his fist.

"What will happen if people hear about the news?" asked Ma Joong.

"That will be a disaster," answered Sergeant Hoong. "Everyone will rush in to recoup his money, and we will soon have only the counterfeits on hand."

"Sergeant Hoong is absolutely right. We must keep this secret until we find a solution. Make sure there's no gossip about it at all!" Judge Dee said.

"I've already told Fan Tong to keep his mouth shut," said Sergeant Hoong.

"Very good," Judge Dee said approvingly. "And from now on we shall watch carefully to see if anyone comes to recoup a large sum of silver."

"When are you going to visit the new abbot at the Sweet Dew Monastery?" asked the gray-bearded sergeant, for he knew that case was also of great importance.

As if reading the sergeant's mind, Judge Dee replied promptly: "Ah ha! I've provoked the Buddha today already," he smiled. "Maybe I've done too much and gone too far!" Noticing the confusion of his colleagues, the judge added: "Do you remember the Taoist teaching that it's better to do less than to try to do too much?" His curt and cryptic reference to Tao only made his associates more confused. They all looked to him for enlightenment.

"I know," explained the judge, "Sergeant Hoong is afraid that I may provoke the Buddhist authorities again. I think I forgot to tell you something. On my way back to the tribunal from my morning exercise, I saw a young monk at the Sweet Dew Monastery who seemed very morose and I asked him why. It turned out he was not only new to the temple, but that he did not even want to be a monk! Since becoming an orphan nine years ago, his uncle has possessed his inheritance. Now he denies that this man is his nephew. Having lost hope, the young man joined the abbey. But he is not as happy as a true Buddhist should be. In fact, he wants to become a Confucian scholar." The judge took a few gulps of his favorite tea and continued, "Although he didn't recognize me as the magistrate, he was willing to take my advice."

"So what did you advise him to do?" asked Chiao Tai anxiously.

"I told him to kick his uncle's butt!"

"No joke! You did?" Ma Joong exclaimed excitedly, grinning from ear to ear. But the others were more puzzled, for such familiarity was totally out of Judge Dee's character.

"I was betting his uncle would take him to court, and bring charges against him as a juvenile offender. That would actually help the young man by establishing an official record of him as the uncle's nephew, wouldn't it?"

"Marvelous!" Ma Joong exclaimed again, and gestured broadly in the air, seeming not sure what to do with his large hands.

"The young monk has promised me one tenth of his father's property if he gets it back," Judge Dee smiled. "I assume he has left the temple by now. In that sense, I've already offended Buddha, for I've cost him a new recruit. According to

Buddhism, everything is in a cause-and-effect chain. Even the Taoist teaching says 'never trouble trouble until trouble troubles you.' Both Taoism and Buddhism share the same wisdom in this matter. But I was following the Confucian training and giving first priority to help other people and maintain justice. Consequently I have to deal with all the troubles ahead. I should have known better, shouldn't I?" Judge Dee laughed mischievously.

The judge's lively humor reassured his associates. More than once they had heard him say, "You must forget about yourself, just as our master Confucius has taught us." They couldn't help but admire him for such mastery of philosophy. Thinking over what the judge had advised the young monk to do, Tao Gan commented thoughtfully: "Yours seems to be a 'fake for fake' strategy, instead of a 'tooth for tooth' one," twisting the few long black hairs which sprouted from the mole on his cheek.

"Exactly," Judge Dee said. "The monk actually doesn't need to beat his uncle, but just to threaten him. As long as that threat looks real, it will work." Judge Dee caressed his long side-whiskers contentedly, congratulating himself on his acumen. All of a sudden, his fist punched his desk and he exclaimed: "Hey! Why don't we use the same trick to get at the swindler who gave us the counterfeits?"

"Same trick?" Sergeant Hoong asked, unable to follow what the judge had said. Neither could any of his lieutenants. Judge Dee sat up in his chair and started to give orders: "Tao Gan and Chiao Tai, I want you to dig a big hole in the wall of the storage vault and secretly move all the valuables to another safe place tonight. Tomorrow morning, Sergeant Hoong, put up as many posters as possible throughout the city telling people about the 'burglary.' It should also say that, in order to help us verify our account books and know exactly what lost treasures to look for, the tribunal is asking each individual who has secured funds at the storage vault to provide detailed descriptions of his own valuables. Assure the public that the tribunal will arrest the burglars and get their valuables back. They should not worry, but their information is most welcome and important. Meanwhile, Ma Joong, send constables to every neighborhood on pretext of searching for the loot. I bet the swindler will immediately appear with information on his deposit, just as anyone else who has deposited something will. With an account on the shape, size, and the amount of each type of deposit, we shall easily be able to detect the criminal, won't we?"

Great laughter broke out in the room, but Chiao Tai still wasn't quite sure.

"How can you be sure that he will tell us the truth?"

"Well, he has to, because he doesn't know that we don't have a detailed record. If he tells the truth and we haven't noticed the counterfeits, he still has a chance."

Chiao Tai nodded once he was fully convinced. Everyone laughed this time, until tears came down his cheeks.

"Well, now I better visit the new abbot and see what he has to say for himself," the judge said as he stood up for the door.

*   *   *   *

Judge Dee had returned to the Sweet Dew Monastery by mid afternoon. Another young novice monk was sweeping the marble stairs leading to the entrance. "I hope he won't get into any trouble in his tribunal," the judge said to himself, thinking of the young monk that he had advised earlier that day.

The judge showed his official card to the new monk. The young man bowed, appeared to take fright, and ran off like a rabbit! Judge Dee didn't have long to wait before the lean elderly monk came out through the gate, followed by the four monks who had accompanied him to the tribunal that morning. The four monks followed their lean elder as quietly as four shadows.

"What a great pleasure to meet Your Honor again," the elderly monk exclaimed. He was cut short before he could say anything more.

"Lead me to your abbot," the judge said curtly.

"Please allow this humble monk to show you the way," the lean, elderly man bowed and proceeded to guide the judge down a long corridor roofed in gray tile. The fragrance of exotic incense reminded Judge Dee of those unpleasant days at the Temple of Boundless Mercy. The fact that the abbot didn't come out to meet him might be quite significant. While the other monks appeared to be almost too well organized the abbot had few friends in the abbey and was probably still ignorant of his arrival. Judge Dee coughed as he speculated about the situation. The incense was quite thick and stung his throat.

The abbot's room had an even stronger odor that mixed the exotic foreign incense with something else equally pungent. Judge Dee's eyes followed his nose as both fell upon a saggy face with a fleshy nose above a thick-lipped mouth. The judge suspected that the other smell was coming from the robe that the abbot was wearing, or it could be from his obese body.

"Welcome," said the abbot after he had read the judge's card, presented to him by the elderly monk. Judge Dee waved his hand to excuse the other five, and stood alone, face to face with the abbot. "Please accept my apology for not visiting you first," said the abbot. Judge Dee noticed some little quaver in the man's voice.

"Your place is certainly more interesting to visit than mine. I would rather meet with you here," the judge spoke with a resonant voice, pointing at the paintings of beautiful landscapes hanging on the walls.

The abbot seemed much relieved to hear such a genuine compliment. "Please be seated, Your Honor, in the best seat over there." The abbot pointed to a spacious couch near the window. He clapped his hands, and a young monk ran in. "Serve us tea, the best tea, of course," the abbot ordered brusquely. A short silence lingered in the room, as the abbot waited for the judge to start the conversation.

Judge Dee cleared his throat and began: "Your Reverence must have already heard what has happened. This morning, you were accused at my tribunal of embezzling the treasure of the abbey. This magistrate had no other choice but to come here for an answer from Your Reverence." Despite his verbal courtesy, Judge Dee looked sternly at the abbot.

With a twist of his thick lips, the abbot murmured, "I don't know how to say this, but...." His voice trailed off as he was searching for the right words.

"Well, let me ask you a simple question, then. When did you arrive here?"

"Exactly a week ago," the abbot answered. Judge Dee noticed the quaver in the abbot's voice again.

"What has happened since then? Did you find anything strange going on at the abbey?" Judge Dee asked encouragingly.

The abbot did find the word "strange" encouraging and he began to speak more freely. "I don't know exactly what you've heard, but I've never seen the gold. All the monks insist that there had been gold, but I truly have not seen it. I simply don't know what they are talking about. I swear to Heaven that I'm speaking the whole truth, nothing but the truth. Yet the monks...." the abbot broke off in the middle of the sentence as he saw the young monk bring in the hot tea.

While Judge Dee was being served tea, he surveyed the room quietly. Beside the pungent smell that he didn't like, something else in the room bothered him. A light coating of dust sat on almost everything: the paintings on walls, the lamps on the tables, and the furniture on the floor. As he looked around, two poems on the walls caught his attention. One read:

> "*Deluded, a Buddha is a perceptive being;*
> *Awakened, a perceptive being is a Buddha.*
> *Ignorant, a Buddha is a perceptive being;*

With wisdom, a perceptive being is a Buddha."
Judge Dee shook his head. He seemed to understand the poem at first blush, but then he wasn't so sure. The style of the poem was tricky. It was called Zen; it looked simple and straightforward but was meant to convey a much richer and deeper meaning. The other poem was written in the same style:

"In our mind itself a Buddha exists,
Our own Buddha is the true Buddha.
If we do not have in ourselves the Buddha mind,
Then where are we to seek Buddha?"

Judge Dee thought he understood this one better, but then he felt unsure again. This was the effect of a Zen poem: the more you read it, the less sure you felt that you fully understood it. Judge Dee became annoyed at himself for wasting his time.

The room remained quiet after tea was served. The young monk had left. Outside the window, dried leaves drifted in the air, reminding the judge of his conversation with the new monk earlier that day. Something struck the judge as ironic. How could he have possibly foretold that the abbot also had a money problem on his hands? A temple was supposed to be a place where a man should not worry about money, wasn't it? Judge Dee smiled. He felt lucky that he had never wanted to become a Buddhist. The silence in the room convinced the judge that he could not get any more information from the abbot. The pungent odor in the room wasn't at all inviting. He hoped he would not have to return.

As the abbot politely accompanied him back to the front gate, Judge Dee saw the five monks in the corridor. Their anxious faces betrayed their curiosity concerning his conversation with the abbot. Judge Dee suddenly felt some sympathy for the abbot. Just like the new monk he had helped that morning, the abbot was quite a stranger here. The two even had something in common in their physical appearance but the judge couldn't tell exactly what. He left the abbey feeling surrounded by more uncertainty than he had felt upon arriving.

When he returned to the tribunal, a constable at the gate told the judge that he had just missed a special tribunal session. A man named Hao Wen had discovered a body in a deep, dried-up well about five miles from the Sweet Dew Monastery. Sergeant Hoong had called in the coroner to examine the body. The coroner was still here and he reported, "Your Honor, this body belonged to a man of about fifty who was well taken care of in his life and hadn't participated in physical labor for years."

Judge Dee scowled, but he didn't interrupt. The coroner went on with his report. "The victim died about a week ago. I didn't find any wounds on his body.

The man wasn't poisoned, and he breathed well before his death. He must have had either a blow or cut on his head or neck. Perhaps that is why the murderer severed the victim's head from its body, cut it low on his neck."

Judge Dee prodded at the ankles of the corpse with a stick. The body had just begun to putrefy. The coroner was right; the murder must have occurred quite recently. The clothes, he thought, looked as if they belonged to a tramp. He put his prod down and signaled to have the gruesome remains removed. He silently watched as the corpse was wrapped in a reed mat, and waited as the coroner cleaned up the floor. Chiao Tai and Ma Joong returned shortly afterward to report that the head was still missing.

For the moment, Judge Dee had to put aside the murder case to remind his associates of their earlier plan. In his office and behind the closed door, they reviewed their plan for the counterfeit "burglary" one more time. Everything had to be done exactly right so that the public would think this was a real break-in. Tao Gan was very excited, as he looked forward to his first "authorized" burglary. The deep dark of night seemed so far off!

By the first light of dawn, Ma Joong already had his constables stirring among quiet neighborhoods throughout the city. Early peddlers at the marketplace gathered in front of many of the notices Sergeant Hoong had posted during the night. Those who could read found this to be an excellent opportunity to demonstrate their highly prized reading skills to the crowd. A great commotion arose as the mood in the crowd shifted from initial shock to worry and then from relief to excitement. Many of the young and more talkative began to count and describe the valuables they had deposited. The older ones mostly just murmured or counted quietly on their fingers.

Hardly had the morning session begun when more than fifty people gathered outside the tribunal gate, waiting to give details about their private deposits. As the fifteenth person, a haggard man wearing a brocade robe, gave his information on his private pledge, Judge Dee knocked his bench with his gavel, the "wood that frightens the hall." He addressed the man sarcastically in his deep and ominous voice: "Thank you for your information, but not for your silver, I'm afraid."

Ma Joong came over with two constables. They brought the ten boat-shaped, silver-looking pieces and twenty palm size coins, and dropped them on the floor. The man's face turned ashen. He knelt down and knocked his forehead on the flagstones of the floor, begging for mercy.

"Well done, scoundrel, you dared to smuggle your counterfeit silver into the public storage vault I set up only a few weeks ago. Our man indeed failed to detect your trick. How smart do you think you can be? Listen carefully. The 'burglary' last night was also a fake, just like yours. We made it up to help you walk in here and betray yourself. You damned fool! Now, speak up, and confess your crime." Judge Dee spoke furiously, holding up his gavel and waiving it in the air.

Surrounded by his counterfeits, the man stood in shock while confessing his crime. "For each of the fakes," Judge Dee said, "you shall receive ten lashes on your back. I would very much like to punish you more severely, but our August Throne has provided specific rules for me to follow. Do you know how much I would be punished for embezzling that money? I could have lost my own head, and you should thank our benevolent ruler for saving your worthless one."

As the judge closed the case, putting down the gavel on his high bench, a few hairs in his long beard was accidentally caught underneath the gavel, pinching his chin. "Ouch!" The judge cried out with an angry scowl. Then he smiled as he recalled what these most favored hairs of his were called by Buddhists: "threads of trouble." No wonder all monks shaved their heads!

*   *   *   *

The noon session of the tribunal began, and its courtyard was once again packed with onlookers. The six palanquins conspicuously waiting outside the tribunal walls had roused great curiosity among the residents of Poo-yang. Their magistrate sitting on the dais behind his high bench addressed them in his usual resonant voice.

"Yesterday, five monks from the Sweet Dew Monastery accused their new abbot of embezzling ten large gold ingots passed on by the late abbot. They said it was the legacy in the abbey that each abbot would save and pass on. I have asked the new abbot, and he told me he never saw the gold. The five monks however, claimed they had seen it in the late abbot's room on the New Year's Eve. I have the five monks waiting outside, each in a palanquin. I gave each monk a pot of clay to model ingots just like the ones he had seen. Each must remain inside his palanquin to do the job. Now let's see what they have produced."

The constables had brought in five small round tables before Ma Joong led the five monks in, followed by the abbot. Each monk held a pot in his hand. The constables took the pots and dumped the contents of each pot onto one of the five tables. The monks had each made completely different things!

Judge Dee smiled, and asked the monks sardonically: "How could each of you remember the same gold you saw in the same place at the same time so differently? Look." The judge left his seat, picked up a boat-shaped piece in his left hand from one table and held up a horseshoe-shaped one in his right hand from another table. Spectators laughed loudly as they now understood their magistrate's subterfuge. "The truth is," the judge continued, "the gold never existed. More exactly, it only exists in the mind of monks as they cultivated their own dogma. On every New Year's Eve the late abbot told the monks that such gold existed so long as they believed it, just as Buddha exists only if he exists in the mind of his believers. The new abbot had no such knowledge, and he was too naïve to understand what was happening."

The judge picked up two rulers from his high bench and dropped them on the floor. "For the lies you told me, each of you should get five lashes on the back as punishment. But considering that this is part of your Buddhist training, I'll punish you with only two lashes each, just to help you remember what has happened. You can believe anything you want. But never try to fool me again. Did you hear me?"

As the five monks knocked their foreheads on the floor to thank the judge for his mercy, Judge Dee suddenly turned to the abbot and questioned him bluntly: "How long have you been a monk?"

Taken aback, the abbot replied: "Seven years, Your Honor."

"Then why do you still have marks on your forehead that could only be left by having worn a cap until very recently?" Judge Dee shouted.

The abbot's face turned ashen. He fell down on the ground motionless. Ma Joong came over and held him up by the collar of his robe.

"You imposter! You killed the abbot on his way to Poo-yang. Where did you put his head? Speak up!"

Onlookers in the courtyard had not heard the like of this before. The hall buzzed with excited murmurs. The man confessed he had been a tramp since he lost all of his land in gambling, but he still wore his cap. A week before, he met a traveling monk on the road. While drinking together at an inn the tramp had learned that the monk was on his way to take up an appointment as an abbot. It suddenly occurred to him that if he killed the monk and posed as the new abbot he could enjoy, once again, a privileged life. The tramp had then murdered the monk with a blow to the head. Having no time to bury the entire corpse, he cut off and buried the head, and pushed the body into a dried-up well. Putting on the abbot's clothes and taking his identification, the imposter was easily accepted as the new abbot. Some monks, however, privately complained about his foul body odor, which resulted from his many years as a tramp. He had quickly made his first and fatal mistake. Too ignorant to understand the discipline and practice among the monks, he bluntly announced that he couldn't find the legendary gold, thus revealing his own ignorance of a Buddhist practice. That had both confused and scared the other monks. They all agreed to get rid of him by charging him with embezzlement. Of course he was innocent of that felony, but for his real crime he had to pay with his life.

Judge Dee and his associates gathered once again in his office after the tribunal session had concluded. The judge changed back to his casual blue robe and black skullcap. He could hardly wait for Sergeant Hoong to serve him a cup of his favorite tea. After a long, slow sip, he began to reveal how he had detected the crime.

"I have to admit that Buddhist wisdom has inspired my investigation this time. It came from the two poems I saw on the walls in the abbot's room. One poem read:

> In our mind itself a Buddha exists,
> Our own Buddha is the true Buddha.
> If we do not have in ourselves the Buddha mind,
> Then where are we to seek Buddha?

I thought I understood the poem but then I felt I didn't. I dislike this kind of obscurantist poetry. It often makes me feel like a fool. But last night it suddenly occurred to me that the monks must have been in some kind of meditative training. You have to believe in Buddha before you can find him. So the monks were told that the gold would always be there as long as they believed in it. Remember the lean elderly monk once told us about seeing the gold on New Year's Eve? But he also said something about polishing the gold and making it shine in their heart. I didn't notice his using the word "heart" until I studied the Zen poem. The imposter knew nothing about the Buddhist philosophy, particularly its doctrine of believing before seeing. So he had earnestly denied seeing the gold, as if it had actually existed!"

"When did you figure out he was a fake?" asked Sergeant Hoong.

"The inspiration also came from a Zen poem in his room:

> Deluded, a Buddha is a perceptive being;
> Awakened, a perceptive being is a Buddha.
> Ignorant, a Buddha is a perceptive being;
> With wisdom, a perceptive being is a Buddha.

That tells me identity is all but interchangeable, and that I should assume nothing. Excellent advice, very wise indeed," the judge nodded, unconsciously glancing at the blue robe he was wearing and his ceremonial robe of shimmering green that he had taken off just a few minutes before.

"My first impression was that the abbot was less learned than I would have expected. Senior monks usually have a solid education. Their knowledge of Buddhism would at least help them to enjoy great conversation with other learned scholars. But this one was not able to converse. He also became nervous when I asked him of the occasion of his arrival. And there was something else that appeared odd. A man of culture cares about his living environment. He may hang a few of his favorite paintings, add some pieces of decoration, or at least rearrange the furniture to suit his own taste. But none of that had occurred, for I saw dust on everything in his room. That told me that his mind was completely preoccupied with other concerns. Yet another thing bothered me. Both the abbot and the new monk I've sent home had something in common in their physical appearance, although I couldn't tell exactly what. It suddenly dawned on me that they both had cap-marks on their foreheads. We all have such marks, as we wear caps all day long. But how could a senior monk, and especially an abbot, still have that mark on his forehead?"

Judge Dee smiled, finishing his report. The quiet of the room seemed charged with unspoken admiration. As he was still enjoying the great sensation that his own acumen had created, a constable arrived to announce a visitor.

"Show him in!" The judge was in such a good mood at the moment that he seemed happy to share it with anyone.

The visitor was no one else but the young man the judge had helped.

"Speak of the devil!" Everyone in the room laughed.

The young man had come to fulfill his promise and give the judge the one-tenth of his late father's property.

"How did you find out who I am? You didn't seem to recognize me yesterday morning," asked the judge curiously.

"Magistrate Lo told me. I followed your advice to threaten my uncle, and he took me to the court. I told the magistrate that I received the advice from a stranger I met in Poo-yang and described you to him. He laughed and said that only the Magistrate of Poo-yang could have come up with an ingenious idea as that."

"Did he punish you at all?"

"No. Instead, he said I should be rewarded. And my uncle got the fifty strikes he has long deserved."

Everyone in the room laughed.

"Here is what I promised you," the young man said, handing the judge a heavy bundle of silver bars.

"I hope they are not counterfeit," Judge Dee said.

Everyone laughed again except the young man.

"I swear they are genuine," he said earnestly.

A louder laughter broke out in the room.

"Do me a favor, young man. Take it to the Sweet Dew Monastery, and tell the monks that I suggested you donate the silver."

Turning towards Sergeant Hoong, Judge Dee asked: "Do you still worry about me having Buddhist authorities as my political enemies?"

"Not anymore! Now you don't need to fear anyone," said the sergeant with a grin.

"Well, it's always a good idea to prepare for a rainy day." Curiously, he glanced up at the young man's forehead, particularly near the edge of his cap, looking for the noticeable mark he had seen before, which was so critical to his solving the case.

CHAPTER 8

▼

CRIMES AND BOATS

"Dad, look what I've made!" his boy rushed into Judge Dee's office, wearing a blue nightgown and carrying a wooden sword in his hand. "A sword just like yours," he exclaimed, comparing his to a treasured sword called Rain Dragon, forged three hundred years before by a legendary sword maker named Three-fingers. For two hundred years, this sword had been an heirloom in Judge Dee's family, passed on to the eldest son. Thanks to this family tradition, Judge Dee had been trained as a skilled swordsman, and that quite distinguished him from all other magistrates. This, in addition to his passionate love for Confucianism and perspicacious understanding of both Taoism and Buddhism, made him unique indeed. Judge Dee took the sword from his son's hand to check the blade and the haft. He nodded approvingly at the craftsmanship of a nine-year-old.

"Did you make that all by yourself?"

"Well, not exactly," the boy said, looking a little embarrassed, glancing away from his father. "I made another one, but Ah-kuei ruined it. With Big Sister's help, I made this new one, and it's much better." He was talking about his younger half-brother and elder half-sister. The latter was born to the Second Lady and was already a teenager. The judge would soon need to find her a suitable husband.

"Do you have a name for your sword?" Judge Dee asked.

"Since yours is named Rain Dragon, I should call mine Fire Dragon. It'll be powerful enough to destroy everything but yours."

"That sounds very suitable to me," Judge Dee said. "Are you going to take good care of it?"

"Sure. I will."

"Have you ever heard the story about a man who lost his treasured sword in a river?"

"No. Tell me about it, Dad."

"Well, it goes like this. Once upon a time, there was a man who had a treasured sword. One day he was traveling on a boat. Suddenly a storm came and a wave caused him to lose his balance. As he stumbled, his sword fell from its sheath and fell into the river. The boatman offered to jump into the water and get the sword back for a nice reward. The man shook his head and said: 'That won't be necessary.' He patted the mark that he had just made a moment before on the side of the boat. 'I'll get it back when the storm is over, and I know where to find it.' The boatman was astounded at such simplemindedness. He laughed and walked away. As soon as the storm was over, the man began to look for his sword in the water, just as he had said he would, but he couldn't find it."

"That man is a fool," the boy exclaimed. "The boat moved during the storm. How could he expect to find his sword by the mark he had made on the side of the boat? I'm not that stupid." Then, he added, "I'll never lose my sword!"

"So you think you are smarter."

"Of course I am."

"The young master is growing up and getting smarter," said Sergeant Hoong, who had followed the boy from the ladies' quarters to the judge's office. "He also runs faster these days, and I am no match for him anymore," the gray-bearded man added. "I was passing by the ladies quarters when the young master jumped out and begged me to accompany him to you. He was eager to show the sword he made."

"Well, he did make a fine sword. But it's time for his sleep. Would you take him back to his mother, Sergeant Hoong?" Judge Dee patted the boy on the head and returned the wooden sword to him. "And when you're done, please return to my office."

Sergeant Hoong realized intuitively that his master had something important to discuss with him. He had worked with the judge for six years as a confidential advisor ever since the latter's first appointment to Peng-lai. The sergeant was always the first to be consulted in any circumstance. The boy left reluctantly with the sergeant, still holding his precious Fire Dragon and with no desire to go to bed.

Judge Dee sat down at his desk and took out the note he had received from the Prefect just before dinner. As he read it through once more, the judge nodded pensively. Sergeant Hoong returned to take a seat opposite the judge. Without looking at him, Judge Dee handed him the note. The sergeant read it carefully, word for word, using his thumb to mark his place. Seeing that the judge still waited, Sergeant Hoong coughed, and prepared to offer his own opinion.

"It states here that the number of crimes on the Grand Canal has been going up recently, a situation that has been brought to the attention of our August Throne. The criminals often managed to escape to another district by water." Putting down the note on the desk, Sergeant Hoong reflected. The Grand Canal ran from north to south through the Poo-yang district on its western side. Although it helped to make the district a center of trade, the canal also brought crimes and trouble, just as the royal note stated. But so it was for the other districts located on the canal. The sergeant wondered how those other districts fared in handling the problem. Glancing at the note again, he shook his head glumly, reflecting his own more morose assessment. "The tone of this note, I'm afraid I have to say, seems also to convey a reprimand to us, suggesting, but not stating explicitly, that we have neglected our duty."

"I did neglect the water region," Judge Dee admitted quickly. "In fact, ever since the spring famine in the northern district, I have scarcely paid a visit to any water area in my district, particularly to its western bank." His hands gripped his desk tightly; evidently he regretted that he couldn't revisit his earlier oversight.

"It also states here that our August Throne has sent an Imperial Censor to travel on the canal incognito. He is going to investigate and report to the Emperor face to face. That doesn't sound good to me either, for the task of the Imperial Censor is not really to catch criminals but to punish those who fail to catch them."

"Exactly! You are quite right, Sergeant Hoong," Judge Dee said, as he waved his hand. The sergeant quickly caught his cue for a pot of hot tea. The gray-bearded man stood up and walked across the room to make it. As he came back to serve the judge, he heard him say: "Imperial Censors are incurably incisive as they are incorruptible. They'll ruthlessly punish those officials who are proven to have neglected their duties. In the days ahead, we may find ourselves in big trouble, if we are not particularly careful."

Sergeant Hoong nodded his head, feeling a chill run down his spine. In his long career he heard of far too many officials being exiled or even beheaded after just such inquiries. "Having said that, however," Judge Dee concluded, "we shall carry out our daily duty as usual. This tribunal should not be distracted by the uncertainty brought by some unknown Imperial Censor. And we mustn't panic!" He sipped his tea, tapped his desk, and then added, "Tomorrow morning, I'll visit the water area with Tao Gan, and see if there is anything I can do to curb this spate of crime."

The night was late and Sergeant Hoong had to leave. At this point, Judge Dee decided he did not want any of his lieutenants to realize the possible risk imposed by this incognito Imperial Censor. For them just to know that a man with such power was arriving would be dreadful enough.

The judge finished his tea and picked up a book from his bookshelf. Reading before sleep had long become his habit. Tonight, he was going to stay in his office and sleep on the couch, without seeking the company of any of his three wives. Although he had been idly dreaming about his Third Lady during his early nap, the note from the Prefect had effectively destroyed his interest in her for the moment.

*   *   *   *

In his first hearing at the morning session, the judge was quite surprised and delighted to hear a traveling silk merchant accuse his boatman of stealing ten silver bars from him. The judge quickly exchanged a glance with his sergeant. A crime aboard a passenger boat was a timely case, indeed; just what he wanted! Caressing his long side-whiskers, he gave both the silk merchant and the boatman a sober appraisal. One was a middle-aged man dressed in a blue silk robe; the other was a barefooted lad, his worn-out pants full of holes. Certainly the judge could not easily suspect that the claim might be fraudulent, because it was so unlikely that a rich merchant would attempt to defraud such an already poverty-stricken boatman. There was simply nothing to squeeze from him.

"Tell me about your whole journey. When and where did you get on board? Did the boat stop at any other place before it arrived here?" Judge Dee asked the merchant.

"Your Honor, this insignificant person got on board yesterday afternoon at three o'clock, to be exact. We stopped only briefly for a late dinner at a place called Three Creeks, best known for its fine cuisine. I was in a hurry to meet with Mr. Liu. He is a silk merchant living in a village down the canal. He said he has a lot of good merchandise, but it was selling fast. I had tipped the boatman to keep on the move at night, and he did. How should I know he would steel my silver overnight? I was a fool, wasn't I?"

"When did you find your silver bars missing?"

"This morning, Your Honor. I woke up at dawn. As I was packing, I couldn't find my leather box. I asked the two other passengers, a nice old couple, if they had seen my silver. They swore they never touched it. I then asked the boatman and he denied taking my silver as well. But I'll bet it's he who has stolen my silver. Please interrogate him with torture."

"Where are the two other passengers now?" asked the judge.

"They are right here as my witnesses, Your Honor." The silk merchant pointed at an old couple standing with a crowd of onlookers in the tribunal courtyard.

Judge Dee took a look at the man and then his wife. They were both dressed in plain blue clothes of cotton, typical of farmers, and they each looked at least sixty years old. The wife was carrying a black and white cat in her hands. "Come over here. Let's hear what you can tell us," the judge commanded.

The old couple shuffled to the judge's high bench and knelt down in front of it. "This insignificant person is named Hoo Too, and this is my wife, Hoo *lee* Mei," the man pointed to the woman at his side. "Our daughter is badly ill, and her in-laws have sent for us. We were really in a hurry. It was fortunate for us the boat didn't stop during the night. Mr. Lee had tipped the boatman and asked him to continue throughout the night. I don't know how to thank him enough! It's a coincidence that my wife's maiden name was also Lee. Five hundred years ago, their forefathers must have been cousins. Heaven sent this man to help us."

Seeing that her husband had strayed from the subject, his wife kowtowed and spoke: "This insignificant woman is Hoo *lee* Mei. Please let us go, Your Honor. I'm afraid we won't see our daughter again." Her voice trailed off as she began to sob and her cat meowed.

Evidently the judge felt pressured to release the old couple, although he really did not want to. "You saw his silver on boat, I assume. When was that?"

"Shortly before the dinner. His leather box was about this big, and filled with silver." Hoo Too gestured with his hands to describe the size of the box, which was larger than a pillow. The judge knew that if the box were filled with silver it would be too heavy for the old man and his wife to carry. The old couple was no longer suspects; the judge could only hope to get some useful information from them.

"Did you see the box again?"

"No. Why would I even look for it? I was comforting my wife all the time. We had no appetite for dinner. I thought we would have to stay for the night on boat, but we arrived in Poo-yang this morning. It was then that he asked me if I had seen his box. Of course I hadn't. Although I didn't sleep a wink, I just didn't pay any attention to his box. He should be more careful with it. You know what? I think he drank too much wine and didn't quite know what he was doing," the old man said, shaking his head as a father would when disapproving his son's behavior.

"Where did each of you go for dinner? You all left the boat, didn't you?" Judge Dee asked.

"No," said the merchant, "dinner was served on board. Neither of us left. I remember seeing the service boy leaving with plates, bowls, and chopsticks. He was only about ten. I don't think he could steal and carry my silver away. Too heavy for him anyway."

Judge Dee turned to the boatman, who had been kneeling quietly on the flagstone floor all the time. "What do you have to say for yourself?"

"I have no idea what he is talking about. Go and search my boat! You can turn it upside down if you want. I swear you will find nothing. May thunder hit me if I ever touched his silver!" The boatman wiped his mouth with the back of his hand. The corner of his mouth had become wet as he swore. His two protruding front teeth had enough stain on them to kill a hungry man's appetite.

"Of course we're going to search your boat!" The judge was much irritated by the man's insolent tone. Turning toward the old couple he said: "The two of you may leave now."

*　　　*　　　*　　　*

Onlookers quickly gathered around the passenger boat as Judge Dee arrived. Most people in the area hadn't seen their magistrate for many months. Parents pointed him out to their children, asking them to be quiet and to behave, while their inconspicuous gestures revealed their respect and awe for his high official status. "Otherwise," they warned in whispering, "the Old Master might have you struck on your bare buttocks with a huge club. He can do that to anyone he wants, even us adults." The children all looked up at the judge in awe and with consternation. To them, a man who could spank another adult must have tremendous power. They all wished they could witness that tall broad-shouldered man demonstrate his immense power.

The passenger boat was about fourteen feet long and three feet wide, and its roof was covered with a black waterproof canvas. Underneath, four people could comfortably sit, or even lie down and sleep in any kind of weather. Judge Dee got on board to search under the roof but found nothing out of the ordinary. Tao Gan followed his master, with the same result. He then used some willow branches to make a big hoop, and moved it outside the entire boat from bow to stern, so that the bottom of the hoop actually passed over the hull under the water. As Tao Gan pulled the hoop from the water, he looked at the judge and shook his head. Nothing had been detected in the water dangling from the boat, but the judge nodded, admiring his lieutenant's smart idea anyway.

He also recalled his conversation with his son. Even a nine-year-old knew that you couldn't retrieve something that had been dropped into the water if the boat were moving. For the same reason the thief couldn't have dropped his booty into the water while the boat was sailing. He must have dropped it when the boat stopped for dinner. All that the judge needed to do was to learn where the boat had anchored the evening before and search at this spot.

"Do you remember where exactly the boat was anchored when dinner was served?" Judge Dee asked the silk merchant.

"I think I do."

Judge Dee ordered the boat back upstream, to the place called Three Creeks. The judge had already asked Ma Joong and Chiao Tai to take care of the routine sessions at the tribunal. He had also asked the politically more experienced sergeant to keep his eyes open to the 'unexpected' arrival of the incognito Imperial Censor. With those official matters presumably well arranged, the judge felt he could now take time to have a closer look at the entire water area that had been neglected for months.

As soon as their boat had arrived at the Three Creeks, dozens of curious onlookers gathered around. Judge Dee gave the order forbidding anyone to swim while the investigation was going on. It took some while and indeed was quite an effort for the silk merchant to locate the exact spot where the boat had been anchored the night before. Judge Dee couldn't help but notice that the boatman wasn't very cooperative. Each time the merchant asked him to move the boat a little he would reluctantly follow or even try to move too much and the merchant would have to ask him to readjust its position again.

The judge brought two constables with him and he asked one of them to keep an eye on the boatman while Tao Gan went ashore with the other one. They needed to recruit more help and find some tools. Judge Dee instructed Tao Gan to get some long poles and to tie hooks onto them. He would rather not hire locals to dive, for he didn't trust any strangers. They might hide the silver for themselves if they found it in the water. Judge Dee only asked them to help find things under the water, but he would not tell them that it was valuable silver bars they were searching for.

Two locals were hired, and with Tao Gan and a constable, the four of them poked under water with their long poles. They worked hard for a while, but found nothing. Judge Dee caressed his long black whiskers and looked around.

"Are you sure this is the pier where you had dinner brought on board?" He asked the merchant.

"I thought so, but now I'm not so sure," said the merchant looking very frustrated. The judge suddenly had an idea, and asked to meet all the dinner peddlers. Shortly after he had given the order, nine young boys were brought to him. It was their job to bring food on board and bring the utensils back to the little restaurants along the shore.

Pointing at the merchant and the boatman, the judge asked the nine boys: "Which of you served this boat last night for a late dinner?"

Each boy looked at the two men and then shook his head. "I didn't," said one boy." "I served so many people. How could I remember their faces," said another. Judge Dee smiled. "Ah, I nearly forgot. There were two other passengers on board last night. They were a couple of farmers, about sixty years old, clad in blue cotton. They also had a black and white cat."

"Now I remember," a boy yelled excitedly. "That cat was so hungry. It jumped at the dishes and scratched my hand. Look!" He showed where his skin was hurt. Judge Dee's face lit up.

"Can you recall where the boat was anchored when you brought food on board?"

The boy looked around and said: "It was on the other side of the pier."

The judge looked at the merchant, who looked quite puzzled. "I was pretty sure we were on this side. Last night we passed the pier and turned right. So today we passed the pier and turned left."

"I see," the judge smiled. "Then we should have gone to the other side. As we're returning to Three Creeks, we should have turned left *before* we passed the pier."

After they had relocated the boat, Tao Gan instructed the constable and the two hired men to their search. The constable stumbled as his pole collided with an obstacle on the bottom. Diving in, he soon surfaced with a leather box! The face of the silk merchant lit up as he opened the box to find all his silver. Judge Dee coughed to signal the arrest of the boatman, and just in time, for he had started to run away as quick as a rabbit. The constables caught him with some onlookers' help and pinned his arms behind his back. They forced him to kneel before the judge. The man kowtowed in fury, begging for mercy, his chin shaking as if he had just been given a dunking in icy water. Judge Dee took his plea as his confession, and ordered a constable to take him back to the tribunal for a public trial, as the law required.

"And take this with you," Judge Dee said, calling to the constable while fumbling around in his own sleeve pocket. He pulled out a silver nugget, tossing it to the constable. "That should be enough to hire another boat and to buy yourself a nice meal." Glancing at the boatman in his ragged pants, the judge added, "and don't keep *him* too hungry either." He felt a little pity for the boatman, for the guy had neither the brain nor guts to deny his crime. His fruitless effort in running away simply proved his guilt. It might have been a challenge for the judge had the boatman accused the service boy or the elder couple of the crime. The merchant bowed low to thank the judge and left happily with his silver. Now he only hoped that Mr. Liu in the village along the canal was still awaiting him with his good silk.

The beautiful sunset told the judge how late it was, and he decided to take Tao Gan and the constable to a nice local restaurant for dinner. As the Three Creeks was renowned for its fine cuisine, it was not difficult to find an elegant-looking restaurant nearby. The one they entered had an ostentatiously decorated archway as its entrance, with a portiere of strings of colored beads hanging from the top. A fan-shaped signpost stood atop of the archway and read: Better seats upstairs. As Judge Dee took a step onto the stairs, he heard the constable speak behind him, "I'll wait for you downstairs." The constable apparently knew quite well that his social status did not qualify him for the upstairs seats, for such elegant seats upstairs were only for people with high social status.

"Eat well," said the judge, "you won't need to pay. Just let the waiter know you're with me."

Tao Gan followed the judge upstairs. As they sat down at a window seat and glanced at the fiery sunset, a waiter came to the table, wearing a large apron and a towel on his shoulder. Surprised to realize who his guests were, he began to speak in the overly flattering phrases that all waiters loved to use: "My lord, the sun must have arisen from the west today. Otherwise how could I have Your Honor patronize my humble restaurant? Which gust of auspicious wind has brought Your Lord here?" Judge Dee put a finger on his mouth, signaling to him to keep quiet. Tao Gan quickly smuggled a tiny silver nugget into his hand and said: "Shut up, you big mouth. Keep quiet about our visit. Just bring the best food you have. And quickly." While waiting for their food, Judge Dee briefed Tao Gan about the increase of crime on the canal and the anticipated secret visit by the Imperial Censor.

From his window, Judge Dee enjoyed an excellent view, especially of the pier where his boat was anchored. He saw that another passenger boat had arrived, with only one passenger in it, and moored right next to his own. Both the passenger and the boatman were walking towards the restaurant. Wearing a bamboo hat and a blue short-sleeved cotton robe, the passenger was a man of about fifty years old with curly whiskers. The boatman was half of his age. Following his passenger by a good distance, he frequently turned to keep an eye on his boat. Judge Dee followed the boatman's glance, but didn't see anything that would warrant the boatman to worry about his boat.

The sunset was now at its most lovely: the afterglow in the sky reflected in the water made the entire horizon look fiery. For a moment, there seemed to be no difference between heaven and earth. The judge recalled a Confucian teaching that humans should live in harmony with nature. He wondered if the great master had gotten his idea from the pleasure of watching a sunset.

The waiter returned, bearing a very heavily laden tray in his left hand. Onto the table he placed a large round pot of hot tea and a somewhat smaller square pot of rice wine. From the tray he lifted four large plates made of porcelain of three colors, a recent innovation in the porcelain making that had just become fashionable. The four dishes were a boiled whole carp stuffed with ground pork, four crabs that had been marinated alive in liquor and salt for weeks, snail meat stir-fried with chives, and shrimp meat stir-fried with bamboo shoots.

The judge noticed the curly-whiskered man come upstairs and take the table next to them. "The sunset is too bright for my eyes," Judge Dee made an excuse and asked to exchange seats with Tao Gan. Now he sat facing the curly-whiskered man, and could observe him from a comfortable distance. He overheard the man ask the waiter: "Do you serve Watermelon Chicken at this time of the year?"

"You've just missed it, Sir. We had it until yesterday. But I'm glad you've asked. You must be a true gourmet. Do you come from the capital?"

"Too bad. My friend had told me that I had to try this local specialty," the man delicately dodged the waiter's question, "Could you tell me how it is cooked?"

"Well, I'm not supposed to tell," the waiter looked around and then whispered, "but here is the secret. You boil the chicken slowly for two hours with salted ham, fragrant sausages, and at least four types of different mushrooms, both dried and fresh. And ginger of course, but you need to use our locally brewed sweet rice wine to marinate the best quality ginger only grown in Peng-lai district, which is a hundred miles away. Then you choose a sweet, ripe watermelon, cut off the top end, and take out the pulp and seeds. You place the chicken and the soup inside the melon, replace the top end and seal it with short bamboo sticks. Finally you steam the melon for half an hour until you can smell the delicious aroma." The waiter wheezed, wiping his mouth in delight at the remembrance of the delicious dish.

Obviously, his vivid elaboration had likewise stimulated the curly-whiskered man's appetite. He sadly shook his head and said, "Well, just give me the best you have. I'll have to visit again next summer to try the dish." Soon, the waiter brought the man the same four dishes he had served to the judge and Tao Gan. The man ate quietly, elegantly using his chopsticks to pick up whatever he wished, but keeping each plate on his table exactly as the waiter had placed them. Judge Dee watched in silence, appreciating the man's table manners. A less-cultured man might have picked up a plate to put some food into his rice bowl, but this man obviously knew better.

As Judge Dee was observing the man at the next table, Tao Gan stared at the judge, trying to figure out what the judge had seen. Failing to understand anything from that face, Tao Gan casually looked out the window. There he saw the boatman returning to his boat. That gave Tao Gan a tingle, and he instantly made a quick decision. He didn't even have a chance to twist his three long black hairs that sprouted from a mole on his cheek, a habit that often occurred when he was trying to think hard. Making an excuse loud enough for the man at the next table to hear, he quickly went downstairs to follow the boatman.

The waiter returned to serve tea. Judge Dee nodded and held up his hand to stop him when the cup was nearly refilled. As the waiter moved on to the other table, the judge saw the man was preoccupied with the beautiful sunset and did not move his hand in the slightest way to acknowledge the service. Judge Dee smiled, sipped his tea, and felt quite satisfied. Now he knew what he wanted to know.

After finishing with more tea, the curly-whiskered man paid for his meal, gave a generous tip and went downstairs. Judge Dee was just about to leave and follow him downstairs when Tao Gan returned with an exciting report. "That boat is going back to Poo-yang tonight, and I've reserved three seats!"

"Bravo!" Judge Dee said.

"It didn't even cost me too much," Tao Gan grinned.

"Well done." The judge tried to sound enthusiastic, as he knew his lieutenant dearly cared about every single coin thus saved. But his tone failed him, showing that he had no interest in this sort of small bargaining. The judge quickly looked away to avoid embarrassing his lieutenant.

"That man must be a robber," Tao Gan whispered to Judge Dee's ear, not in the least disturbed by the judge's lukewarm praising. As they went downstairs, he added, "Although dressed plainly, he seems quite wealthy. He has shrewd and stern eyes. Don't expect any mercy from him. I would not." Tao Gan made a gesture, passing his hand across his neck quickly to indicate decapitation.

Judge Dee grinned and shook his head. "The man must be the Imperial Censor incognito." Tao Gan was dumbfounded. He had never seen an Imperial Censor or any high-ranking officials from the Imperial Court. The sheer power of such a man alarmed him, making him stick out his tongue in consternation. Twisting the few long black hairs that sprouted from the mole on his cheek helped to quiet him down.

"How do you know?" he asked.

"His table manners have betrayed him. He never moved a single plate on the table, and he is quite accustomed to personal service. He is too cultured to be a robber. I'm sure he is the Imperial Censor. We must be extremely cautious."

"Then why do we follow him?" Tao Gan asked, confused and protesting.

"I'm not following *him*. It's the boat that has me interested. I still can't figure out what's odd about that boat. But we'll soon find out. That's why I'm so glad you have reserved seats for us."

Tao Gan gave Judge Dee a bewildered look. Although he had worked for the judge for several years, he could still miss some cues by huge margins. He had thought that the man with curly whiskers was a primary crime suspect. It had never occurred to him that it was the boatman and his boat that the judge in fact suspected.

The constable rejoined them downstairs. His face made it clear that he had drunk a lot more than he should. As Judge Dee got on board, he overheard the tail end of a conversation in which the boatman had happily informed his passenger that they would be having three more passengers. The man was not as pleased as the boatman seemed to be. Judge Dee figured that neither had yet guessed him to be a magistrate. He turned around and whispered to Tao Gan and the constable, asking them to keep him incognito.

The sun had disappeared beneath the horizon. In the remaining twilight, Judge Dee saw a quilt hanging from a pole at the stern of the boat. Its front side was made of orange-colored silk; from its rumpled back cover of plain white cotton cloth, the judge ascertained that it had been washed and then dried earlier that day. As people would normally wash the covers only, leaving the cotton wadding dry, the judge began to wonder what particular reason the boatman had to wash the whole quilt. He also noticed several flies around that seemed to love a certain spot on the quilt. As the judge was just about to speculate the reason why, the boatman came to fold the quilt and put it away.

The judge still couldn't figure out what made the boat appear somewhat different from the other passenger boat that he had boarded earlier in the day. Although each boat carried four passengers and both were typical of the commercial boats on the canal, something nagged him. Surveying the cabin, he also saw a sword conspicuously lying under the seat of the curly-whiskered man. Now the judge understood why the boatman appeared to be so happy to have more passengers. He must have also taken the curly-whiskered man as a robber, just as Tao Gan had. The other passenger also saw that Judge Dee noticed his sword. As if to respond to any question of curiosity, the man said, "I heard that lately it hasn't been very safe to travel on the canal, so I have my sword with me." As he spoke, he unconsciously glanced at the boatman. He must have suspected the boatman to be a robber! Judge Dee almost chuckled. Luckily I didn't bring my Rain Dragon, he thought. Otherwise, both men would have been even more nervous.

"Such rumor will soon be dispelled as people realize that no criminal can get away with his crime," the judge responded in a casual and relaxed tone. "Earlier today, at the place called Three Creeks, a boatman was arrested for stealing ten silver bars from a passenger on his boat." Judge Dee had noticed that the curly-whiskered man seemed to be encouraged by the news. "I don't blame you for being more than cautious. As for myself, I have some good company," he spoke of Tao Gan as he glanced at his fellow passenger. He also thought he detected a tremor on the face of the boatman as the word "boatman" was mentioned. But perhaps even that proved nothing. In fact, it might be quite natural for a person to feel a little uncomfortable if someone in the same trade were apprehended for a crime.

The constable had indeed drunk too much wine at dinner. He quickly fell asleep and snored loudly. Tao Gan was still a little nervous about being so close to an Imperial Censor. But he was relieved that the man was not a robber. Tao Gan had not taken his eyes off the boatman since boarding, but he had not yet detected anything wrong.

Soon, as they heard noisy splashing from behind, a ship laden with soldiers caught up to them and then passed them. Judge Dee and Tao Gan exchanged glances. "It seems that we have some very good company on the water," said the curly-whiskered man. Even though his comment sounded casual, it made the boatman more nervous than ever.

The water quieted again as the soldiers' ship moved ahead. The constable continued his snoring. Tao Gan gave him a good nudge in the ribs and stopped him. "Good night," Judge Dee said, as he lay down to get some sleep.

A peaceful air and bright full moon accompanied them for the whole night, and Judge Dee woke up at the first light of dawn. He yawned, and stretched his legs. As he sat up, he was in one of the rare and most beautiful moments of the day; the sun appeared suddenly to jump into the sky. It would indeed be another lovely day. As the boat arrived at Poo-yang and the boatman was busy anchoring the boat, Judge Dee stood beside him, eager to be the first to get off. Suddenly, he frowned. He had not expected he would have to step up so steeply to the landing. Up nearly an extra foot! It took only another second for him to understand its implication. He tapped his forehead, and slowly turned around, smiling. "I nearly forgot. As the magistrate of Poo-yang and your host on this land, I invite both of you to breakfast." The sudden revelation of his true identity surprised both men. Before they could ask any questions, a commotion occurred on the bank, as people had recognized their "parental official." They bowed low and greeted him loudly: "Good morning, Your Honor!"

"Morning!" Judge Dee responded curtly and turned around to speak with Tao Gan and then went ashore to await both his guests. Tao Gan took the constable aside, instructing him to take the boatman off for a nice breakfast. He himself followed the judge and their fellow passenger to a restaurant. As they sat down at a table Judge Dee whispered again to Tao Gan. The lieutenant seemed shocked and his eyes opened widely. Politely, he bowed to the guest and left in a hurry.

As soon as Tao Gan was out of sight, Judge Dee stood up and bowed low to his guest. "Your Honor, the magistrate of Poo-yang is honored to receive you in his district. I'm truly regretful that I couldn't receive you in a more proper and official manner. But right now I'm in the middle of an investigation, and I believe we'll be able to close the case when my lieutenant returns momentarily."

"How did you know I came from the capital?" asked the man, both surprised and crestfallen with a slight hint of hostility in his tone. Judge Dee bowed again and said: "It is not difficult to tell a crane from chickens." The man smiled, and tapped his fingers on the table. A waiter came to serve hot tea. Before they had the chance to finish their first cup, Tao Gan returned, panting excitedly: "I found it! Just like you predicted. It's all in the bottom. And I've checked the quilt too." He handed the judge a gold bar.

"Go to guard the boat and have the constable arrest the boatman. I'll be back at the tribunal as soon as we finish our breakfast," Judge Dee ordered.

"Don't you think you owe me some explanation, my magistrate?" asked the curly-whiskered man after Tao Gan had left.

"Surely I do. But since it's a long story and part of it is still ongoing, I think it's best to let you observe our next tribunal session for yourself," said Judge Dee. "I hope you don't find offense in my humble proposal," Judge Dee added politely, putting his offer forward as a courtesy that would not be easy to reject. Judge Dee ordered a local specialty as a treat for his guest: rice wine with rice still in it but mixed with additional dates, resins, and the fruit of wolf-berry that looked bright red in the white wine.

As they arrived at his office, Judge Dee let the curly-whiskered man take his desk and knelt down in front of him. "Please allow me, Your Honor, to formally receive you at my tribunal. It is the wish of all the people in the Poo-yang district that our August Throne have a long, long life." He knocked his forehead on the floor and waited for instructions.

"You, too, may be seated now," the man replied, surveying the room to point at a humble drum-shaped stool.

The gray-bearded sergeant shuffled in. "Sergeant Hoong of the Poo-yang tribunal reports his personal service to Your Honor." As the sergeant knocked his forehead on the floor, everyone heard three booming strikes of the gong at the tribunal entrance.

"You may stand up now," said the curly-whiskered man.

"May I serve you a cup of tea, Your Honor?" Sergeant Hoong asked.

The man responded with the briefest of gestures. A man of his status did not need reply a sergeant even when spoken to. The sergeant, however, thought he had detected a most subtle inclination of the head, and thus commenced to serve the tea. Judge Dee excused himself to don his official robe, adjusting his winged judge's cap in front of the standing silver mirror. "Please make yourself comfortable, Your Honor. I'll leave the screen a little open between this office and the court-hall. You can easily overhear the session from here," said the judge as he left.

Soon after the judge sat behind his high bench on the dais, constables brought in the boatman. The man looked around before he knelt down.

"Speak up!" Judge Dee's voice was as loud as usual. At the moment, he was representing the law and therefore the highest authority, ignoring the fact that a superior imperial official was sitting in his office watching.

The boatman knocked his forehead on the floor and said: "This insignificant person is named Foo Hoo." His name was barely audible as the way it was pronounced.

"Speak louder!" shouted the judge.

"This insignificant person is named Foo Hoo. I'm a boatman and have just arrived in town. In fact, it is Your Honor who has invited me to shore and treated me to a nice breakfast. Don't you remember?" The man looked at the judge, and then looked around at the crowds of onlookers in the courtyard, to see if his statement had made any effect on them. It did, and several people shook their heads, as they could not understand why their magistrate had arrested his own guest.

"That's because I wanted to have your boat thoroughly searched, you moron. We've found everything." He raised his hand with a gold bar in it.

"You did?" The man's face instantly turned ashen.

Judge Dee waved the gold in the air.

"I got it through a robbery," the man confessed, referring to the gold.

"What about the murder?" Judge Dee yelled.

"The murder!" the man collapsed on the ground.

"Who did you kill and how did you do it? Speak up, if you don't want me to apply any of those," Judge Dee pointed at the tools of torture in the hands of constables standing by.

The man gave in. "I had a partner in the robbery. His name is Tan Chai. We put the gold bars at the bottom of the boat and covered them with a board to make it look like the normal flooring of a boat. While we were on the water, I killed him when he was sleeping soundly, so that I could have all the gold myself. I tied our swords to his body and dropped him in the water. The two swords made the corpse sink quickly."

After the man put his thumb mark on the court recording as his confession, the judge announced the inevitable death sentence. Back in his office, he bowed low as his official guest asked him eagerly: "How did you know there was gold on that boat?"

"It actually took me a while to figure it out. I didn't realize that the boat was that heavy until this morning as I was about to land. To get off, I had to raise my foot nearly a foot!"

"How did you know there was a murder, then?"

"I saw a quilt at the end of the boat as I got on board. Several things appeared odd about that quilt. Its silk cover was too expensive for a boatman to own. Thus I knew he was not 'just' a boatman. Flies perched on it, a possible sign of blood. And the entire quilt was washed which is not the conventional way of washing a quilt. Thus I knew he must have had reasons to wash it in a hurry, probably to get rid of blood. He should have thrown it away with the body and the swords, but he was too afraid that it would stay afloat. I guess Your Honor got on board yesterday early in the afternoon. As he had already skipped his breakfast, he couldn't also skip his lunch. Otherwise he wouldn't have taken the boat to shore, and you wouldn't have been taken on as a passenger. He was very much afraid of you, because you had your sword while he had lost his. That's why he was happy to take us as passengers last night. He thought you might be a robber, too."

"How do you know I'm not a robber? Eh?" the man suddenly grabbed his sword, withdrew it from its sheath, and placed its blade next to the judge's throat. As he dropped the sheath on the floor and twisted his curly whiskers with his left hand, he was grimacing.

"Well," Judge Dee said as he stood still, calmly looking the Censor in the eye. "The excellence of Your Honor's table manners revealed your high status," he said.

At that moment, Ma Joong and Chiao Tai showed up at the door to announce the arrival of a squad of Imperial soldiers at the tribunal. They were shocked to see the man point his sword at their magistrate's throat.

"Send them to the courtyard and ask them to wait for me there," the man ordered. He gave a tepid smile and returned his sword to its sheath. "I certainly must report favorably about you to our August Throne," he said, but his tone made Judge Dee wonder. After all, I might have just won a battle but lost a war, thought the judge. Evidently, the Imperial Censor's ego was much bruised by someone who could so easily detect not only a robbery but also a murder on the very boat on which he had been a passenger. Judge Dee recalled that his son had named his toy sword Fire Dragon, with an understanding that his father's sword was named Rain Dragon, fire being inferior to rain. How appropriate that was! The judge felt a little uneasy now about his own performance. Clear-cut success was almost like proclaiming that the Imperial Censor was only second best, or the Fire Dragon!

If he had let the man discover the murderer first, however, he would most certainly have been charged with negligence of his duty. Sometimes you had to choose the lesser of the two evils, the judge thought. Yet, how might it be possible to convince such a man that, although both were clever, that the Censor was wiser? Judge Dee turned his eyes to the wall where the Rain Dragon was elegantly hanging. It was quite a challenge.

He closed his eyes, and engaged in silent conversation with the spirit of his late father. He felt he still shared something with his father, for example, the moon. The mysterious patterns of shadows on the moon had inspired numerous beautiful legends, and he could still remember many of them as his father had told him. He knew that the moonlight shining on him tonight would not be the same as that which his father had seen, but that the present moon had surely shone over the head of that wise man, whom he had admired and called "Dad" for so many years in his childhood. How he would love to call "Dad" once again, simply to let that man take over and help him out.

CHAPTER 9

▼

PROPERTIES AND PAPER

Fall had arrived, at long last. Judge Dee was most grateful that the hot humid summer had passed. But it annoyed him to have so many mosquitoes still abuzz and flying around. This is much worse than last year, he thought. Humans had learned to fight off many wild beasts or to tame them or to keep them at bay; but they had never won the battle against mosquitoes! Neither kings nor beggars could escape these annoying creatures. "Poo-," the judge sighed, as he failed once again to catch an elusive one, slashing empty-handed in the air. What a humiliating experience!

He scratched a newly acquired itch on his left ear, and shook his head. None of his repertoire of several classical philosophies seemed to help. Taoism didn't help. Unlike the killing of a few bees that would likely bring a greater number in retribution, killing a mosquito would not cause more mosquitoes to venture near. Therefore, doing the less as Tao had advocated wouldn't reduce their further infestation. The reincarnation theory of Buddhism couldn't help either. There was no self-evident chain of reward or punishment to consider. And Judge Dee definitely did not want to become a mosquito in his next life. Even his great master, Confucius, provided little consolation. Neither the principle of benevolence or that of justice could help.

In Judge Dee's house, just like others, the practical method of dealing with mosquitoes was to burn a special type of incense in every room, but the effect was minimal. Four tapers of incense burned together in his office, and the judge was still getting bitten. That made him quite irritated.

While scratching his ankle where he had been bitten the previous night, he found he couldn't break himself away from a poem he had just read. He had the habit of reading a few poems before his nap. Not really an admirer of most poetry, he usually just used it to help him fall asleep. Besides, he felt poems were too sentimental. He hated to be carried away by strong emotions, and liked to remain cool-headed all the time. Today, however, the poem he was reading caught his attention.

> "*This water, since when, its flow?*
> *This mountain, since when, its being?*
> *Man's fate changes from this to that!*
> *These forms alone stay forever.*"

The poet presented a strong contrast between the eternity of nature and the transience of human life, particularly an individual's unpredictable fate and fortune. The recent incident of outsmarting the Imperial Censor had somehow cast a considerable shadow upon Judge Dee's heart. He understood it had invited unwanted envy. But how could this be avoided? The poem he was reading reinforced his sense of unease; a deep 'blue' mood grew in him and made him drink too much wine at lunch. In fact, he even spilled a whole glass of wine on the tablecloth.

As the judge returned to the poem with greater attention, he began to copy it, practicing the use of a variety of calligraphic scripts. As each such copy was done, he put it aside on top of his desk. Because it took a fair while for the ink to dry, these scraps were soon spread side by side on the table. As the earlier ones dried he laid the new ones on top. In no time, he had accumulated quite a large pile of paper on his desk. Just looking at that mess depressed him even more. He put down his brush-pen and lay on his couch. Soon he fell asleep.

Normally he would sleep for only half an hour. Today, the wine helped him sleep longer. Three hours later, a gusting autumn wind came in through the open window and blew the pieces of paper off his desk onto the floor, scattering them about. Some settled on one of the incense burners intended to keep away mosquitoes. Blue smoke and orange flames arose. The whirling gusts inside the room blew the burning paper back to the desk and whirling about its legs. The tablecloth draped over one of the legs caught fire first. Then, larger flames burst forth as his poetry book caught on fire.

The judge woke up just in time to snatch away what was left of his poetry book, dropped it on the floor behind him, and quickly stomped out the flames.

He rushed to the wall to draw the Rain Dragon from its sheath, and returned to fight the larger fire. With a few swift movements he chopped the burning desk into half a dozen pieces, spreading them out at his feet. The judge watched the fire engulf the wood. The flames gradually changed color, from orange to red and black, and were finally extinguished. The smoke irritated both his throat and eyes, making him cough and his eyes to tear.

At just that moment Sergeant Hoong came in. "Good Heavens! What's going on here?" he exclaimed. "I've just put out quite a fire," Judge Dee answered, somewhat stoically, staring at the black ashes that were still smoldering. The white smoke coming from the incense joined the black smoke, and mingled into a shape that looked like a dancing dragon.

"What happened to your desk?" the sergeant asked in surprise. Judge Dee ruefully pointed out its remains in the fire with the Rain Dragon. As the gray-bearded man stood by amazed, the judge merely smiled and returned his sword to its sheath on the wall.

The sergeant called in several constables to help douse the embers. While they were cleaning up, the judge indicated he wished them to leave the burned poetry book alone. For some reason, the judge felt he wanted to keep it. Perhaps the poem still had its grip on him. Or, perhaps it was that the book had originally belonged to his father, and it was difficult for him to lose it. The judge scraped the ashes off the covers of the book and returned it to the bottom shelf in his bookcase.

The room still reeked of smoke. Judge Dee began to don his official robe and his winged cap for the afternoon tribunal session. As he was adjusting his official cap in front of the standing silver mirror, he heard the familiar three booms of the gong.

Before leaving his office, Judge Dee glanced at what remained of the poetry book, now much burned and no more than the half its original size. The book must have been at least thirty years old; time had turned all of its pages brown. Now that the burned part had been partially cleaned, a white edge appeared on each page, in contrast to the older brown surface. Judge Dee suddenly realized that for all these years the inner side of each piece of paper had actually remained quite white. An exciting new idea occurred to him. "Remember the case of a land dispute?" he asked Sergeant Hoong.

"Sure," the sergeant answered as he recalled the case quite vividly. A poor man had a small piece of land next to the much larger acreage of a rich landlord. Twenty years before, according to the poor man, the rich landlord had proposed a deal. The landlord had said, "You have only a small piece of land, but you still have to pay the minimum property tax on it. Why don't you let me handle it as if it were mine? Adding your land to mine won't increase my taxes. If you allow me to claim it for you, you won't need to pay any taxes at all. But of course the land is still yours." The poor farmer had been grateful to his rich neighbor. He had accepted the suggestion and had stopped paying the tax. Twenty years later, however, the rich landlord denied having had this conversation, and claimed that the land had been his ever since he had started paying its taxes. He even presented the tribunal an old deed showing the transaction of the land. The thumb marks on the deed were barely readable, but the color of the paper was convincingly brown to prove its old age.

"Go and fetch the deed in the dossier," Judge Dee ordered, "and bring it to me in the court-hall." Before leaving the room, the judge took the poetry book and put it capaciously inside his sleeve pocket.

Judge Dee entered the court-hall and sat behind his high bench. The constables brought in two men to kneel before it. One of the men introduced himself as Tao Mei and complained, "How unfortunate I am to have this vicious scoundrel for a neighbor! I woke up this morning and looked out my window. I saw him standing in my yard, picking pears from my trees. I rushed to stop him, but he ran away like a rabbit. I followed him to his yard where he claimed all the pears in his basket were from his own trees. We quarreled and many of our neighbors came to listen, but the scoundrel kept denying his theft. I have to come here for justice."

"Your Honor," the other man, introducing himself as Ma Fan, had his own complaint. "It must be the accumulated bad luck of at least eight generations that has made me live next door to this hooligan. This morning I was picking pears in my own yard. All of a sudden, he came in and claimed that all the pears in my basket were from his trees. Why should I bother with his? My own trees have produced plenty. His accusation made no sense. Your Honor can surely see that. Please give me my due."

The man knocked his forehead on the floor several times to show his respect for the court. Unfortunately, the judge wasn't even looking. While the two men were presenting their case, he had been completely distracted, waiting for Sergeant Hoong to bring him the old deed concerning the land in dispute. His face lit up as he saw the sergeant, and he anxiously took the deed from the latter's hand. He quickly tore the paper checking the edges carefully where the paper was torn. Smiling, he whispered to the sergeant and pointed to Ma Joong. The sergeant nodded, beckoning Ma Joong, and quietly they left the court together. A constable replaced Ma Joong to help hold one of the two big signposts that read: "Be silent," and "Be serious."

Judge Dee put down the deed to look at the two men kneeling in front of him. This time he noticed that one of them was bald and that the other one had shifty eyes. The judge also noticed a basket full of pears on the floor between the two kneeling men. Some pears were fairly big and some were very small.

"What brought you here? Speak up!" Judge Dee said.

His words surprised and confused both men. They looked at him blankly. As soon as the words went out of his mouth, the judge realized his error. He apologized, "I'm sorry that I've entirely failed to hear your case. My mind has been much preoccupied with a previous one, brought in some days ago concerning a land dispute. You may have heard of that one."

Onlookers in the courtyard nodded. They all remembered the case to which the judge had referred. He spoke to the two men kneeling in front of him again. "Your case involves property of much less value, but justice should prevail. Let me assure you that I'll be fair, and I'll address your issues just as seriously. The law protects everyone's property, no matter how small it is. Everyone should understand that nothing is too trivial for the tribunal, as far as justice is concerned. Now proceed. Who has which complaint?"

This time Ma Fan complained first. He knocked his forehead on the floor and said, "Your Honor, this insignificant person, Ma Fan, is a hardworking man, but I have the ill luck of having this hooligan as my next door neighbor. I got up early this morning to pick pears from the trees in my yard. But before I carried them home, he came and grabbed my arm, yelling at me and accusing me of stealing his pears. What nonsense! They are all mine, from my own yard. I won't even try his stinking pears." The man's eyeballs seemed to slip even more deeply in corners of his eyes as he glanced at the man kneeling next to him.

"Watch your tongue." Judge Dee snapped.

"Your Honor," the baldheaded man finally had a chance to restate his case. "This insignificant person is Tao Mei. This morning I woke up and found this scoundrel picking pears from the trees in my yard. I put on my clothes and ran out to catch him but he sneaked back to his own yard. We quarreled nearly all day, and many neighbors came to listen, but no one could resolve our dispute. That's why I'm here. For justice, Your Honor," Tao Mei knocked his forehead on the floor.

This was clearly a case of "he said" vs. "he said," as neither had produced any conclusive evidence. A basketful of pears did not seem to have much value, but some people were just mean enough as to want to steal anything. The judge sighed sadly and looked at the two peasants, thinking it all through in his head: Do I have any proof? Yes. I have this basket full of pears. But how can I make it talk? Which trees did these pears come from? Are the pears left on the trees any different? Ah ha! Judge Dee suddenly got an idea.

He ordered the constables to give both Tao Mei and Ma Fan a piece of paper and asked them to draw the large-sized, the small-sized and the typically full-sized pear on their own trees. The curious spectators in the courtyard tried to figure out what their judge was up to. A smart-aleck loudmouth exclaimed that it was a size 'assize.' "If they don't fit, he has to acquit," he said, referring to the papers in Tao Mei and Ma Fan's hands. The crowd missed his point and asked the loudmouth to explain. Scratching his ears, the guy admitted he actually didn't know how a size test would work. As the crowd laughed at his ignorance the man blushed, covering his face with both hands. Most spectators wondered if the two peasants could even draw something to resemble a pear. One frankly admitted that under such pressure he would wet his pants. Everybody laughed at his candor, and enjoyed the fun of such public teasing. A tribunal session often generated this kind of fun, and people loved it.

The gossiping quickly stopped as two constables took the drawings from Tao Mei and Ma Fan and handed them to the judge. He looked at the papers and the pears, respectively. Suddenly, he threw the paper at Ma Fan and rapped his high bench with the oblong gavel known as "the wood that frightens the hall." Everyone in the courtyard held his breath, waiting for the judge to reveal his finding.

"You stole the pears and yet expect to get away with it. Trying to fool this tribunal? Not a fat chance, as long as I am the magistrate! Speak up."

Ma Fan's voice began to quiver as he tried to deny his guilt. "I didn't do anything wrong, Your Honor. I only picked pears from trees in my own yard."

"Nonsense. Look at your drawings here. And compare them with the pears over there. Can't you see how you betrayed yourself? You pathetic fool! Look, so many of these pears are much smaller than the typical pear you drew. Why would someone pick pears when they're not yet ripe, if the trees indeed belonged to him? You must have been stealing, and in quite a hurry, too. That's how the small ones got into the basket, isn't it? I can easily prove my words by sending a constable to fetch some of your pears. It's really disgusting that you still wanted to steal when you have better pears.

Ma Fan had to admit his larceny. Blinking, he slapped himself twice, first on the left and then on the right cheek. As he bowed to ask for mercy, Judge Dee ordered five strikes on his bare buttocks as punishment for the theft. The crowd in the courtyard was much impressed by the judge's reasoning and his gift of quick detection. "See. I told you it's going to be a size assize," the smarty-pants piped up again. Others sneered at him and asked sarcastically, "Oh, really? Did you tell us who the thief was then? Why aren't you the magistrate in the first place?" Another round of laughter broke out.

Just then Ma Joong and Sergeant Hoong returned with the two farmers involved in the land dispute. The rich landlord introduced himself as Jiao Hua. "I have been in possession of that piece of land for twenty years: you can check my tax record. I gave Your Honor an old deed. What else do you want from me?"

Judge Dee smiled, but he didn't say anything.

The other man introduced himself as Shang Tang, the poor neighbor. He repeated his story that twenty years before his rich neighbor had offered to pay his taxes for him and how happily he had accepted the offer and had never thought about the consequences.

Judge Dee roared at Shang Tang, "Don't you know that you have committed a crime?"

"I know, I know," the man pleaded, knocking his forehead on the floor many times over. "This is like a pest on the monk's head; everyone can see it when someone points it out. I confess, but I didn't feel it was a crime at the time. I thought he just did me a favor, and never thought about the loss to the tribunal. Now I see his greedy intentions. What a fool I was!"

"You have to repay a pound of silver to this tribunal right now," said Judge Dee.

"A pound of silver! Isn't that too much?" cried Shang Tang. "But how about the land? Is it still mine?" he spoke anxiously and flecks of foam showed at the corner of his mouth.

"You idiot! A fine of a pound of silver has already proved that, hasn't it?" said Judge Dee, wondering at what a simpleton the man appeared to be.

"So it *is* mine," the man grinned broadly, and knocked his forehead on the floor to thank the judge.

Jiao Hua blinked his eyes, not believing that he had lost. "Haven't I paid the taxes all these years? How could the land still be his?" asked the rich man.

Instead of answering the questions, Judge Dee asked one of his own, in a familiar and curious tone, almost like asking an old friend: "How could a piece of paper look so old when it isn't? Tell me your secret."

Jiao Hua's face grew pale. His hands shook and his forearms quivered.

Judge Dee smiled. Then, his resonant voice thundered in the court-hall. "You damned fool. Who do you try to cheat at this tribunal? Don't even think of it! Look at this." The judge took out the burned poetry book from his sleeve pocket and held it up in the air. "This poetry book belonged to my father more than thirty years ago. The outside of the paper has turned brown. But look, the inside still has its original white color."

Judge Dee beckoned two onlookers in the courtyard to come nearer, and he showed them the white color appearing on the inner edge of the ruined pages in his poetry book. Then he pointed to the deed Jiao Hua had produced.

"Well, this is what his faked deed looks like." He showed them the place that had been deliberately torn apart. Nothing was white. The paper was completely brown all the way through.

"Tell me the trick you used to turn the paper brown. Or do we need to do you to a nice brown turn!" Judge Dee glanced at his six constables, who held tools of torture in hand. "Are we ready?" the judge raised his voice in a yet more emphatic tone.

"Yes, Your Honor." The voices of the six constables and the various ominous noises they made with the torture tools in their hands prompted the landlord to give in.

"No torture please! I confess. Here's how I did it. I soaked the paper in a pot of tea for a few minutes and took it out. As the paper dried, it appeared brown and looked as if it were many years old. I thought it would convince Your Honor that I've owned the land for twenty years. But I was only fooling myself. As a proverb says, adding a pair of feet to the drawing of a snake destroys the whole picture. I'm such a fool, and Your Honor is truly a wise man!" The landlord knocked his forehead on the ground for mercy.

Judge Dee ordered twenty strikes on his bare buttocks as punishment and closed the tribunal.

*   *   *   *

A week after the accidental fire in his office Judge Dee received three brand new desks. One made of Korean pine came from Magistrate Lo of Chin-hua. Another made of Northeast China ash came from Magistrate Pan at the Woo-yee district. The last one made of the most expensive mahogany came from the Prefect.

These unexpected gifts created quite a festive atmosphere at the judge's house. As each desk arrived, the ensuing commotion inspired yet more jubilation. Generous tips went to those who delivered the desks, and Judge Dee wrote letters of thanks to each of those who had sent them. The judge was not surprised to receive such gifts from Magistrates Lo and Pan, for both owed him such favor.

The desk from the Prefect, however, came as a really sweet surprise. Quite flattered, the judge was unable to conceal his joy and self-congratulations.

The messenger from the Prefect announced that a conference of the six magistrates of the prefecture would be held at the Prefect's office in two days. This is an excellent chance to thank the Prefect and Magistrates Lo and Pan in person, Judge Dee thought. He also wondered how they had each heard about the fire in his office so quickly. Just as a proverb said, "good news tends to stay home while bad news has hundreds of legs and runs thousands of miles." It was amazing how much of his private life was actually under public scrutiny. He couldn't help but admire how Magistrate Lo could successfully go out incognito. The man could have fun with any sort of woman he wanted, because he knew all kinds of tricks to disguise himself. Judge Dee had often disguised himself as a physician, either in an investigation or simply to get a sense of a more ordinary life. When he carried his "physician's box" of red-lacquered pigskin and walked along a crowded street, many patients stopped him and asked for help. The judge had enough medical knowledge to write appropriate prescriptions or to refer them to the real physicians they needed. But more than once he had been recognized as the magistrate while he was pretending to be a physician walking on the street. How embarrassing and awkward to appear in 'disguise' to people who actually knew who he was. The judge caressed his long side-whiskers as he reflected on those several embarrassments. How did that podgy fellow manage to disguise himself so well? Judge Dee wondered with a curious envy.

The judge ordered the mahogany desk to be put in the exact place where his old desk had been, and the desks from his two colleagues put next to it. The Korean pine desk on the right, and the Northeast China ash desk on the left, the three desks formed three sides of a square. Judge Dee assigned Ma Joong and Chiao Tai to sit to his right and Sergeant Hoong and Tao Gan to his left. The four of them sat comfortably at their seats, somewhat overwhelmed by their unexpected new status.

It was mid afternoon, and most of the sunlight had already left the room. But a stray ray of light shone on the black mole on Tao Gan's face, and made the few long black hairs sprouting from it appear silver. As usual, Judge Dee discussed the pending cases with his associates.

"So, what do you think of the case a Mr. Wei brought against another Mr. Wei?" Judge Dee was referring to a case brought in by Mr. Wei Min against Mr. Wei Tan. They both lived in the Village of Weis where all the villagers were related and shared the same family name of Wei.

According to Wei Min, his neighbor Wei Tan had forged his signature on a deed transferring a piece of his land to Wei Tan. Wei Min said that he had thought the price was too low and had not signed the deal.

"Wei Min seems to be an honest man. I don't think he lied to us," said Sergeant Hoong, "although Wei Tan has shown us the paper."

"That's exactly the problem," Tao Gan said. "I've compared the signatures and I honestly couldn't say if Wei Min's signature was forged."

"Wei Min said that he wanted to sell the land because his father was very ill," Chiao Tai said off-handily, scratching his ear. "He needed the money to buy better food for his father, who hasn't tasted meat for three years. But Wei Min said he refused to sell the land so cheaply."

"The poor old man will die anyway if he learns the land is lost," said Tao Gan, twisting the long hairs sprouting from his mole.

"The old man has no chance to survive unless the land is returned. That's why I don't believe the paper at all," Sergeant Hoong said.

Ma Joong drummed the glossy surface of his new desk with his large fists, not used to sitting at it yet. "I visited the Village of Weis yesterday," he said. That surprised everyone else in the room, for no one had expected him to be so interested in a case that appeared to have no females involved.

"I saw a group of women washing clothes at a pond near where the two men live. One of them seemed attractive. Pretending I had lost my way and needed directions, I chatted with an older woman and discovered that the young wench was Wei Min's wife."

"That's interesting, Well done, Ma Joong!" exclaimed the judge.

"Yes," Sergeant Hoong followed. "That may lead us somewhere we haven't been before. I knew that piece of paper is worthless." His long beard was shaking as he became more emotional.

"This reminds me of something," Chiao Tai said. "Didn't someone mention yesterday that Wei Min's father has the same disease that Wei Tan's late wife had? As a widower, Wei Tan might be having an affair with Wei Min's wife."

"That is certainly a possibility. But what does that have to do with the forged signature?" Sergeant Hoong asked.

"Well," Tao Gan said, "if that's the case, it helps a lot, for it explains why Wei Tan could have forged Wei Min's signature so well. The man would have had plenty of access to the examples of the signature."

"Why didn't I think of that before?" Judge Dee exclaimed. He waved his hand for Sergeant Hoong to pour him a cup of hot tea. The excitement suddenly made him feel thirsty.

"Look into our dossiers to find both men's signatures," the judge ordered. Sergeant Hoong took up the task and left the room.

Turning to his three lieutenants, Judge Dee said, "As you all know, I'm going to attend a conference of magistrates in our Prefect's office. I have no idea how long it will last. I'll go by myself and leave the entire tribunal affairs to you three and the sergeant from tomorrow on. I know this is not the first time that you have covered for me, but please remain alert and be careful. One thing for sure: Don't start a fire!"

Everyone in the room laughed.

"I'm not kidding," said the judge. "If we have another fire, the desks won't be replaced, but *we* will."

Sergeant Hoong returned; his smile told everyone that he had found what Judge Dee had wanted. As he sat down, he extracted two pieces of paper from his sleeve pocket. One had Wei Min's signature on it, and the other had Wei Tan's. Judge Dee's face lit up. He asked Ma Joong to fetch the two men, saying he knew how to close the case. This surprised his associates. Hadn't he just been sitting with them? How could he have completed his investigation? They all had great confidence in him, however, and were anxious to learn of his findings.

Judge Dee started the afternoon session announcing his anticipated absence for a few days. After Ma Joong brought in Wei Min and Wei Tan they both knelt humbly to introduce themselves to the court. The judge gave Wei Tan a stern look. "Are you sure you didn't forge his signature?" he asked.

The man's chin twitched unconsciously as he denied doing so. "I swear to Heaven I didn't forge any signature. We had a deal."

"For heaven's sake, I hope you didn't take advantage of the fact that his father is ill and needs money badly. You are neighbors and both live in the Village of Weis. Don't you share the same forefathers? Most villagers are cousins, aren't they? As the local proverb says, you can't write another Wei without repeating yourself, and all Weis on earth are brothers. Please remember that as a fact." The crowd of onlookers in the courtyard all nodded in agreement. Some shook their heads in disapproval of such litigation in the first place.

The judge beckoned to Wei Tan to come near his high bench. "Come over here and look at this signature. Are you sure this isn't yours?" he asked.

Wei Tan stood up and came over to the high bench. What he saw was a piece of paper, most of it covered by other things that usually stayed on the judge's bench: rulers, ink stone and ink, brush-pens, and a piece of brown, hard wood of oblong moldings known as the "wood that frightens the hall." The only part that remained uncovered was "Wei," the surname of everyone in the Village of Weis.

"I've never forged his signature. There is no doubt it is his," claimed Wei Tan as he pointed to the signature.

"What are you talking about?" Judge Dee removed the wood and other things on the paper, which turned out to be a deed that Wei Tan had filed in the tribunal's record when he had purchased a large piece of land several years before. Wei Tan blushed as he realized his mistake.

"How can you deny your own signature? You could quite easily lose all your land if you keep this up," Judge Dee said.

Wei Tan pleaded in his quivering voice as he kowtowed, "Please forgive me, Your Honor. I'll be more careful." Judge Dee rearranged things on his high bench and beckoned to him again. "This time you better be more careful. Are you sure this signature is yours?" the judge looked at him sternly.

Again, the paper was completely covered except for the word "Wei" in the signature. Wei Tan stared at it and fell silent. Being fooled once, he had to be very cautious, and he wasn't sure what was awaiting him this time. He stared for quite a long while. Finally he said, "I'm pretty sure this is mine. Look here, this last stroke from left to right. It's the new fashion in writing to move back a little towards the left after completing a stroke from left to right. I do it that way now, but few in my village have learned the fashion yet. Look here. The brush obviously moved back, although for some reason it has been stopped and didn't go further. Maybe it was out of ink."

"Thank you for clarifying it. You have been most helpful. No one could have helped me more. You surely have learned the new style. The reason you suddenly stopped your brush was because you were trying to forge someone else's signature, when you remembered that few in the village had yet learned the fashion." As he was speaking, Judge Dee removed all the obstacles covering the paper, and it turned out to be the very deed in question with the alleged signature of Wei Min. Dumbfounded, Wei Tan had to confess and he soon got exactly what he deserved. Twenty strikes on the bare buttocks.

*   *   *   *

Five days later, Judge Dee returned from the magistrates' conference. Apparently he was in a good mood, bringing home a gift for each of his wives and a toy for each of his children. In a cheerful tone, he told his lieutenants and Sergeant Hoong about his meeting.

"The Conference of Magistrates was quite a success, and we learned a lot from each other's experience. The most exciting event, though, was to receive a special message from our August Throne."

Judge Dee sipped his favorite "Hairy Tiptop" tea and revealed more details. A property dispute had occurred in the royal family. The father of one of the Emperor's favorite concubines had died, and all of his wealth was to be divided equally between his two sons. The Imperial Court sent an envoy to facilitate the transaction, but no matter how the property was divided, neither brother was satisfied. They each complained that the other had been given the larger share. The mission failed and the envoy reported to the Emperor, asking that he be punished for his incompetence. Although quite upset, the Emperor forgave the failure of his envoy and decided to ask local officials to resolve the dispute.

"As the brothers happen to live in one of our neighboring districts, our Prefect was the one asked to help solve the problem." Judge Dee stopped in the middle of his story and drank up his tea. Sergeant Hoong got up to refill his cup.

Back at his own chair, the gray-bearded sergeant slowly commented, "I'm afraid our Prefect may not be quite so lucky. If he fails, our August Throne is likely to be more upset, and someone has to be blamed."

"Did the Prefect ask you for help?" Chiao Tai asked.

"Surely he did," the judge answered.

"What did you do?" asked Ma Joong and Tao Gan almost simultaneously.

The judge smiled but remained quiet.

"You solved the case, didn't you?" asked Chiao Tai in excitement. His liking and admiration for the judge made him believe that Judge Dee could work his way out of any such tangle.

Looking at his three excited lieutenants, Judge Dee smiled. "This is what I suggested that our Prefect should do. Have the brothers switch all the things they got from their late father. If each brother thought the other one got more, tell him he should be happy to have what the other one had. There should be no more quarrels. It would be just as simple as that!"

"Bravo!" Ma Joong hit the desk with his large fist and Tao Gan clapped his own delicate but deft hands quite loudly. Chiao Tai didn't make any noise, but he nodded, equally satisfied. His affection for the judge had also grown tremendously. Only Sergeant Hoong withheld his praise for such acumen. He muttered pensively, "So you literally resolved a dispute among two members of the royal family the minute you heard it." Judge Dee laughed self-indulgently. "And you did it in front of other magistrates and our Prefect, as well as the Imperial Messenger," the sergeant's voice trailed off.

Judge Dee laughed even louder, but he frowned, as he suddenly realized what Sergeant Hoong really meant. The gray-bearded sergeant turned his head towards the Rain Dragon hanging on the wall and murmured, "If the late Old Master had to resolve such a case, he wouldn't have announced his solution so publicly, and nor in such haste." The sergeant caressed his beard after he stopped his mumbling. Judge Dee sat up in his chair and fell into silence. He picked up a brush-pen and started writing quite furiously on his desk without ink.

The three lieutenants began to notice that something had gone awry, although they didn't understand what was wrong. They knew, however, that it was better to leave the judge and the sergeant alone. And so they filed out, one by one. As Sergeant Hoong started to follow them out, Judge Dee stopped him. "Thank you, sergeant, for your reference to my late father."

The sergeant turned around. "I'm the only person who knows more things about your father than you do. I'm sorry that I have to remind you...." Judge Dee interrupted him, "You don't need to say any more, and please do not apologize. I do realize my mistake now. I shouldn't have been so brash. It will have made other magistrates jealous, and I'll also embarrass our Prefect. What would the Imperial Messenger say to the Emperor? I've found some smarty-pants in Poo-yang? I can't believe I was that imprudent!" The judge punched his forehead with his fist. "I shouldn't be so careless. As if outwitting an Imperial Censor on a boat weren't bad enough, I now may have even offended my own Prefect," Judge Dee laughed ruefully. He then recalled the poem from his father's poetry book and began to write it on his desk with his brush-pen, yet again without any ink:

"*This water, since when, its flow?*
This mountain, since when, its being?
Man's fate changes from this to that!
These forms alone stay forever."

As he stopped writing, the judge kept his pen in his hand but slowly pressed his thumb against his fingers with the pen in between. The lightly made bamboo tool soon gave way and broke. Sergeant Hoong stood quietly against the door, watching and listening. Then, all of a sudden, Judge Dee heard the buzz of a mosquito!

CHAPTER 10

▼

A SIGNIFICANT LIFE

Judge Dee was quite ill; in fact he had not been so sick since he was eight years old. Even Sergeant Hoong had not seen him so sick before; he had begun to serve the judge's father about a year after his son had recovered. The sergeant heard about the strange illness second-hand. As a young boy, the judge had had a high fever for three weeks and had not been able to recognize anyone. Not even his parents. The doctors had all but given him up, advising the parents to order his coffin. The drama that happened afterwards became a family legend that everyone seemed to remember somewhat differently.

Sergeant Hoong's favorite version was that someone recommended an eccentric blind masseur known as "Da Mo," who had two thumbs on each hand. The blind man dressed in the robe of a Buddhist monk but wore the cap of a Taoist priest. He cursed both monks and priests, calling them murderers, because so many families sent their sick members, especially their children, to their temples and monasteries as a last resort, and never again saw them alive. As he touched the pulse of this deathly sick eight year old, the four-thumbed masseur exclaimed: "If you hadn't found me, this boy would surely be dead by midnight!"

The blind man ordered the family to take down one of their largest doors and to lay the boy upon it. That provided a flat platform for his treatment. He selected a few pressure points on the boy's body, starting at the middle of the forehead. The masseur pressed the boy's head with his thin knuckles, moving to the boy's eyebrows and then working slowly towards his hair. He repeated this procedure fifty times. His next motion moved from the inner ends of the eyebrows to the temples. Again, he repeated the movements fifty times. Then he placed his hands behind the boy's ears and massaged fifty times. Finally, he pinched the tips of the boy's ring fingers three hundred times! The boy suddenly opened his eyes and cried out loud. He had survived by a miracle.

Now the judge had similar symptoms once again. Even after three weeks of quiet rest, lying in bed in his First Lady's room day and night, he still had a very high fever, and could not recognize his family. His three wives were in tears all day long, kneeling at his side. His three children cried outside his chamber, for the adults wouldn't allow them into the room where they might disturb their father. His three lieutenants and Sergeant Hoong gathered in the judge's private office, feeling helpless and useless.

Occasionally the sergeant would bring an update on the judge's condition, for he was the only outsider allowed to enter the First Lady's room. Ma Joong had been in charge of the tribunal for the past weeks. He felt fortunate that he hadn't had any very tough cases to solve. He and his colleagues spent most of their time sitting in the judge's office, just as they were now. Everyone waited anxiously, but no one knew how he might help the Judge.

Chiao Tai sat very quietly at his desk. His deep loyalty made him feel guilty that he was unable to do anything for the judge. Tao Gan had collected dozens of secret prescriptions that were supposed to provide miracle cures. Sergeant Hoong often shook his head, as he didn't know which one to recommend to the First Lady. Ma Joong sat next to Chiao Tai, staring at his own large fists, motionless atop the gleaming surface of his desk; he was still not used to the desk, and often bumped his knees against its legs.

A constable came in, presenting a note from Magistrate Lo of the neighboring Chin-hwa district. Their cheerful neighbor had heard of the sad news in Poo-yang and sent his trusted physician. In his note, Magistrate Lo highly recommended the doctor; he was over seventy years old, had been in practice for more than fifty years, and was the third generation in the family to practice medicine. The old man had always had a cure for any disease, according to Magistrate Lo,...but all of his patients had been the young women whose company the magistrate so often enjoyed.

The offer by Magistrate Lo raised their hopes but these hopes dimmed quickly when they considered the nature of the doctor's practice. Ma Joong frowned. Why would that podgy imbecile send a doctor who specialized in women's diseases for Judge Dee? Wasn't that simply a poor practical joke in the worst taste?

"Should we give it a try?" asked Chiao Tai.

"Let him in," said Sergeant Hoong.

The constable ushered in a man clad in a white cotton robe carrying a flat box of red-lacquered pigskin. Every physician had this kind of box. Even children knew that a doctor always carried a pigskin box, with his notepad and brush-pen for his prescriptions. Judge Dee had a box like this to use when he disguised himself as a physician.

The old man had long white whiskers and a beard. Stroking them with his thin knuckles, he introduced himself as "the humble servant from Chin-hwa, who is ready to serve the Magistrate of Poo-yang." His voice was unexpectedly shrill; Ma Joong reached up to cover his ears with his large hands.

Sergeant Hoong served the old man a cup of hot tea and politely asked: "Please forgive me for my ignorance, but I must ask you a question. Why do you think you can help? Dozens of doctors have proved quite useless. I hear that you specialize in treating female diseases, but our master is a strong broad-shouldered man who is six feet tall. How can you convince us you are better than those we have tried before?"

"In all humility, I refuse to speak a single word about the patient before I examine him. Even then, I won't offer my help if I don't have complete confidence in my ability to help him. Lead me to the patient, please." The white hair in his long beard quivered as he spoke through its tangle in his high-pitched voice.

Ma Joong and Chiao Tai glanced at each other. They were surprised by the old man's self-confidence; his humility barely disguised his self-esteem. Chiao Tai stood up and quietly led the way, as if obeying his own master. Ma Joong and Sergeant Hoong followed, and Tao Gan reluctantly accompanied his colleagues with much hesitation, doubting there could be any secret left undiscovered, since he had already undertaken a thorough search of all known miracle cures.

Together, the group stopped outside the First Lady's apartment. Sergeant Hoong went in alone. Soon he came and beckoned the old physician to enter. The doctor followed, stepping quickly into the main bedroom. The space had been cleared; no maid or other woman was in sight. The old man sat on the side of the bed, holding two fingers to the judge's left wrist to feel his pulse. The man closed his eyes while feeling the pulse quietly for three long minutes. He then held up the judge's hand and examined his palm. The old man nodded as he detected a deep line running across the palm from the ring finger to the wrist.

"Look. This line here is usually indiscernible in the palm of a healthy person," the old man spoke to Sergeant Hoong standing behind him with some condescension as if he were speaking to his own apprentice. He forced open the judge's mouth with his thin but powerful hands, and looked at the judge's tongue. An awful smell leaped from the mouth. "What a completely blackened tongue!" the white-haired man exclaimed and quickly covered his nose.

"In two more days there will be no help for him! He's lucky that I'm here today." The old man stood up and left the room. The three lieutenants and Sergeant Hoong followed him back to the judge's office.

"Can you do it?" asked Ma Joong. He was so anxious that he didn't even wait for the old man to sit down.

The old man didn't answer. He opened his red-lacquered pigskin box and pulled out a piece of paper. Sergeant Hoong quickly prepared ink for him, and the man wrote with his own brush. He prescribed about a dozen items, mostly herbal, but two or three were insect or animal parts traditionally used in medicine. Reviewing the list one more time, he added a few more items. Finally, he wrote a number next to each of them, indicating the amount he wanted used in his treatment. He handed his prescription to Sergeant Hoong and said: "It'll take four weeks for him to recover. Right now he is extremely weak, just like a woman after childbirth. He is a man of exceptional strength, and probably has never been sick as an adult. A poison in the air, or an evil spirit, as most people call it, hit him at his most vulnerable moment. He is now as weak as a new-born baby."

Tao Gan made a face, and with a tug at Sergeant Hoong's sleeve, appeared not to believe a single word of the old man's story. Ma Joong and Chiao Tai glanced at each other, unsure that they could accept such diagnosis. Only Sergeant Hoong nodded in agreement, recalling the story of the judge's illness as a child. The judge had never been so sick since his childhood episode. Thus, the old man had this part right. It was unpleasant to think of Judge Dee as vulnerable as a woman after childbirth, but the analogy helped the sergeant understand the situation. Perhaps the judge did need to recharge his energy, thought the sergeant. There had been so many stressful events recently!

Sergeant Hoong decided to recommend the prescription to the First Lady. And indeed, what miracles then occurred! Half an hour after she had given him some of the medicine, the First Lady saw the judge open his eyes for the first time in days. And after only three doses, the judge moved his head and was able to recognize his family. As his three wives shed tears of relief at his bedside, Sergeant Hoong eagerly shared the good news with his colleagues in the judge's office. Ma Joong played a pleasant tattoo on his desktop as if it were a toy drum from his childhood, and Chiao Tai and Tao Gan went about the room unembarrassed by their own wide grins. Even the constables cheered up as they heard of the rapid progress.

Within three days, the judge could sit up in bed. The room was again cleared of women, to allow Sergeant Hoong to bring in Ma Joong, Chiao Tai, and Tao Gan. They sat near to the judge, looking at him closely, as they hadn't been able to do for quite some time. They were overjoyed and much relieved.

"How nice to see you getting better!" Ma Joong's voice trailed off as he began to lose some of his usual self-control. Others shed tears too. Despite the social taboos that usually prevented men from crying in front of each other, they felt they just could no longer withhold their feelings.

Judge Dee was still quite delicate. If the doctor's analogy held, the judge was now as weak as a woman after childbirth. There were many superstitious beliefs about woman after childbirth. If she talked too much in the period of her recovery from labor, it was believed that she might hurt her throat and thus risk having a harsh voice for the rest of her life. Or, if she read for too long, she might injure her eyes and weaken them permanently. If she stood for a long time, her heels could trouble her in the days to come. And if she ventured outdoors, the exposure to chill wind might give her a chronic headache. After labor a woman was expected to remain confined to her bed for at least four weeks, and so it was to be for the judge.

During those four weeks, he was incredibly bored, of course. All that he could do was to revisit the memories of everything he had done throughout his life. Thus, he recalled many episodes from his childhood that he had long forgotten. Now, as before, he had no idea how he had become so sick. He remembered that he had had a dream one night, and the first two cases he solved in Poo-yang somehow returned to haunt him. Those were the rapes at the Temple of Boundless Mercy and the case of the vicious Cantonese merchant who had caused more than a dozen deaths in three provinces.[1]

Both cases had connections with powerful groups. Behind the monks of the Temple of Boundless Mercy were the Buddhist authorities in the capital, and behind the merchant were other wealthy merchants in Canton who had powerful friends in the royal court. Sooner or later, it seemed likely to the judge that these forces would attack him. His imprudence in showing off in front of the Prefect and Imperial Messenger might also have consequences. Even worse, he had also shown himself to be smarter than the Imperial Censor, who was extremely jeal-

---

1. For more about those two cases, namely the rapes at the Temple of
   Boundless Mercy and deaths caused by a vicious Cantonese merchant, please
   read *The Chinese Bell Murders* by Robert van Gulik, Harper & Row,
   Publishers, Inc., 1958.

ous. All these worries had recently caused him much distress. Perhaps it was during his sleep, when a person is most vulnerable, that the poison in the air found him and penetrated his body, as the old doctor from Chin-hwa had suggested.

Judge Dee smiled. He opened his left hand to stare at his palm. For a moment he felt he could see himself as a tiny young boy sitting in the middle of his palm! With his fingers and thumb encircled, that boy seemed to feel threatened. "The sky is falling down!" Judge Dee heard the boy scream. He sighed, closed his eyes, and shook his head, trying to shake off such unpleasant memories.

*   *   *   *

After another full month of rest, Judge Dee finally left his bed in his First Lady's room and returned to his private office to meet with his colleagues. Sergeant Hoong served him a cup of his favorite tea, and made it with only half the accustomed amount of tealeaves, as his body was only strong enough for tea of half strength. The judge sat at his desk, surveying the room that he had missed for nearly two months. He knew he was still too weak for tribunal sessions. The dignity of the tribunal required a person of considerable strength in both body and mind.

As Ma Joong reported the tribunal affairs, Judge Dee appeared to be quite satisfied. Only one case had not been resolved. A merchant named Feng Gang living on the bank of the canal had accused his neighbor of having an adulterous affair with his wife. The woman denied it, of course. The only evidence that the husband could provide was that of a boatman who testified that he had witnessed the intimacy as he past by the window of their house on the water. But the neighbor's wife had testified that her husband had been at home at the time. Ma Joong wasn't sure whether to believe her or the boatman whom he had temporarily detained. "He has plenty to eat in jail, so he's happy," laughed Ma Joong. "It's much better than his home, that stinking little boat. He even asked the warden to buy him a few drinks. Ha, ha, ha..."

Judge Dee frowned. "Bring him here," he said. After a second thought he asked them to keep a record of the interview.

A constable brought in a man in a short robe and wide pants. He knelt in front of the judge and introduced himself, "This insignificant person is named Yin Yang."

"Where do you come from?"

"From the north."

"How old are you?"

"Thirty-eight."

"Is your home in a city or the countryside?"

"In a city."

"How old are your parents?"

"They both are deceased."

"Do you have brothers?"

"Two younger ones."

"Are you married?"

"Yes. I have two sons. The elder one is nine, and the younger one is seven."

Judge Dee sent the man back to jail without further questioning. His lieutenants and Sergeant Hoong were quite disappointed. They had hoped to find the judge as incisive and quick as he had been before. Had the illness weakened him to the point that he could ask only pointless questions?

The next day, Judge Dee and his colleagues gathered again in his private office. He ordered a whole ham for lunch. He also bought a big vase of amber-colored sweet wine made from glutinous rice. Both were local specialties of the Chin-hwa district. "I haven't tasted meat or wine for ages. Let's all eat what we can." His associates grinned, as they were glad to see him regaining a good appetite. "To your health," they cheered, toasting with their wine cups.

Suddenly, the judge asked that the boatman be brought before himself again. "Listen to our conversation, and record it as carefully as last time," he ordered. The three lieutenants and Sergeant Hoong glanced at each other, wondering what their judge was up to.

The boatman was brought in, and the smell in the room made his mouth water. As he knelt in the middle of the room, he glanced frequently at both the ham and wine. Judge Dee started asking his simple questions again.

"How old are you?"

"Thirty-nine. I'll be forty after the New Year."

"How long have you been jailed?" the judge asked.

"Thirteen days."

"Do you miss home?"

"Yes, of course," said the man, who glanced at the meat and wine again.

"How big is your family?"

"Well, my father has died. I have two elder brothers. My wife gave birth to two boys. They are three and five now."

Judge Dee asked that the man be given some meat and wine. The man devoured his plateful in no time. The judge resumed his questions:

"Do you come from the north?"

"Yes."

"From a city or the countryside?"

"From the countryside."

"Have you ever before tasted ham this good?"

"Never! This is the best meat I've ever had. Even at a rich men's kitchen in my hometown I've never tasted meat so delicious." The man wiped the corner of his mouth with the back of his hand; he appeared to drool from just the memory of the delicious meat.

Judge Dee smiled. He waved his hand and sent the man away with a little more meat. The man grabbed another cup of wine before he left the room. Ma Joong and Chiao Tai glanced at each other. Their judge behaved so strangely. He was far too long-winded, almost as tiresome as a gossiping woman. Sergeant Hoong and Tao Gan murmured their doubts to each other: Could the change in the judge's behavior be due to the medicine he had been given? Had that old doctor from Chin-hwa given him what was suitable only for women, and thereby affected the judge's character? "To your health," the four associates toasted. As they held up their wine cups, they all wished the best for their judge.

Tackling quite a large chunk of ham, Ma Joong began talking about a case that he had just solved during the noon session of the tribunal a few minutes before. "You won't believe this," he said, wiping his greasy hands on his pants.

A man came to the tribunal to accuse his next-door neighbor of seducing both his wife and his concubine. On his way home for lunch he saw his neighbor come out of his house. The neighbor grinned at him and said, "I've had a great time at your house."

"What do you mean?" The man was upset and suspicious.

"I've had fun with your wife and concubine."

"Damn you! I curse your tongue."

"I'm not kidding," the neighbor grinned.

"Prove it," the man demanded.

"Well, what if I tell you that your wife's breasts are warm and your concubine's buttocks are cold?"

The man turned pale. He didn't stay to hear another word, and ran home. His wife was cooking and his concubine was washing clothes, sitting on a stone stool. He put his hands inside their dresses; his neighbor was damned right! The husband was outraged and ran out the door. He caught up with his neighbor, and accused him of adultery. The neighbor laughed and said he was only joking. The man wouldn't listen, and brought him to the tribunal.

After carefully listening to the long and vivid narrative by Ma Joong, Judge Dee smiled and began to tease. "What did you do? You can't wait to summon the women. Right?"

Others laughed as Ma Joong blushed. "Come on. Of course I know better. It's so obvious. I punished that dirty rotten neighbor right away."

"For what?" Judge Dee asked.

"For adultery with the women, of course."

The judge shook his head and said: "He should only be punished for making a lewd joke."

"He wasn't merely joking! He knew quite intimate details about both women. How could he be joking?"

Judge Dee chuckled. "I know what you mean by such intimate details. Look! I also know the wife had warm breasts and the concubine had a cold rump. Does that mean I am guilty too?"

"How do you know that?" Ma Joong scratched his ears.

"You've just told me," the judge snickered. The others laughed again.

"I mean…" Ma Joong was embarrassed and unable to reply, "…you know what I mean…"

"I know you were fooled, just like the husband," said the judge.

Ma Joong blinked, wanting to hear more.

Judge Dee smiled and stroked his long side-whiskers. "Let me ask you this. What were those two women doing when the husband ran home?"

"His wife was cooking and his concubine was washing."

"There you go. His wife was standing over the stove and his concubine was sitting on a stone stool."

"So?"

"So what should be warm, and what should be cold? I thought you knew a woman's body better than that, for heaven's sake!"

The others in the room broke into loud laughter. Ma Joong slapped his forehead and exclaimed: "What a fool I am!" They all laughed, and turned again to the good Chin-hwa ham and wine.

*   *   *   *

The next morning, Judge Dee finally felt able to appear at the tribunal session, and ordered the boatman brought forward. For the first time in two months, the judge wore his ceremonial robe and the black winged cap, although his robe looked baggy because he had lost so much weight. The moment he rapped his gavel on his bench, he felt his normal strength and resolution. His resonant voice resounded and thundered in the tile-roofed court-hall as he announced the opening of the tribunal session.

"You came from the south, right?" the judge asked casually, as the boatman knelt on the flagstone floor.

"Yes," the boatman answered, smiling vacuously at no one in particular. His eyes moved aimlessly as if he was only half-awake. A hiccup brought forth a terrible smell of liquor.

"How old are you?" the judge continued, with one hand covering his mouth.

"I was forty last year, and I'm forty-one now."

"Do you live in a city or the countryside?"

"Sometimes in a city and sometimes in the countryside."

"Do you have brothers?"

"Two twin brothers. Both died as infants."

"How about your parents?"

"My mother died at my birth, and my father is still alive."

"Are you married?"

"No kidding. I'm a father already. My baby can smile when you hold him."

"Hold on," Judge Dee rapped his bench with the gavel. "What a shameless liar! How can you be a trustworthy witness? I talked with you three times, and your stories change each time. You can't even keep your age straight. Here are the records of our last two conversations. The first time you said you were thirty-eight, then you said you were thirty-nine going on forty, and today you say you are forty-one. You probably count each day in jail as a year gone by. You're a big drunk and you keep making up stories about your kids, siblings and even your parents. What else do you lie about? Speak up! Why have you made yourself a false witness?"

"I didn't lie. How would I dare? I have an aging mother to support."

"Nonsense. Didn't you just tell us a moment ago that she died at your birth?" Loud laughter broke out in the court-hall.

"How much did you get from Feng Gang to lie for him?"

"One piece of silver," the boatman groaned.

"Are you sure he didn't give you two pieces of silver?"

The man mumbled and put out two fingers.

"Was it three or two?"

The man looked frightened, vehemently shaking his head and waving his hand to deny everything.

"You're useless, even when you're not drunk. There's only one thing you didn't lie about. That is that you've never tasted any better meat than I gave you yesterday. You are not worthy to testify about anything." Turning towards his constables, the judge said, "Take this rogue out and bring in that ruffian."

The constables brought in the merchant and made him kneel in front of the judge.

"I know you've bribed the boatman. But he's such a poor liar he couldn't even tell the same story twice. Now let's hear you tell the truth!" The judge rapped his bench with his gavel. Once again, he felt that he was as strong as he had ever been.

The merchant lay like a lump of jelly on the floor, promptly confessing that he had made up the story in order to divorce his wife. Any man could eject his wife from his house if she was proven unfaithful. So, with two pieces of silver he had bribed the boatman to testify against her.

Judge Dee ordered ten strokes on the bare buttocks of each man, and thus closed his first tribunal session since his recovery. Now, as the familiar sound of corporeal punishment came from the courtyard, his two months absence from the court seemed only a blink of an eye.

*   *   *   *

That evening, Judge Dee enjoyed a delicious dinner with his three wives in the quiet dining room, as the full moon sent its soft light through the windows. The dinner dishes had just been cleared, and he and his three wives were ready for a domino game. Months had passed without these evening games. Judge Dee was thrilled to touch these game-pieces once again. He and his three wives sat around the square mahogany table after a servant set an extra light on it. Although a legacy from his father, the table originally had come from his mother as part of her dowry. The judge had it in mind for his own daughter when she married.

The First Lady sat opposite the judge. As usual, her hair was arranged in three coils held by a thin gold hairpin. The Second Lady sat on Judge Dee's right and the Third Lady on his left. The maids brought in tea, watermelon seeds, and dried fruits. Their presence reminded the First Lady that she had hired two additional servants during the months her husband had been so sick, to sit at his bed in case he needed anything at night. Since his recovery, she thought of letting them go, but they kept pleading with her to let them stay on. Tonight, with so many maids around, she knew it was long past the time to let these extra maids go.

Before they had a chance to finish their first game, they heard a commotion outside. Sergeant Hoong rushed in, panting. "An Imperial Messenger has arrived, accompanied by six constables. They are waiting for you at your office." The sergeant brought him the ceremonial robe and the black winged cap that had been left in the office. As the judge hurried to put them on, the sergeant helped him make sure that the wings on the cap were also properly aligned. The women left the dining room, quickly retreating to their own quarters. Sergeant Hoong accompanied the judge to his office.

"The Magistrate of Poo-yang arrives!" announced the sergeant outside the door of the judge's office.

As Judge Dee entered the room, he saw an Imperial Messenger holding a scroll of golden brocade above his head. His six constables stood at his side in two rows, each quite rigid at the expression on his face. The atmosphere became as serious as in the Imperial Court. "The Magistrate of Poo-yang now humbly receives the order from our August Throne," the Imperial Messenger announced in a thunderous voice. Just like the Messenger the judge had met earlier at the Prefect's office, this man had a pair of remarkably powerful lungs.

Judge Dee knelt down to knock his forehead to the floor, awestruck. The Imperial Messenger moved his hands to the ends of the golden scroll, to let it unroll. The unfurling and snap of the scroll caused such a sudden puff of air that Judge Dee blinked hard. When he reopened his eyes he found himself staring at the personal calligraphy of the Emperor, written in the First Hand with the Vermilion Brush.

The Imperial Messenger declaimed the content of the scroll: "In this third year of His Majesty's own calendar named Zong Zhang, His Excellency of the Great Tang Empire gives his irrevocable executive order as follows. Immediately remove Dee Jen-djieh from the office of the Magistrate of Poo-yang, and...." The rumbling of the declamation brought Sergeant Hoong to his knees as he listened outside the door. His eyes blurred and his heart thumped against his ribs. His ears became so full of that booming voice that he could not hear anything else. The sergeant never expected Judge Dee's career to end so abruptly. It was true that the judge might have offended someone and might have more than a few political enemies, but his local popularity should at least secure him his current position as the Magistrate of Poo-yang. The sergeant bit his thumb to make sure that he was not dreaming. Sure now that he was awake, the gray-bearded man clenched his fist and pounded upon his chest, as sad tears sprang to his eyes.

The door opened, and the Imperial Messenger stepped out, followed by the six constables. Sergeant Hoong bowed low and dared not to look at any of them.

When he found enough strength in his legs to enter the room, he saw the judge still kneeling on the floor. The sergeant quietly knelt down at his side.

"Give me the map, and let's find this place called Lan-fang." The sudden request from the judge quite surprised the disheartened sergeant. For a moment, he didn't know how to respond.

"Didn't you hear me?" the judge asked impatiently as he stood up and smoothed the wrinkles in his ceremonial robe. "I have the impression that it's a district in the extreme west."

"What? You, you,…you're exiled to Lan-fang?" The sergeant couldn't believe his ears, and his tongue failed him. Staring at the black winged cap on the judge's head, he wondered why the judge was still wearing it. The Imperial Messenger would have surely removed it if the judge had been ordered into exile.

"What are you talking about, sergeant?" Judge Dee grumbled. "Didn't you hear the order of our August Throne? I've been appointed the Magistrate of Lan-fang, and we are supposed to leave Poo-yang in three days. We have lots of things to do, and we don't have much time."

Now the sergeant realized he was quite the fool. He hadn't listened to the complete order of the Emperor when the Imperial Messenger proclaimed it! What a relief! But he soon started to wonder again. Why Lan-fang? As he went to fetch the map, he recalled that this was only their second year in Poo-yang. Usually a magistrate was expected to work for three years. The abrupt removal of Judge Dee from his current office did not seem at all fair, particularly as Poo-yang was such a wonderfully prosperous district. And where was that Lan-fang? If the judge was right and Lan-fang was indeed on the frontier in the west, life there would be very difficult. Few crops grew in that barren soil. Most people would rather be an ordinary citizen in Poo-yang than a magistrate of Lan-fang.

As he returned with the map, Sergeant Hoong overheard Judge Dee's excited voice outside the door: "I knew I was right!" The judge looked up at the sergeant and pointed at a book in his hand. "Lan-fang is the district on the extreme western frontier. It used to be the gateway to the Silk Road. Fifty years ago commercial travelers switched to another route, and Lan-fang was abandoned. But it's still there. It's a border town where one has to expect sudden attacks from the western barbarians." The judge tapped the book to show the sergeant where he had found his information.

Sergeant Hoong's silence made the judge realize that the sergeant was not nearly as excited as he was about the transfer. The judge sighed. "I know. Maybe it seems that the Buddhist authorities in the capital and the friends of the Cantonese merchants have decided upon my transfer long before my term of office in

Poo-yang has expired. Perhaps you're right that even our Prefect is glad to see me go elsewhere at this point. But think about it. I'll still be a magistrate. As long as our August Throne has placed his trust in me, I have to live up to that trust. Besides, it will be most instructive to serve as magistrate in an outlying district like Lan-fang. Doubtless we shall find interesting problems there that would not occur in the larger cities of the interior."

The judge's upbeat attitude finally persuaded the sergeant. He nodded and said: "As long as you don't mind, I won't either."

Judge Dee raised his eyebrows and looked at Sergeant Hoong. "That reminds me. You have always been with me as I've moved around. But Ma Joong and Chiao Tai joined me at Peng-lai and Tao Gan started working for me at Han-yuan. I shouldn't assume that they all want to follow me to Lan-fang. I'll tell them tomorrow and ask each of them to decide for himself."

"I bet they'll all follow you, Your Honor."

"I hope you're right. As you probably know, I don't want to lose any of you." Judge Dee smiled, but his smile faded as he thought of another difficulty: "I will also have to break the news to my wives. I hope it won't break their hearts."

*   *   *   *

Standing at the doorway to his First Lady's room, Judge Dee frowned as he heard weeping inside. As he entered the room he saw his wives sobbing together. The Second Lady broke out into a loud cry when she saw him. Before Judge Dee could open his mouth she wailed: "Why should I always be the unlucky one? What can I do now? My daughter is already sixteen. I told you to find her a husband when we got here last year, but you didn't listen. You said it was still too early and we had plenty of time. I listened to you, and thought we would be here for three years. Now what? We're leaving for a place no one knows. You're not marrying her to a barbarian Uighur, are you?" She threw herself into the arms of the judge and cried even louder.

Judge Dee felt his heart sink. He didn't like her wailing, but she certainly had a point. If they stayed in Lan-fang for three years, his daughter would be nineteen. Most responsible parents would marry their daughters well before they turned eighteen. Not having found her a husband in Poo-yang, he might have lost his best opportunity. He had not thought about this problem, and now he found it difficult to deal with. Definitely he would not marry his daughter to anyone in Lan-fang, and then leave her behind in that barren land.

The Third Lady came over and stood by the Second Lady. Patting her shoulder to comfort her, she said, "Please look at the bright side, my Second Elder Sister. At least you'll have her with you for a few more years, and won't have to miss her living apart from you thousands of miles away." She lent her silk handkerchief to the Second Lady, to wipe the tears off her cheeks and save her makeup.

"It could be worse, you know," said the First Lady. "Her father is still a magistrate. We can try to find her a suitable husband here even after we leave. And we may find one in the capital too." She spoke with a man's conviction as well as a woman's heart. Her excellent qualities always gave the judge strength, especially in difficult situations.

"How did you hear of our move before I had a chance to break the news?" Judge Dee suddenly asked.

"The new maids I hired during your illness eavesdropped and told us everything. I will let them go now. I should have done it sooner, but just found it difficult. After all, life in the house is much easier than to work in the fields. But since we're leaving, it's much easier for me now. Tomorrow morning they'll be sent home."

Judge Dee nodded and then asked his other wives to go to their own rooms. It had been a long day and an unusual evening, and he was really tired. Before his First Lady had time to undo her hair, the judge fell sound asleep.

The next morning Judge Dee was awakened by a cry from his First Lady. She couldn't find her gold hairpin! The judge didn't give it too much thought, for he was more concerned about whether his lieutenants would decide to follow him to Lan-fang or not. He much hoped that Sergeant Hoong's instinctive guess was right.

As soon as his three lieutenants gathered in his office he told them about his transfer to Lan-fang. They were dumbfounded. Judge Dee asked them to decide for themselves if they would come with him.

"I'll follow you wherever you go," said Chiao Tai. His military training helped him make his decision quite quickly.

Ma Joong smiled as he made his answer into a question, "Isn't this an opportunity to understand barbarian women?"

Tao Gan pulled his long black hairs from the mole on his cheek, and said, "I'll have nothing to do here after you're all gone. So I better follow you."

Judge Dee looked around and felt much relieved. He glanced at the sergeant and said: "Sergeant Hoong was right when he said that you would all come with me. I deeply appreciate your loyalty. I understand the sacrifices you're making. I myself will miss this lovely place. If nothing else, I will miss the ham from

Chin-hwa. Our two years here in Poo-yang have given us many good memories. Tonight we will commemorate these years with a festive dinner at the "Four Springs a Year."

*   *   *   *

Two months later, Judge Dee was still on his way to Lan-fang. A team of four carts slowly wended its way through the western mountains. In the first cart Judge Dee sat on a bedroll, leaning back against a large package of books. Sergeant Hoong sat opposite him on a bale of cloth. The road was rough and the bedroll and bale provided scant protection from the constant jostling.

Behind followed a large cart with silk curtains on its windows. Inside were the judge's wives, children, and maids, three of each. Trying to snatch some sleep, they curled up among pillows and padded quilts. The two other carts were loaded with luggage. Some servants perched precariously on top of the bales and boxes. Others preferred to walk beside the over-worked horses. Ma Joong and Chiao Tai rode at the head of the procession and Tao Gan brought up the rear.

"According to the map," Sergeant Hoong said, "we'll arrive in Lan-fang in two days. When do you think we'll have our first case in the new district?" The two months on the road had proven tedious, and the gray-bearded sergeant was looking forward to something refreshing and challenging.

Judge Dee didn't answer. He had been reflecting on the cases he had solved in Poo-yang. Except for the two major criminal cases he solved shortly after his arrival, the rest of them consisted of insignificant cases not much worth remembering, particularly the very last one. He chuckled as he remembered the sorry-looking maid who stole his First Lady's thin gold hairpin on the night she gave her and another maid their notice of dismissal. The next morning, his Lady couldn't find her hairpin anywhere in the house. Judge Dee hadn't paid much attention at first, but by that afternoon he realized that it had probably been taken by one of the maids as a kind of petty retaliation. She must have felt angry that she couldn't keep her job.

The First Lady had said she felt more sorry for the maid than upset at the loss of her hairpin, and she had asked him not to punish the maid. The judge, however, was disinclined to leave anyone with the impression that it was possible to get away with a larceny, no matter how unimportant it might be. Besides, it was a challenge to discover and prove which of the two maids had stolen it.

Judge Dee's silence and the smile on his face made Sergeant Hoong curious. "What's so funny?" he asked.

"Remember the reed mats I sent to the maids two days before we left Poo-yang?"

"That is indeed a hilarious story. I'm afraid we won't have such fun in Lan-fang. You sent identical reed mats to the maids as a gift from the First Lady. But you also told them that whoever had stolen the hairpin would see her mat magically grow an inch larger the following day. Each mat had an edge of blue cloth, so it seemed impossible that its size could change. Nevertheless, you warned the maids that you would send your constables to their houses to measure the mats. And you did. One of the mats was one inch shorter! The guilty maid must have been afraid that the mat might actually grow. The poor girl had decided to trim the mat just in case. Think about it! The trouble it must have been to trim the mat and then restore the blue edge." The sergeant couldn't help laughing as he remembered her embarrassment when she was told how she betrayed herself.

"It served my purpose perfectly, and my First Lady got her gold hairpin back. She gave each of the maids a pair of silver hairpins instead. I hope that maid has learned her lesson, though," the judge smiled.

As he reflected on the episode, the judge felt he had learned a broader lesson. Life was often unfair, and sometimes not what one hoped for. The maid wanted to keep her job but she couldn't. The judge would like to have completed his service in Poo-yang, but he had been reassigned early. Nevertheless, it would have been pointless to act foolishly in retaliation.

A sudden jolt of the cart interrupted his train of thought. Judge Dee looked out his window at the barren, sandy expanse. He lowered his head, trying to think of someone to whose son he could marry his very fetching and eligible daughter. Somehow, this seemed much more difficult than court investigations. How much he wished that everything in life were just as simple as the cases he had solved in Poo-yang!

Bibliography

100 Judicial Cases from Ancient China, selected and translated by K. L. Kiu, Published & Printed in Hong Kong by the Commerce Publishing in 1991.

Chinese Poetry, Yip, Wai-lim, Duke University Press, 1997.

Dee Goong An: Three Murder Cases Solved by Judge Dee, Robert van Gulik, Toppan Printing Company, Tokyo, 1949, reprinted by Arno Press Inc., 1976.

Gu An Li Xuan Pin, (Commentary on Selected Ancient Cases), Wu Han University Press, 1985.

Gu Dai Qi An Yi Zhu, (Translation and Annotation of Ancient Wonder Cases), Qin Hai People's Press, 1982.

Jing Shi Qi Mo, (Wonderful Strategies in Life Struggles), compiled in the Min Dynasty and recently reprinted and translated into modern Chinese, Beijing Yan Shan Press, 1995.

Judge Dee At Work, Robert van Gulik, Charles Scribner's Sons, New York, 1967, paperback by The University of Chicago Press, 1992.

Ming Qing An Yu Gu Shi Xuan, (Selected Stories of Criminal Cases in Ming and Qing Dynasties), The Mass Press, Beijing, 1983.

Murder in Canton, Robert van Gulik. Originally published in 1966, paperback by The University of Chicago Press, 1993.

Necklace and Calabash, Robert van Gulik, Charles Scribner's Sons, New York, 1967, paperback by The University of Chicago Press, 1992.

Poets and Murder, Robert van Gulik, Charles Scribner's Sons: New York, 1968, paperback by The University of Chicago Press, 1996.

Red Pavilion, Robert van Gulik, Charles Scribner's Sons, New York, 1961, paperback by The University of Chicago Press, 1994.

The Chinese Bell Murders, Robert van Gulik, Harper & Row, Publishers, Inc., 1958, paperback by The University of Chicago Press, 1977.

The Chinese Gold Murders, Robert van Gulik, Harper & Row, Publishers, Inc., 1959, paperback by The University of Chicago Press, 1979.

The Chinese Lake Murders, Robert van Gulik, Harper & Row, Publishers, Inc., 1960, paperback by The University of Chicago Press, 1979.

The Chinese Maze Murders, Robert van Gulik, 1952.

The Chinese Nail Murders, Robert van Gulik, Harper & Row, Publishers, Inc., 1961, paperback by The University of Chicago Press, 1977.

The Emperor's Pearl, Robert van Gulik, Charles Scribner's Sons: New York, 1963, paperback by The University of Chicago Press, 1994.

The Given Day, Robert van Gulik, Dennis McMillan Publications, 1986.

The Lacquer Screen, Robert van Gulik, Charles Scribner's Sons, New York, 1962, paperback by The University of Chicago Press, 1992.

The Monkey and The Tiger, Robert van Gulik, Charles Scribner's Sons, New York, 1965, paperback by The University of Chicago Press, 1992.

The Phantom of the Temple, Robert van Gulik, Charles Scribner's Sons, 1966, paperback by The University of Chicago Press, 1995.

Willow Pattern, Robert van Gulik. Originally published in 1965, paperback by The University of Chicago Press, 1993.

Zen Poems, Selected and edited by Peter Harris, Alfred A. Knopf, New York, 1999.

Zhong Guo Gu Dai Zhi Fa Duan An Shi Hua, (Historical Stories of Lawsuit Settlement and Law Enforcement in Ancient China), Ji Lin People's Press, 1981.

Zhong-Guo-Qi-An-Gu-Shi-Jing-Xuan (*Selected Stories of Chinese Wonder Cases*), Edited by Wang Yi and Sheng Rui-yu, Ming Chuang Publishing Limited, Hong Kong, 1996.